I0716075

LIES THAT BLEED

THE EMBER WAR SERIES
BOOK 1

LEIA STONE

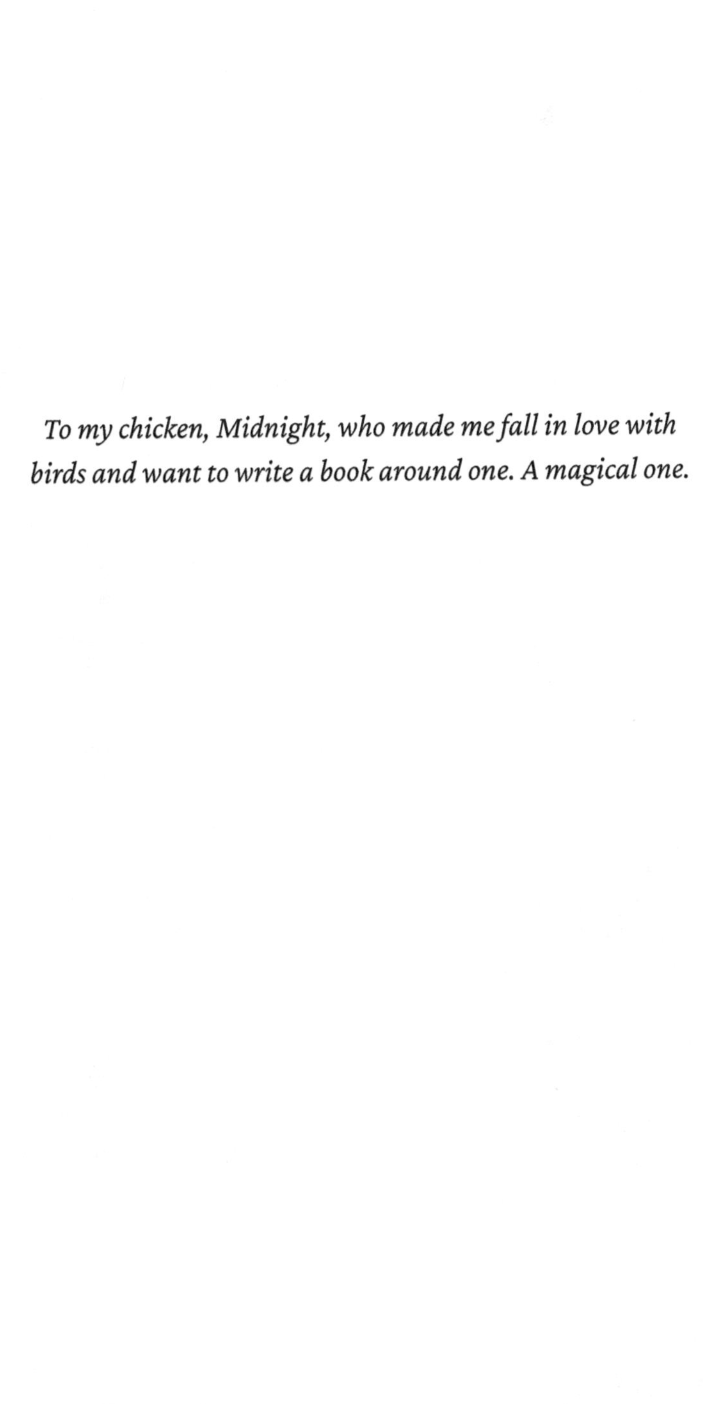

To my chicken, Midnight, who made me fall in love with birds and want to write a book around one. A magical one.

SPECIAL NOTE

This book is unique for me in that there are songs that inspired certain characters or scenes in the book. If you want to listen to them, here is a Spotify playlist: https://smarturl.it/LiesThatBleedPlaylist

LUSKA
THE WALL

THUNDER CLIFF

SKY REACH

EVERGREEN

GOLDEN HILLS
CEDAR CREEK
AMERSEA

MARBLE SHORES

THE COVE

RIVERINE

STORM HAVEN

Imbria
The Wilds

My governess knocked on the open door to my room and I peered up at her, picking at my nails as nerves ate a hole into my stomach.

As the emperor's eldest daughter, I had trained for this day since I was four years old. I normally had guts of steel. I couldn't remember the last time I'd cried or gotten upset, but today wasn't just a regular day.

Today was the Lottery, a drawing in which I knew my name was already chosen—as was my right as the emperor's daughter at the age of nineteen.

"I'm ready," I told Elaine, but my voice cracked, revealing my weakness.

She stepped into the room, a frown pulling at her mulberry-colored lips. Her russet brown hair was the same color as Vespa, her fox creature that stood beside her, mirroring her movements as she crossed the carpet.

"Claiming a creature of great strength and power is what is expected of you so that you can rule the empire." She appraised me, looking over my Fleet-issued fatigues, likely making sure everything was tucked in properly. Today I represented my entire family, and if one boot lace was untied it would be a stain on the Everhart name. Even Vespa cocked his head to the side, as if checking me over one last time, and I couldn't help but stare at his bright pink ember marks. They ran the length of his back in three jagged lines, glowing like they contained fire. Normally a fox would be seen as a more timid creature but not Vespa. He was twice the normal size of your average fox and had sharpened claws and huge fanged teeth.

I nodded and stood. "Yes, ma'am." I assumed a military position, back straight, hands held behind me, fingers overlapping. Elaine served eight years in my father's Imperial Fleet before she left to become our governess. In those eight years, she achieved the rank of first lieutenant. My father wasn't going to hire just anyone to raise his daughters. No. He needed someone who knew how to kill a man with their bare hands.

Elaine walked over to me with Vespa trailing right beside her, and I took in my governess for what might be the last time. Elaine always wore her hair in a tight bun at the nape of her neck. She told me when I was younger that it was because long hair left untied could be used against her. I didn't understand what she meant until she grabbed my long black braid in a sparring session and slammed my face to the floor with it. I never sparred with my hair in a braid or ponytail again, always a bun.

Elaine had been with me all of my nineteen years. Once a spritely young twenty-eight-year-old, she was now pushing fifty, and yet was every bit a badass as the young warriors in the Imperial Fleet.

She saw to it that I bathed each night, that I went to all my lessons, that I showed respect to my master teachers. She disciplined me when needed, and showed little affection when appropriate. She was for all intents and purposes a mother figure. But she was never one to show much emotion. She was even-keeled and stiff-upper-lipped, much like her employer, my father.

So it shocked me when she swam into view suddenly with unshed tears lining her eyes. "Claiming a great creature is what is expected of you," she repeated herself. "But coming back alive will do." Her voice shook with emotion.

My mouth popped open in surprise, then she opened her arms and pulled me in for a stiff hug. My heart burst to life in my chest at her sudden show of sentiment. I wrapped my arms around her, breathing in her lavender and coconut shampoo. That smell was home, and I would miss it when I went to boot camp. Assuming I survived The Wilds.

"I promise to come back with something powerful or not at all," I told her, knowing my father would kill me if I limped out of The Wilds with a ferret at my side. I'd be better off dead.

She pulled away from me, wiping her eyes to erase all evidence that she had showed too much emotion. "That's what I'm afraid of," she said, reaching out to take hold of my shoulders. "Have I been too hard on you? Too much pressure to claim a powerful creature could send you home in a body bag," she warned.

I frowned. Where was this coming from? For my entire life, Elaine had drilled into me that I was Aisling Everhart, future empress, eldest of the ruler of Amersea himself, and the most badass woman in all the world.

I tried to hide the hurt that crossed my face. "You don't think I can do it?"

Elaine sighed. "Of course you can. You're cut from the same cloth as your father. I just... there will be many creatures to choose from. Not choosing too low, or too high, is a gift. And, Aisling, you can be..."

"Cocky." I grinned, placing a hand on my hip.

She let out an exasperated sigh and shook me slightly. "Yes! And a puma, lion, or a bear will be good enough. What I am trying to tell you is... if you see one, don't go for the *Talanagi*."

She slipped into the old tongue and chills raced up

my arms. The Talanagi were so rare they were almost myths. Dragons, griffins, firebirds, creatures of such great power; they killed ninety-nine percent of those who tried to bond with them. Unless you were Luskin. Those bastards seemed to have no problem bonding the ancient creatures. The word was hard to translate from the old language; it was like *magical ancient*, but that wasn't quite right.

I chuckled. "Don't worry. If I see a Talanagi, I'm running the other way. I'm not stupid."

Elaine pursed her lips as if she disagreed with that. "Just remember, you look into the creature's eyes first, and you will feel if the bonding is good. If the creature looks away too quickly—"

"It's too weak," I told her.

She nodded. "If you feel the need to look away too quickly?" she quizzed.

"It's too strong for me," I answered.

She nodded as if she felt satisfied with that and released my shoulders.

"Well, I have to wake your sisters. So..." She lingered as if she didn't want to let me go yet. I'd never told her I loved her, though I did. It wasn't something that was verbalized in my family. We loved by taking care of each other, not flinging around useless phrases. But the three words burned on my tongue now.

"Wish me luck," I said instead, holding out my arm for the age-old ritual.

She grinned, reaching out and pinching me lightly on the forearm for good luck. "Good luck, Aisling. May the stars look after you."

With a nod, I grabbed my three-day pack. I needed to get out of here before I cracked under all this emotion. I wasn't used to seeing Elaine like this.

"See you at the ceremony!" she called as she and Vespa left the room and split up, each going to a different bedroom down the hall to wake my fourteen-year-old triplet sisters, Virtue, Valor, and Victory. My mother was into weird names and I kind of liked that we were all unique in that way. My name might be spelled strangely but was pronounced *Ash-ling*. My close friends called me Ash.

Reaching out, I touched the locket at my neck, the one that held the picture of my mother, and rubbed it for good luck. It was weird to love someone you barely remembered. I was only five when she died in childbirth with the triplets. But in every story I had heard about her, every picture of her, she brightened the room, and I felt connected to her even though she was no longer in this world.

Slinging my bag over my shoulder, I grabbed a muffin from the kitchen, where Tonia was cooking up a huge feast, and snuck out before she could see me. There was no way I could eat eggs and bacon on Lottery Day. I would yak the second they called my name.

Every Amersean citizen was invited to put their name into the Lottery at nineteen years old. From that batch, once a year, only twenty percent were called at the ceremony and given a chance to enter The Wilds. Because I was the emperor's daughter and future leader of Amersea, I automatically got chosen. Of the cohort of chosen lottery candidates who went into The Wilds in the hopes of claiming a creature of awesome power, only around five percent came out alive. The odds were not good.

My stomach soured at the thought of the statistic and I chucked the muffin on the entry table as I moved to the front door. I needed to see Jace, my boyfriend, who would know how to calm my nerves.

"I thought you were riding with me to the Lottery ceremony," my father's voice came down the hall, and I stilled with my hand on the knob.

Turning, I kept my back erect and chin up. "Yes, sir, I will be back in time. I just wanted to go check in with Jace first."

My father's creature, a black puma with orange glowing ember marks, stalked towards me, sniffing my leg. I stilled, wondering what Zuri was smelling me for. She was the most ruthless creature known to our kind, other than the Talanagi. Her magic was unique in that she could not only breathe fire but she had awoken the power in my father to teleport *through* her fire, allowing him to jump from one end of the world to another in the blink of an eye. He could be on the battlefield at The Wall and home for dinner on the same night.

My father strode over to me, wearing his battle uniform. The sleek black leather with gold shoulder caps and a gold puma crest on his chest reminded me of the glowing embers that fell from the sky and glowed on the creatures we brought back from The Wilds. This same ember powered our houses and motorized cars, our factories and trains. Our entire society ran on it, which made it more valuable than gold, more valuable than anything.

My father's inky black hair was slicked back perfectly without a strand out of place. Only in the past year did I notice the slight grays coming in at the sides, which he quickly dyed over to cover. My father would never want to be perceived as old. To him, getting old was a weakness he would stave off as long as he could.

He glanced down at me. The normally stoic emotions that he held softened when he gazed at me.

"You know, when you were born, I was sad that I didn't have a son first to fill the role of successor and heir."

My father was not one to mince words. He told you what was on his mind, even if it hurt.

I nodded. "I know. You've told me before."

The firstborn, whether male or female, would be the next ruler when he died or stepped down.

My father grasped my shoulders, and a proud

smile graced his face. "Little did I know you would be everything I wanted in an heir, daughter or not."

I swallowed hard, fighting a grin. That was a high compliment coming from him.

Bowing my head deeply, I cleared my throat. "Thank you, sir. I won't let you down."

He squeezed my shoulders before letting go. "Just claim the most powerful creature you can find and then we'll have nothing to worry about."

Those words were in stark contrast to Elaine's. She just wanted me to come back alive. My father wanted me to come back only if I bonded to a creature powerful enough to bring his legacy into a new age. I wasn't surprised though. He expected perfection.

"Even if it's a Talanagi?" I asked, meeting his gaze. I didn't know why I said it. It was almost taboo to talk about them and I regretted it the moment his brows drew downward.

"I'm not sure claiming an animal *that* powerful is smart." He laughed off my comment.

What he'd implied was that claiming a creature more powerful than Zuri would not be smart. I needed to be powerful enough to take over for my father, but not more powerful than him.

I swallowed hard.

"Yes, Father." I bowed my head lightly and then turned to leave, shifting my pack to my other shoulder on the way out.

"Tell Jace I said hello," he called as I shut the door behind me.

I crossed the well-manicured garden and slid my leg over my motorbike. My father loved Jace. He would arrange our marriage right now if I'd allow it. As the son of the commander of my father's fleet, Jace was a prime candidate to be my husband one day—something I was not quite ready for. At nineteen years old, marriage was not uncommon in our culture but it was reserved for the working class of society. Unless of course you were the emperor's heir, then you should be married by twenty with a male heir on the way. I knew it would be expected of me soon, and I loved Jace, but we had a little more time, so I wanted to enjoy life just dating for now.

I sat there for a second, surveying our fifty-acre property affectionately deemed "the emperor's palace" by the locals. It sat on top of a hill and looked out over the entire city. I could even see the Imperial Fleet Training Center from here. Inside, among the many bedrooms and bathrooms, we had a bowling alley, a library, and a salon. All fully staffed. Then outside were the horse barns, riding arena, and archery corner. It was amazing and yet never really felt like home to me. I often longed for our smaller country house in Cedar Creek, nestled among the forest in a quiet village.

I rode my bike through Riverine, the capital city of Amersea, with the wind in my hair and a smile on my face. This bike was a present from Elaine for my seventeenth birthday, and the freedom it gave me was something I treasured. The small chunk of ember, about the size of a marble, that powered the bike glowed within the motor against my calf.

After turning down Jace's street, I waved to his security guard, Yuri, who stood at the entrance of his property. He waved back, pushing the button to open the giant wrought-iron gates for me. Jace's father's estate was beautiful, with well-manicured lawns, a swimming pool, and a grand guesthouse that Jace now lived in. When we eventually married, we would likely buy a house in this area of town. It had enough security to be safe for us but wasn't overly pretentious like my father's place.

I parked my bike and hopped off of it, taking long strides through the garden to his guesthouse. Jace moved out of the main house last year and it afforded him freedoms I could only dream of. No governess, no parents asking where he was going, and he threw some killer weekend parties.

I wanted to surprise him on Lottery Day with the news my father had told me last night. He'd promised to rig the Lottery in favor of Jace's name being picked so that we could go to The Wilds together. It was frowned upon to pre-pick names, but as son of the commander of the Imperial Fleet, Jace would need to bond with a creature of great power to take after his father. He would never get that chance without getting picked in the Lottery.

The back door of Jace's guesthouse opened and I smiled, ready to greet him, when a young girl about my age, with long messy blonde hair, stepped out. She was wearing jeans with a shirt that was half tucked in and she had one boot on. She leaned down to put the other on when Jace stepped out, shirtless, and pulled her up for a face-eating kiss.

My soul left my body in that moment.

A whimper escaped my throat and Jace yanked his head away from the girl and met my gaze from across the yard.

"Shit," he grumbled.

The girl looked at me wide-eyed and wisely bolted in the opposite direction, limping as she fought to get her boot on the other foot.

My heart shriveled into dust and died right then and there, but somehow I kept breathing. How was I still alive? It felt like a hole had opened up inside of my chest and I just wanted it to swallow me up and eat me alive.

Jace cheated. He cheated on me, I told myself as I processed what was happening.

Jace ran for me, hands out as if trying to calm a raging bear. "Aisling... this was nothing—"

Him calling cheating on me "nothing" made my sorrow morph to red-hot rage in a millisecond.

I will kill him. I will rip out his guts and decorate that blonde chick's house with his entrails!

When he got within range, I punched him in the balls as hard as I could. Which was pretty damn hard. Elaine would be proud.

He fell to his knees with a groan, keeling forward, grasping between his legs and sucking in lungfuls of air.

Jace peered up at me in misery, his angelic blond hair swept over one beautiful blue eye. "Aisling, men have needs," he managed to get out. "She was the scratch to an itch. It meant nothing. I love you."

That *bastard!* He knew as future empress I was not allowed to bed a man until marriage. It ruined all prospects. Every year when I went to the doctor, my father had purity checks done on me. Being the emperor's daughter came with a huge responsibility. Jace had said he was fine with it, that he loved me and would wait, but clearly that wasn't true.

He was curled in the fetal position on the grass, and I stooped low and pressed my lips to his ear. "I trusted you with my entire heart," I breathed, each word threatening to drown me in sorrow. "I hope your dick rots off and you die in The Wilds." I growled the last part and stood, storming away from him.

"Aisling! Come on. You can't break up with me over this!" he bellowed after me, still curled in a ball on the lawn.

I was on my bike and halfway down his driveway when the first tear threatened to fall.

No. I was an Everhart. The daughter of the emperor of Amersea. I wouldn't let this derail my future. I wouldn't let Jace make me cry. I had a Lottery ceremony to attend. The entire country would be watching me to lead them. Every little girl would look to me when my name was called to go into The Wilds. I had to give them the confident smile that they deserved.

Jace Ledger was dead to me.

CHAPTER

TWO

Citizens came from all over Amersea to attend the Lottery: from the sea towns of the Marble Shores to the Evergreen Forest, and even from the former rival nation of Imbria. Imbria was once its own territory, with its own leader. A king. They had a completely different language and customs. They ate spicy food, drank tea with herbs in it, and the men wore colorful clothing without embarrassment. It wasn't until the Great Blackout fifteen years ago that our two sides fought and Amersea won, overtaking the terrorist nation and absorbing them. Imbria was now considered a state within Amersea, all under the control of my father.

I watched from the Lottery stage as the Imbrians poured into the great hall. They clustered together as if they were one. The women wore bright colored silk wrap dresses that were their custom. The men wore long tunic shirts that hung past their knees, and tight leggings of bright colors. It was said that the Imbrian people were particularly beautiful, and I had to admit that was true. Bronzed skin, eye color that varied from chocolate brown to honey yellow, to a rare light blue. They were tall, athletic and particularly lethal. Brought up in the ways of the warrior since they could walk, I knew better than to mistake the women's polite smiles for weakness. Their culture was a hospitable one, but they would cut your throat in your sleep if they deemed it necessary.

Because they were a nation that had been taken over by force, the Imbrian people had gone from one of the richest lands to an impoverished desert overnight. I didn't pity them though, it was their own fault. *They* caused the Blackout on our city, *they* attacked in the middle of the night, killing thousands of Amerseans without cause. They became greedy and they got what they deserved.

Now they bowed to *my* father, they paid taxes to *our* household, and they spoke our language. They were lucky we allowed them into the Lottery at all. Though only a small amount of Imbrians were permitted to enroll in it. We couldn't let them get too powerful. They might try to take us over again.

My gaze locked with one particularly tall and handsome Imbrian. He was built like a bear, as if he lifted weights in his sleep. His brown skin was covered in tattoos and small scars, and his black silky hair hung across his forehead in a glossy swoop as he glared at me with piercing blue eyes.

"Kohen Badshah," Elaine whispered beside me, and my stomach dropped.

That was Kohen Badshah? Son of the former king of Imbria? It was rumored that after losing his father to the war, and his privileged life, he'd taken to the streets and started a gang to survive. Leader of the Avasan gang, he was said to do anything for money, including stealing your organs and selling them on the black market.

I swallowed hard and glanced around the room some more. When I spied Jace groveling by his best friend Tucker, I rolled my eyes. He was giving me weepy puppy dog eyes, and I wanted to run over and beg my father to take his name out of the Lottery. But if I did that, I knew he would ask questions, and it wasn't becoming of a woman of my title to do something so emotional. So I sucked it up and then looked for my best friend, my only friend, Tetra. You might think being the future empress would have gained me popularity and an amazing social life. It did not. People either avoided me for fear they would piss me off, or they were fake nice because they wanted something from me. Tetra was the realest person I ever met. She told me my hair looked bad one day in third grade and the rest was history.

When my gaze landed on my blonde bestie, she

raised her cane high into the air and whooped loudly. "Go, Aisling!"

Heat rushed to my cheeks in embarrassment. I glanced at my father to see him roll his eyes. He wasn't a huge fan of Tetra. She was far too lower-middle class for him. Which was everything I loved about her. She brought a normalcy to my life that I craved.

I gave her a small wave and then used a hand sign language we'd invented in fifth grade, letting her know I needed to talk to her after, that it was important. She nodded, appearing concerned. I hadn't had time to tell her about Jace cheating on me. I'd had to go right from that back to my house to ride here with my father. I couldn't wait to hear her plans for a salacious revenge plot after the Lottery was over. When the sun set tonight, all of the candidates would go into The Wilds to claim their creature of choice, and I needed to know that if I died in there Tetra would shave Jace's head in his sleep or feed him herbs that made his balls fall off.

The Imperial Fleet song played out of the speakers and I brought my hand up in a salute as I stared at the Amersean flag. The two white stars on a black backdrop caused pride to swell within me. One star represented Amersea and the other Imbria. We'd been through a lot as a people, but were finally united under one flag after years of in-fighting—bonded by our shared common enemy to the north, Luska.

When the anthem stopped, Elaine bowed slightly

to me and then took her place beside my sisters offstage.

I lowered my hand and my father stood, walking over to the podium with Zuri by his side. "Today, you will be given the chance to become heroes, future leaders of the Imperial Fleet, defenders of Amersea against the Luskin tyrants."

The crowd burst into applause, but I noticed the Imbrians gave a modest, halfhearted clap while the others were shouting and even jumping up from their chairs. It had been over a decade since we'd conquered them and wounds still needed to heal. Maybe with the next generation.

My father gave a charismatic laugh. "Now I know you're excited, but only some of you will be chosen today."

The sound of groans filled the space and he nodded. "Good luck to all. Make us proud." He saluted and everyone saluted him back.

Next was my father's assistant. Lucinda was a young, excitable little thing who spoke in a shrill voice and smiled constantly. She'd been hired about five years ago to improve his public image, and at that point she took over the Lottery ceremony announcements.

I liked her well enough, when she wasn't talking too much.

"Hello, my beautiful Amerseans!" she called in a high-pitched voice. "You must be so excited to have this opportunity." Her creature, a beautiful peacock with electric blue glowing ember lines throughout his tail feathers, pranced on stage behind her.

Most creatures had really badass powers, and they endowed their human to have powers as well. Lucinda's was no different. Her peacock, Carlyle, could camouflage himself to his surroundings so that he could listen in on conversations without being seen. He had a mental link to Lucinda to tell her everything he heard. She was basically a spy, which I think was another reason my father hired her.

"Before we start the Lottery, we have a special candidate." She looked over at me and I stood at attention. "Miss Aisling Everhart, emperor heir, who by right of birth can bypass the Lottery system, will be given the opportunity to go into The Wilds and represent her family." She glanced to my father, who nodded once, and then to my sisters off stage, who clapped excitedly with Elaine by their side. The triplets wore matching purple dresses with white heels, ever the perfect ladies in public even at fourteen years old.

The crowd erupted into applause and I moved to stand in the front of the candidate line. For some reason, in that moment, my gaze flicked to Kohen Badshah. He didn't clap for me, though he watched me with a cocked head and keen expression.

I peered straight ahead and kept a military stance. Sometimes lottery candidates had a scarcity mentality in The Wilds. Thinking that all of the good creatures would get taken, they killed the weak candidates off first. I wanted anyone watching to know that I was military trained and wouldn't take any crap from any of them.

"Alright, let's see who else gets this amazing opportunity!" Lucinda called out through the microphone as she walked over to a giant glass ball at the side of the stage. It had a big crank on the left, and she reached out and spun it, watching the little white paper names tumble inside and mix around. The Lottery was voluntary, and even though you could die in The Wilds, we still had to cap the number of entrants each year. Citizens were clamoring for the opportunity to bond with a creature which would lead to a hefty sign-on bonus and a great job within the military. This would give them a steady income for the rest of their life. We'd been at war with the Luskins for four decades. This was solid and steady work which wouldn't be going away anytime soon.

I watched the crowd as they wiggled nervously in their seats. The entire stadium was packed with over two thousand potential candidates. No family members or friends were allowed as there just wasn't enough room, but they all waited outside to hear the results. I'd barely been able to sneak Tetra in for moral support.

Lucinda pulled the first name. My gaze flicked over to the small white paper to see that it was Angeline Sawyer. I didn't know her.

"Oh, how wonderful! Riverine's very own Jace Ledger!" Lucinda trilled, smiling as she then threw Angeline's name into a small incinerator beside the glass ball. A poof of smoke destroyed the evidence.

So that's how they rigged it. I had always wondered.

The crowd clapped wildly as my lying, cheating ex-boyfriend smiled proudly and stepped onto the stage to stand beside me.

"Stand at the end," I said to him under my breath without moving my lips.

"Aisling..." he pleaded.

I turned to him with a giant smile that hopefully the crowd would think was genuine, but it was my eyes that I infused with murder vibes.

He got the message and waved at everyone as he moved ten feet away from me to stand at the end of the white dotted line of the first row.

"Okay," Lucinda laughed nervously, clearly thrown by our little display. "Next is..." She reached into the glass bowl and I had to control my reaction when I saw the name Kohen Badshah.

My gaze flicked to his. He leaned forward in his seat as if anticipating. Would Lucinda read the real name? She glanced at my father and he gave her the smallest, barely perceptible nod.

"Kohen Badshah." Her voice was flat, void of any excitement. The crowd gave a polite clap, nothing overly rambunctious like they had for Jace and I.

My father was allowing the ex-prince of Imbria to go into The Wilds and possibly bond with a creature and become more powerful? Why would he do that? My mind scrambled for a reason. My father didn't do anything without thinking it through. Making the heir of Imbria more powerful so that he could possibly one day take back his country and go against us was stupid.

I eyed the Imperial Fleet officers, dressed in their black and gold uniforms, all stationed around the edges of the room, and noticed how their bodies tensed as Kohen walked across the front of the stage and towards the stairs that would bring him up here. As he got closer, I realized that he was massive, taller than I had previously thought, and more handsome too. He stepped right up next to me and peered down at me. "Am I allowed to stand next to you or should I go be with him?" He jerked his head towards Jace.

I clenched my jaw at the question, keeping my posture straight and erect. "Do whatever you want," I growled under my breath.

He nodded, stepping up directly beside me, arms hooked behind his back in a posture that mimicked mine, and that's when it hit me. My father was letting him in The Wilds because he was going to have him killed. If the prince of Imbria got taken out on the streets, there would be hell to pay, but in The Wilds, where ninety-five percent of us would die anyway, it would be considered normal.

My father was a genius.

Lucinda called the next name, and the next. One by one, candidates made their way to the stage. Most of them were cheering and smiling, but every once in a while you got a crier. Someone who didn't want to risk their life for their country was rare, but it happened. They were the first to die in The Wilds, too weak to even fend off a dog if it tried to bond with them. Their families were usually very poor and had begged them to enter for the money they might get if they made it out and survived boot camp. It was quite sad when you thought about it.

I began to drown out Lucinda's voice. This ceremony was taking forever, and I'd been to every single one since I was six years old. It got monotonous. I was quite surprised by how many Imbrians were being called up, and I was trying and failing not to be attracted to the sandalwood and honey scent coming off of Kohen Badshah. I should have told him he couldn't stand next to me. It was affecting my thoughts. Boys who smelled good were my weakness. I just wanted to stick my nose against his throat and inhale.

"Tetra Thindrel." Lucinda's voice snapped me back to the present and a collective gasp rang throughout the crowd.

I broke my military posture and dropped my arms, taking one step forward and out of the line. I glanced at Lucinda, who'd just read the name, and then at my best friend in the crowd. Tetra was frowning in disbelief, eyes as wide as an owl's.

I then looked back at my father. You put your name in the Lottery at the door. Tetra never would have put her name in there; she was given special permission to be here today just to support me. My father appeared alarmed, like some mistake had been made. People were watching, waiting to see what would happen. If anyone found out that these lotteries were rigged, it would start a civil war. By Tetra being here, they would assume she had put her name in, as family and friends were not permitted to come just to support each other, other than my sisters of course as they were future heirs. I wondered now if there had been a mix-up at the entrance and a guard had put her name in.

My father started to clap, smiling as if he had just heard the best news in the world, and my stomach sank. He was going to let it happen. He had to go along with it now that her name had been called or the Lottery would look suspect. Everyone else mirrored my father's clapping, but in a lower tone much like they did for when the Imbrian names were called.

I peered at Tetra in fear as she struggled with her cane, trying to make her way out of the aisle. Her right foot dragged limply behind her as she slowly moved over to the stairs. Everyone fell silent as they watched her struggle to mount the steps, her shoe squeaking as it trailed behind her.

My breath came out in ragged gasps as I fought for control and slipped back into my line. Beside me, Kohen suddenly backed away and I snapped my head in his direction as he took a place at the back row of candidates, leaving the spot next to me open for Tetra to slide into.

I frowned in confusion, wondering why he would do that.

Tetra was shaking like a leaf by the time she reached me, so I slid my hand into hers and squeezed, trying to convey to her that it would be okay, that I would die in The Wilds protecting her before I let anything happen to her.

More names were read, until finally the stage was full. Four hundred of us in all, crammed like cattle in a kill pen.

Which was probably what we were now.

For tonight, we either lived or died in The Wilds. Nothing else mattered.

THREE

"You're going to be okay," I told Tetra as I paced the changing room. She was struggling to get her uniform over her twisted foot. I wanted to help her but I knew she hated that. She'd been painfully silent since the Lottery. I'd begged my father afterwards to reverse the decision, but he told me it was done, witnessed in front of so many people. It would cause a rebellion to show preference to his daughter's best friend.

"I told my father to make sure the soldiers let you in as a visitor only, not to put your name in," I mentioned under my breath. "He promised. Someone screwed up and they will pay with their life."

She looked up at me then. Her deep brown eyes were in such contrast to her moonlight-colored hair. "Why should I get special treatment?" She shrugged and I frowned.

"Because you're my best *damn* friend and I won't let anything happen to you," I promised her.

She stared at the floor, avoiding my gaze. "I know how this works, Aisling. If you are distracted in The Wilds trying to keep me alive, you put yourself at risk. I won't let that happen. Just... make sure my mom is taken care of when I die."

I gasped at her resignation. "No!" I shoved her and she almost fell over. "Make sure yourself when we both walk out of The Wilds with creatures bound to us," I shot back.

She stood in her underwear, one leg in her black, issued pants, glaring at me with anger.

"There's the Tetra I know. The badass who won't let anyone put her down," I told her.

Her glare turned to a smirk. "Push me again and I'll punch you in the boob."

I grinned. My bestie was back, aggressive sarcasm and all. She was going to be fine. She had to be. I couldn't imagine a world without her in it.

"We're a team, Tetra. You and me. We can do this." She wasn't good with hand-to-hand combat, but she aced archery, and you were allowed endless weapons, so if she could get a bow and arrows somehow, we had a shot at keeping her alive.

She relented, reaching out to use me to steady herself so she could get her pants on. Now she was dressed like everyone else, excluding me. I wore the black military jumpsuit everyone else had on, but the golden puma emperor patch over my left breast signi-fied my station as successor to my father's rule.

"I didn't pack a bag," she informed me.

I nodded. "There's time. You go out and keep your mother calm. Tell her I'm going to make sure you survive this and I'll get you a three-day pack."

She released the breath she'd been holding. "Ais-ling, even if you protect me from other candidates, you can't keep me safe from the creatures."

"Watch me," I growled.

Her face softened as if she were talking to a child. "There are only two ways to leave The Wilds. In a body bag, or bonded to a creature."

"I know that," I said through clenched teeth. Why was she pushing this and being negative? I didn't want to talk about this right now. I wanted to believe it was possible for both of us to get out of this alive and bonded.

"The second a creature sees my limp, they will take me out. Too weak to bond," she said, and I reached up and plugged my ears like one of my little sisters.

Tears filled my eyes but I blinked them back. Ever-harts didn't cry.

"It's okay," she said, as she pulled my hands away from my ears. "I just want you to know that whatever happens in The Wilds... I'm okay with it."

"Stop," I begged, my voice nearly a whimper. We were crammed in a small changing room and I knew the girls around us could probably hear at this point.

How the hell had we gotten here? My best friend with the bum foot was going into The Wilds. It hurt worse than Jace's cheating. It hurt worse than anything I could think of.

She changed the subject: "What did you want to tell me after? It was big news?"

Oh right. Maybe we needed a subject change.

"Jace cheated on me. We need to plot a big revenge."

Her eyes flew wide. "That bastard. I'll kill him in The Wilds myself." She gripped her cane to illustrate her point.

I grinned. "Just keep that attitude and you're going to do fine. All you need is one creature to see that fighting spirit and—"

"Take pity on me?" she interrupted.

I shook my head. "See your true worth."

I noticed that my words made a difference. Tetra stood a little taller then and I pulled back the curtain to exit the dressing room. "Finish getting ready and then go talk to your mom. I'll be back with a three-day pack for you."

She nodded and I slipped out of the dressing room. Sure enough, the other girls avoided my gaze as I passed, which told me that they were totally listening to the louder parts of our fragile conversation.

"If any of you tries to pick her off as an easy kill in The Wilds, I'll have my father make sure your families work in the iron mines for the rest of their lives," I said boldly.

All of the girls looked farther down at their feet, except for one. An Imbrian. She laughed.

"What's so funny?" I stepped over to her, not in the mood for any crap right now.

"My family already works in the mines," she said casually, and her friend chuckled. I recognized her; she had been sitting with Kohen Badshah earlier. She had four piercings in each ear, and the right side of her head was shaved. Her long brown hair was in a braid over one shoulder, and I couldn't help but remark on her beauty. She must be in Kohen's little Avasan gang.

I lowered my voice, knowing I had to stop this insubordination right now or it would grow. "Well, then, I'll have to think up a special punishment for them. How does that sound?"

The grin was wiped from her face, and for a moment I felt bad for saying it, but I would do anything to keep Tetra safe. If people thought she was an easy target, they were going to be sorely mistaken.

"Relax, princess," she said. "I don't bite unless provoked." She then gave me her back, a disrespectful move, but one I didn't care about. I had more pressing matters at hand, like keeping my best friend alive.

Every candidate who came to the Lottery packed a three-day bag for their time out in The Wilds should they be picked. This pack would keep you alive out there while you hunted your creature... or they hunted you. Tetra hadn't brought one because I'd told her that she wouldn't be picked, and now the buses were leaving to take us out to the border lands and if I didn't get a pack for her she was as good as dead.

I burst from the dressing room with my own pack on my back and ran outside, where the families of those who were not picked had gathered. They now walked away en masse with their children, heading across Emberlane Park to the underground train station that would lead them north, probably to Cedar Creek where they lived.

I scanned the crowd in panic, searching for any face I knew.

Come on. Come on.

"Charline!" I screamed across the park and she turned, her mother, father, and three siblings in tow.

Taking great strides, I bolted across Main Street and into the park named after the very valuable substance that fueled the trains, buses, and factories that ran our city.

Charline was a strong girl. She would have made an amazing candidate to go into The Wilds. I knew she had aspirations to join the Imperial Fleet, and because she was not chosen and would not bond with a creature, she would have to join as a human and would live her life in a grunt position. Her face was downcast; I knew she was disappointed about not being chosen. We'd gone to school together at the Imperial Fleet Academy from grade six to twelve and she was a decent person. She didn't kiss my ass based on who my father was, and also didn't seem scared of me.

"Sorry about your name not being chosen," I told her.

She nodded sadly. "Thanks, Aisling. Good luck out there."

I eyed the pack on her back. "Hey, Tetra wasn't prepared for her name to be called..."

Dawning understanding shone on Charline's face and she gripped the straps of her pack tightly. "I would, I mean I want to help Tetra, but this stuff was expensive. I was going to give it to Truly for her Lottery." She looked at her fourteen-year-old sister.

Truly and my sisters were friends.

Charline's family wasn't well off. Her father worked in a machine factory and her mother cleaned houses on the weekends.

I reached up and ripped the emperor's patch off my chest, causing the garment to tear slightly, and handed it to her. "These threads are made with real gold. It should cover the cost of the pack and more, but if not, you can go to my house, ask for my governess, Elaine. Show her the patch and she will pay you in imperial coin if you prefer."

Her eyes widened and she peered back at her mother and father.

The horn sounded for the bus caravan leaving for The Wilds and I rocked on my heels, praying to the stars that she would say yes. I had no other options.

I drove my point home: "Elaine will pay you whatever amount you ask. Triple what you spent on the pack. *And* you can keep the patch." Elaine would. She would see the patch and know that I had given it freely. Charline was strong, but not strong enough to rip it from my chest.

Her mother nodded, and I sighed in relief as Charline unslung the pack.

"Is there a hunting knife?" I asked her.

She bobbed her head. "Water canteen, two days' clothes, tarp for sleeping, dried meats, matches, a tourniquet. It's fully loaded, we've been building it all year." Her eyes welled with tears and my heart pinched.

"Hey, enroll in the Imperial Fleet anyway and work your way up. Even without a creature you can get a good paying station. Especially with how talented you are with a blade," I counseled her. She was damned good with a dagger.

She brightened at that. "You think so?"

I nodded. "When I'm empress one day, I'll even hire you on my personal guard." It was a promise. I never gave someone my word if I didn't intend to keep it. Charline was amazing with a blade and loyal to Amersea, and as my father taught me, loyalty was invaluable.

She stood a little straighter then. "O-okay."

Her mother and father smiled, looking pleased.

The word of the emperor's daughter was as good as a signed job contract.

I saluted her and she saluted me back. Taking the pack on one shoulder, now carrying two, I wished her well and then ran as fast as I could to the line of a dozen sleek silver buses, large chunks of ember glowing under the hoods.

Everyone was already inside with only a few stragglers making their way in the open doors. I groaned under the weight of two packs, but pushed through the pain of my burning muscles. Tetra waved me over to one bus from the window where she sat inside, and I made it just in time to toss both of our packs in the storage compartment under the bus and then slip in line.

Jace's voice came from beside me. "Aisling, let me explain this morning…"

I growled. Was he serious? We were about to go and fight for our lives in just hours and he wanted to talk about why he'd cheated on me?

I pulled the blade from the holster on my thigh and held it up to his throat, causing his eyes to go wide.

"Jace Ledger, if you attempt to explain your man whoring *one* more time, I swear to every star in the sky I will gut you like a fish the second we get to The Wilds, just to shut you up."

Hurt flashed across his face and then his gaze fell to my lips. "But—"

I pushed the blade deeper until one drop of blood trickled down his neck.

His gaze darkened and he snapped his mouth shut and wisely stepped away from me, moving past me to get onto the bus. The second he left, I was staring down Kohen Badshah, who had just heard every word of what I'd said and was apparently standing right behind Jace.

I swallowed hard, sheathing my blade as I tried to read his expression. It was blank, like he either had no emotions or he was good at hiding them. I was guessing the latter.

Why had he stepped out of line during the Lottery so Tetra could stand next to me? It didn't make sense. Unless he had some ulterior motive…

I raised one eyebrow. "Enjoying the show?"

His tongue swiped out and licked his lips, causing my stomach to warm at the sight. He was undoubtably the most handsome man I'd ever laid eyes on—and completely untouchable to me. My father would murder me and make Valor his heir without hesitation.

He stepped closer, cocking his head to the side, and peered at the opening of the bus where Jace had just entered. "If you want me to, I can make him disappear."

Surprise rushed through my body, which was quickly doused in fear. I had been joking about killing Jace to shut him up. I still cared about the bastard, I just didn't want to hear his excuses for why he was screwing some blonde on Lottery Day when we had been saving ourselves for each other.

"No thanks," I said and turned, confused.

I got onto the bus and found Tetra. She had saved me a spot, and I slunk into the seat beside her. My mind was still spinning with what had just happened outside.

"Got you a pack. How did your mom take it?" I asked her.

"She said she would start saving for my funeral costs."

I barked out a laugh. That sounded like Bethel. Brutally honest and sarcastic. I loved her like my own mother. "But seriously, did you assure her that I would take care of you?" I turned to face my bestie.

She shook her head. "I didn't need to. She said she knew that we would either both come out alive or there would be two body bags when our name was called."

I grinned, happy that Bethel had confidence in me to keep Tetra safe.

The bus started on its journey and a short girl with pink dyed hair that I didn't recognize as being from Riverine walked over to our seat and crouched down.

She met my gaze. "We are forming an alliance. You want in?" she asked me.

Though she was small, I could see her arms were

stacked with muscle, and she had an eyebrow and lip ring for whatever that was worth.

"Who is we?" I asked her.

She flicked her head to the back of the bus where there was a group of meatheads speaking in hushed tones, Jace being one of them.

"Pass," I told her. We needed an alliance if we wanted to survive, but I wasn't so desperate to join Jace and his idiot friends.

Her face fell. "We can protect your friend." She flicked her gaze to Tetra, who crossed her arms in annoyance. She didn't like being talked about like she was fragile, and normally she wasn't, but in this case she was.

"So can we," a familiar female voice called from the seat in front of me, and I looked up to see the Imbrian girl from the locker room. The one with the four earrings who had laughed at me.

"I'm Anika." She held out a fist and I frowned. Reaching out, I bumped her fist but glared at her.

She peered at the pink-haired chick. "You can run along now. She passed."

I liked her attitude when it wasn't aimed at me.

The girl with the pink hair growled but took off, walking back to the end of the bus.

Anika tipped her head over to front of the bus, where seven people were huddled and talking. "We want to keep our alliance small, but we have room for two more people. We plan to sleep in shifts and watch each others' back during creature fights."

I stared at the group she had indicated. Five of them looked to be in Kohen's gang, six including Anika, but two of them I recognized as top students at the Imperial Fleet Academy where I went to school. Roc and Alek had the power and skills of ten men combined. I sat a little straighter then, seriously considering this. But then my gaze locked with Kohen and he tipped his head as if telling me he agreed with Anika's choice to invite me.

I snort-laughed then. "You realize I'm the heir to the emperor's throne, right?"

She looked at me like I was an idiot. "Yeah, that's why we want you."

I crossed my arms and sighed. "I can't be in an alliance with Kohen Badshah."

It was bad enough the group was made up of mostly Imbrians. Though they were lethal and respected fighters, they could not be trusted not to slit my throat in my sleep for the retaliation my father had inflicted on their land after the Great Blackout.

Was she insane? Was Kohen insane? My father *killed* his father in the Blackout War. He was probably planning to poison me in my sleep.

She scrunched up her face at that. "We don't care about politics, princess. We just want to survive the night."

I peered at Tetra, who was picking the skin of her fingernails. Right now on this bus with heat and sunlight, everything seemed great, but when we entered The Wilds and the sun dipped over the horizon, all manner of hell would unleash and an alliance would be smart. The right alliance.

"I can't, I'm sorry. I'm not an idiot. I know Kohen probably wants me dead," I told her. I'd be better off tucking tail and begging Jace's group to form an alliance.

She glared at me, teeth clenched as she leaned forward and got right in my face. "You don't know shit about Kohen Badshah."

Then she pushed off the seat and went back to the group, shaking her head.

Whoa. Possessive much? Maybe they were dating.

Tetra peered at me. "That was the right choice. You wouldn't be able to sleep knowing Kohen and his gang were watching your back. It sounds like a trap."

I sighed in relief that she agreed with me. "Maybe I should go back over and talk to Jace—"

"Stars no! That bastard doesn't deserve to be in an alliance with you. It's taking every ounce of self-control I have not to shove this cane up his ass." She shook the giant pearlescent ball of her cane in my face and I grinned.

"I love you. Please tell me you've started a revenge plot for when we survive this."

She nodded. "I have. It all starts with hair remover cream in his shampoo bottle."

I barked out in laughter, so loud that several people looked my way, including Kohen and his friends. I narrowed my gaze at him but he kept his face calm, betraying nothing. I hated when a guy was hard to read.

He broke away from his group and walked towards us, causing the breath to hitch in my throat. I grasped the hilt of my dagger and swallowed hard as he walked right over to me, looming over both Tetra and I.

"Can I speak to you privately, Aisling?" he asked.

I glanced at Tetra and she shrugged, as if saying, *You're in charge.*

I sighed, curious as to what he might say.

Standing, I met him face to face, or more like face to chest because he was so tall, but he didn't back up as one might expect and so we were inches from each other. I could feel his warm breath splash over me and inhaled the scent of cardamom and ginger. *Spiced tea.* The Imbrians were known for it.

After an agonizing few seconds he stepped to the side and walked over to a few empty seats. He sat first, against the window, and gestured that I sit next to him in the aisle seat.

I looked left and right, knowing this would start rumors I didn't need. Instead of sitting, I knelt on one knee so that I was still visible to everyone. I didn't need anyone saying something happened between Aisling Everhart and Kohen Badshah that didn't.

"What?" I asked in low tones.

He looked up at me with a vulnerable expression, the first time he'd let any of his cards show. "If I leave the alliance, will you join? I know you have to be careful with your image."

I frowned. Was he serious? "Why would you do that?"

He swallowed hard. His Adam's apple was covered by part of a snake tattoo which moved when he swallowed, and gave off some serious *I've been to prison* vibes.

"I want Anika, Nikhil, Meera, Dev, and Kian to be safe. They're like family to me." His timbre had changed from the cold tones he was using earlier, and with each name he listed of his friends, the emotion built in his voice.

Against my better judgment, I dropped to sit beside him and almost regretted it immediately. His scent washed over me, along with the heat of his body and my thighs clenched in response. "You seem perfectly capable of protecting them," I told him, eyeing his gigantic muscles which pulled at the fabric of his shirt.

He nodded. "Normally yes." He met my gaze then and I nearly lost myself in his ice-blue eyes. "But I know your father will have plans to assassinate me in there, and when I'm gone they will need a strong leader to get them out alive. Someone like you. Someone trained for this."

I couldn't help the sharp intake of breath that pulled through my lips. "I—"

"Don't bother denying it. It's what I would do," he said, facing forward this time, staring at the leather seatback in front of him as if it held some important information.

He knew my father's plan was to kill him... and he was trying to look out for his friends?

"You won't stand a chance without an alliance," I informed him.

He nodded. "I'll make one with the weaker candidates. It will buy me time to maybe bond with a creature, but if the emperor wants me dead, I will only be a danger to my friends."

He was right. If my father wanted him dead, he'd have his spies in The Wilds take out his entire alliance.

"And why do you think I would do you a favor?" I asked, sizing him up. He just said he would do the same as my father, meaning he would take out his competition and keep them from getting stronger. And how the hell was I even entertaining this conversation? It felt borderline treasonous.

He looked at me again. "Because of how you reacted when they called your friend's name. You would do anything to protect her, right?"

My heart was in my throat. I simply nodded.

"I need someone like that looking out for my

family, and in return they will make sure not a *single* hair on your friend's head is touched."

I had to control my breathing. It felt like he was staring into my soul. He saw me, like *really* saw me for who I was, and I wasn't sure what he thought.

"Okay," I blurted out before I could lose my nerve. "For Tetra. But if I join the team I want to be in charge. It's the only way I can ensure things will run smoothly and we get out alive."

He dipped his head. "Done. I have heard that Amerseans are a people of their word. That to go back on your word would drive you to a shame so deep you would kill yourself."

It was true. Our custom was that we gave our word, and shook on it, and the deal was done. No need for contracts or signatures.

I nodded. "That's right. You have my word. I will protect your family to the best of my ability." I used the word *family* because he had.

Reaching out, he extended his hand in the Amersean way. I took his warm fingers in mine, ignoring the way his touch made my heart beat a mile a minute. We shook, and then I left the seat before rumors could start.

"Get up," I told Tetra, and jerked my head to the front of the bus. "We're joining an alliance."

As we made our way to the front, Kohen started to speak to the stragglers in the middle, grouping them up into a large alliance of over twenty people.

I met his gaze from across the bus and he subtly nodded. All emotion gone from his face; he was back to looking like a ruthless warrior. Did I just play into a trap?

What the stars did I just do?

FOUR

We reached the outer edge of the city that led to The Wilds just before sunset. The long stretch of road suddenly went from sparse trees to lush forest. The Wilds were like a vein running right through the center of Amersea and Imbria on either side of the river. It had been there since the dawn of time, and the creatures inside could not leave it unless they were bound to one of us. If they tried, they died at the border, gasping for air as if suddenly deprived of oxygen. They needed their bond to us to be free and move around the world, and we needed them to become more powerful in the war. It was a win-win. Some old tales said that The Wilds didn't exist until one day a giant star fell from the sky and cracked into the earth. They said it split the sky open, which was what caused the ember to rain down, only over The Wilds, and then the star brought the creatures down to the earth. But the story was told in so many different fantastical ways I never knew what to believe. All I knew was the bond was what allowed the creatures to live outside The Wilds and we needed them in the war.

One thing that always amazed me when I came to this part of the country that held The Wilds was the ember. I peered out the window up at the fire sky as we approached. Everywhere else in the country the sky was blue, but here, over The Wilds, it was an angry orange and yellow. The ember rained from the fire sky in varying sizes, from small glowing flakes to huge chunks the size of marbles—to the biggest one we ever found, the size of a melon. That melon-sized ember still powered our steel factory today, and it was found over a hundred years ago. Though now it was more like the size of a walnut, slowly shrinking each year with energy expenditure. It burned clean and wasn't combustible if struck, so there was no danger in that. You could heat your entire house for a whole winter with one ember flake the size of a sunflower seed. I'd put a chunk into my motorbike the year I got it and it still hadn't run out.

Ember was what fueled our society, more precious than all gold and silver, and The Wilds was teeming with it. A large portion of our Imperial Fleet went to guarding The Wilds from ember thieves. The soldiers stood every ten yards along the perimeter on both the Imbrian and Amersean sides. It was a well-known practice among candidates to take one piece of ember you found on your trip in The Wilds. My father allowed it for all candidates, but it was otherwise strictly prohibited unless you were an embersmith. The embersmith's were checked before and after their ember collection shift and all ember found was given to the emperor for sorting, assuming they made it out alive. My father divvied out portions to keep the city running, but it was a big responsibility. But for the candidates, willing to risk their lives to keep fighting in the war, he allowed them to take the biggest piece they could find. It was a little nest egg you could share with your family when you got it—if you made it out.

Though finding ember was at the back of our minds. First and foremost, we needed to be tracking creatures and staying alive. The bus approached the border of The Wilds and I instinctively held my breath as we drove through the almost clear barrier that created a bubble of sorts, like walls from the ground to the fire sky, all the way around The Wilds. To the trained eye it was obvious and I'd been here with my father plenty of times but my fellow Lottery winners didn't seem to notice that we had just officially entered The Wilds. Our scientist thought it was what kept the habitat safe for the creatures, but it didn't harm us. We could breathe just fine inside the almost invisible wall.

As if my very thinking had brought it up, I stared at the small flakes of ember, no larger than a winter snowflake, as they fell to the ground outside the bus. It glowed its magnificent orange hue, like it contained living fire.

"Ember!" someone screamed, and everyone ran to that side of the bus to watch the flecks sprinkle from the sky. The windows to the bus opened and the candidates reached their arms out, trying to grasp the small particles.

I glanced at Anika, noticing she was the only one from our alliance, other than Tetra, who didn't rush to see the ember.

"Aren't you interested in what it looks like up close?" Tetra asked her.

She flicked her gaze at my friend and held up her hand. I hadn't noticed it before but she was missing the pinky finger of her right hand. "I've held more ember than anyone on this bus. My father is an ember-smith, and my mother and I worked in the sorting center."

Tetra peered down at her lap submissively and my gut tightened. When Anika had said her family worked in the mines, I had assumed the iron or copper mines in the northeastern mountains of Imbria. But now I knew she meant the ember sorting facility, commonly referred to as the ember mine among the people. The facilities were placed inside of the mountains around our region, with only one entrance for security purposes. Though ember was not carved out of a mountain, the sorting facility felt very much like a mine, with no sunlight and little ventilation. The working conditions there were grueling, and most didn't survive more than twenty years in that line of work without getting repeated lung infections.

"You stole?" I asked her, eyeing the missing finger. It was common practice in the sorting facilities to take a finger from a thief who tried to bring ember home in their pockets. They had creatures who could smell it on you, even the tiniest piece. First offense finger, second offense hand, third offense your life.

She growled at me but said nothing.

I rolled my eyes. The thief got what she deserved. I wasn't going to feel sorry for her. All ember was owned by the emperor, my father, and if she stole from him she stole from me and our entire country. It cost more than she could ever imagine to keep our beautiful nation running the way it was. Free school until twelfth grade, free healthcare for all regardless of station, work programs for the poor, an elite army, clean water, and prosperous farmland. Did she think if we let everyone steal the ember that she would have such a nice life?

Even Imbria, which had been reduced to rubble over a decade ago in the war, had been built back up to its former beauty in most places. Yes, there were still pockets of poverty and slums, but my father invested a lot of coin to take care of the newest members of our country, and if she stole from him then she was ungrateful.

Fool!

I crossed my arms and gave her my back. I was doing this to keep Tetra alive. I just needed to focus on the task at hand and remain unemotional like Elaine had taught me.

I whistled and called our group back over. There were nine of us in all.

I introduced myself to each one and learned their names. The males Dev, Kian, and Nikhil, were stacked with muscle and tattoos, much like Kohen, and looked like experienced fighters. Anika was clearly a badass if I were going on personality and attitude alone, but I worried about Meera.

I eyed the weaker-looking Imbrian. She was scrawny and shy, and seemed like she couldn't even heft a sword. "When we move in The Wilds, we move as a team," I told everyone. "We walk in a circle with Meera and Tetra in the center."

Meera made a noise in her throat as if she was offended, but Anika nodded as if she agreed with me.

"Now, imperial law states that murder in The Wilds is legal, so don't think anyone is going to be scared of being carted off to prison," I stated.

A somber mood fell on our group. It was claimed that in order to get the best creature you had to sometimes fight a fellow candidate, and death resulted. But the rule had blurred into it being okay to murder under any grounds. All I knew was that I was going to watch my back, even among this alliance. I'd practiced for this my entire life. I could go forty-eight hours without sleep if I had to. I brought coffee satchels for just that. This could all be a ruse to get Kohen's friends to kill me. But I had to partner up with someone for Tetra's sake, so why not them? The Avasan gang was notorious for the brutal way in which they dealt with their enemies. I didn't know how much was rumor and how much was true, but the scars on the knuckles of every Imbrian here told me most were probably true.

"Alright, we are almost there. List your talents quickly so I know how to use you. Anything that will help us survive." I started with one of my ex-classmates, Roc. He was a brute nearly Kohen's size, with a shaved head of brown hair and hazel eyes. He'd proudly slept with half the school, but he was really talented with hand-to-hand combat and hunting.

"Hand-to-hand combat, compound bow hunting, pleasing women," he said, and waggled his eyebrows at Anika.

A few of our group burst into snickers, but Anika wasn't fazed. She just gave him her middle finger and rolled her eyes. I actually kind of liked her. Her bitchiness was comforting. I hated fake-nice people.

Alek was next, another of my former classmates. His bright blond hair and blue eyes always put him in the pretty boy category for me. He was good with swordsmanship, foraging, and animal tracking. The Imbrians went next.

"Removing organs with a kitchen knife," Nikhil said with an eerie smile.

My eyebrows shot up and he and all the others burst into laughter.

I sighed. "Alright, you had me. Come on. Get serious."

"Street fighting. I don't need a fancy weapon, I can remove your eyes with a stick," he said. "And also pleasing the ladies." He winked at Tetra, who grinned. She liked bad boys. We were in trouble.

Roc reached out and fist-bumped Nikhil.

"Next," I sighed, wondering if these guys knew that they were literally never going to get laid again if they died in here.

"I'm fast, and good with throwing knives," Dev said, opening his jacket to reveal over twenty throwing knives. That was helpful.

"I like to blow things up," Kian said with a straight face.

I eyed his pack. "Did you bring a bomb or something?"

He just grinned in response.

Geez, these people were kind of maniacs. I was glad I was with them.

I peered at Anika.

She yawned as if bored. "I can kill a man with my bare hands and he won't even see me coming."

Now it was my time to roll my eyes. Egomaniac. *Whatever.*

I pointed to Tetra. "She won't admit it but she's amazing with a bow and has more courage than anyone here. She also has extensive knowledge of military strategy and logistics."

Tetra smiled at me gratefully. I knew she wouldn't want to talk about herself. Especially with no combat military training. She went to the Imperial Fleet Academy with us but only because my father got her accepted on account of my begging. She didn't take any physical battle classes and majored in war theory, sticking to the books and academic side of things. She was extremely intelligent, which wouldn't do her much good in The Wilds.

"And how about you, princess?" Anika asked. I wasn't sure yet if the *princess* thing was an insult. I was pretty sure it was. The Imbrians had royalty in their leadership, so calling me a princess was making me an equal to Kohen, their prince. My father stripped him of that title when he took over Imbria, but his people still considered him as such.

"I'm good with anything sharp, hand-to-hand combat, and leading teams. I've also taken survival training to live off the land and endure extreme situations," I said as casually as I could. Stating your strengths was weird.

Meera raised her hand and I realized I'd completely forgotten her. I nodded, giving her permission to speak: "I know how to make an odorless and tasteless poison from herbs found in The Wilds." She smiled.

I shared a look with Tetra. We were definitely with the most lethal alliance in this cohort.

"Remind me not to put you on cooking duty," I told her.

She nodded seriously, not getting my joke, but I saw Anika crack a smile.

The bus slowed then and pulled to a stop in a line of other buses.

This was it. Most would fall on the first night from creature attacks and fellow candidates. If you made it to night two, you would likely be weakened, injured, and exhausted. It was on that night you needed to bond with your creature, because going to night three was never really an option. We packed for three days, but no one lasted that long in The Wilds. It was too intense.

"Alright, let's move out," I ordered my team, catching Kohen's gaze as we passed.

I was going to treat this like an exercise at the Imperial Fleet Academy. I was squadron leader and these were my teammates. Goal number one: keep everyone alive. Goal number two: bond with a creature. Goal number three: survive said bonding and make it out in one piece.

I wished I felt more confident. Truth be told, I didn't have many weaknesses, I was raised not to. But

I hadn't expected Tetra to be here with me. Her friend-ship was my weakness, and I feared Kohen had exploited it and tricked me into falling right into his trap.

There was only one way to find out if that were true...

CHAPTER
FIVE

"You will walk, not run, into The Wilds!" Brigita, an Imperial Fleet captain, shouted to the amassed candidates. She wore Fleet-issued fatigues that looked like they'd seen recent battle. The hem of her pant leg was shredded, and a small bloody cut had dried on her cheek.

Her creature, Sandor, was a lioness, and she prowled behind her, staring us all down like we were prey. Orange glowing ember stripes ran down the length of her back.

We were technically already inside The Wilds, with the fire sky above us and the thick trees all around us, but there wasn't much action at these outer edges. My father had too many soldiers out here. The creatures knew to stay away; they didn't want to test the boundaries for fear of dying.

"Once you are in there," she said, "you are on your

own. We are not permitted to help, as this would defeat the purpose of only allowing the strongest into boot camp."

Boot camp, commonly referred to as *hell month*. It was four weeks of training that brought candidates to mental and physical exhaustion, and the envy of everyone my age from the Marble Shores of Amersea to the Northeastern Mountains of Imbria. We all wanted in, and the only way you could gain entrance was to be chosen in the Lottery and bonded to a creature here in The Wilds. If you graduated, you were guaranteed a top posting in the Imperial Fleet and a paycheck every week.

"My brother is stationed at Thunder Cliff base," one girl said beside us, "so I'm hoping to bond with a water creature."

Thunder Cliff sat just at the front of the war and saw the most action. They were right on the edge of the water, and those who bonded to a water creature were automatically sent there so they could slink into the ocean and spy on the Luskins. My father would kill me if I went and bonded with a creature that would cause me to be bound to water. No thank you.

Brigita cleared her throat. "Stay alert, stay alive, and good luck." She pushed a button on her airhorn and everyone began walking quickly through the giant trees and into the darkness that was The Wilds.

I began to walk at Tetra's pace as she struggled to use her cane while stumbling over the uneven footing. People pressed around us and the landscape got rockier. As I passed Brigita, her hand snaked out and grasped me by the upper arm. She pulled me close to her, narrowing her gaze on the Imbrians in my group.

Leaning into my ear, she whispered, "Steer clear of Kohen Badshah," and then released me.

I frowned, but gave her a nod and then we kept walking.

What did that mean? Had she already heard that we'd spoken on the bus, or did she just see that my alliance included some of his people and wanted to warn me that he was bad news? Or was she warning me that my father put a hit out on him and she didn't want me hurt when that went down?

I eyed Kohen. He was walking with all the rejects from the bus. Small, lanky, and awkward candidates followed him like puppy dogs after their master. Kohen was pointing to trees and people and things on the ground, giving them some lessons on how to survive, I presumed.

"He's not who you think he is," Anika said, watching me study him.

I snort-laughed. "He's probably worse."

We stopped at a sign planted right in front of the road, the place where all of our packs had been lined up in a row.

You are entering The Wilds. Entrance without a bonded creature is forbidden unless you are a candidate.

And if you are a candidate, good luck. May the stars guide your way.

"Bond or body bag. Let's do this," Roc said, rolling out his neck and hefting his pack.

"Need help?" I asked Tetra as she readjusted her pack, while trying to balance on her cane.

She shot me a glare. "Are you going to wipe my ass, too, Aisling?"

I swallowed hard. Point taken. I was babying her too much.

I backed off, tightening the straps of my own pack, and kept walking.

The imperial soldiers that we passed gave me a salute of respect.

"Make us proud," one of them said.

No pressure.

If I came out bonded to a Labrador, my father would definitely be disowning me. And the people of Amersea right along with them. They expected a powerful creature to bond with me—but not too powerful so that I overshadowed my father.

I sighed. Everything was political when you were the emperor's daughter.

I led my group past the sign and into The Wilds, peering up at the fire sky in awe. Little glowing specks rained down around us, almost too small for the eye to see. Still, there was value in them if you gathered enough. I'd been to the edge of The Wilds with my father over a dozen times but never had I walked into the belly of the beast.

"I want hands on weapons. We could be attacked at any moment by an offended creature," I snapped, after I noticed at least half of my group walked lazily and without a care. Tetra included.

They remedied the issue and I relaxed a little.

"Wouldn't they only attack us if it was to bond?" Tetra asked.

She never paid attention in creature class. She assumed her entire life that she wouldn't be getting one.

I opened my mouth to speak when Anika started talking: "Creatures in The Wilds will kill you because they don't like the way you smell, or because you got close to their nest of eggs, or a hundred different reasons."

I nodded in agreement with her. "And sometimes you can use the opportunity to submit that creature to your will and bond with them."

"And others will kill you because your weakness offends them and they want to prove they are more dominant," Anika added.

Dammit, I liked her the more I got to know her. She was smart, no nonsense, and knew her stuff. In another lifetime we might have been friends.

The deeper into the forest we walked, the more a supernatural darkness fell upon us. The temperature dropped, and wide thin slices of ember floated from the sky like falling feathers.

Dev's hand snaked out and grabbed one, only to drop it on the floor as he hissed in pain, retracting his fingers to his mouth. It was smoking.

Anika grinned. "The big pieces are hot as they fall. You have to wait a few minutes for them to cool off. You should see my father's fingers, scarred from nail to wrist with burn marks."

He frowned, eyeing the chunk on the ground with its mystical orange and yellow glow, black charred marks at the edges almost like coal coming out of a hot fire.

"We keep moving," I announced. "There will be plenty of time to grab some ember before we leave," I assured them.

A twig snapped beside me and I flung out with my sword, stopping only when I recognized the person. The tip of my blade rested at Kohen's throat.

His eyes were stormy as they stared into mine. "Well, it's good to know I left them in capable hands."

I pulled the blade back, exhaling. "What the hell are you doing sneaking up on us like that?"

He held out a small, gray cloth zipper case and peered over at Anika. "These somehow got in my pack." There was worry in his gaze, and I looked over at Anika to see fear flash in her eyes.

She snatched it from him and stuffed it in her bag. "Thanks," she muttered.

"Good luck, everyone," Kohen told them, and then disappeared into the woods.

"What's in that?" I asked her as we started to walk again, Tetra and Meera in the middle like we'd discussed.

"None of your business," she snapped.

I rolled my eyes but kept walking, scanning the trees for threats. She wouldn't be stupid enough to bring drugs into The Wilds. The last thing you wanted was to be inebriated during an attack. Maybe they were tampons or something embarrassing.

A hair-raising scream echoed throughout The Wilds and we all froze for a second.

"Nothing we can do. Move on. Worry about your own teammates," I coached. It felt heartless, but running through the forest in the direction of that yell might get us killed.

After an hour of walking, the sound of trickling water pulled my attention up ahead and I immediately began to push our group north and to the left. Nothing good lived in that water, just creatures of untold power that would take you out as you attempted to wash your face.

"Anyone dying to be posted at Thunder Cliff?" I asked. Bonding with a water creature was generally frowned upon as it really restricted your movements.

"Nope," was the resounding answer.

The sounds of The Wilds seemed to only get louder the farther we walked. Growls, chitters, caws, slithers.

It had my heart fluttering in my chest and all of my senses on heightened alert.

Something skittered across the leaves up ahead and I held up my fist. Our group stopped walking. I could hear another team talking farther in the woods, but about ten feet to our right, behind a thick fern, was the purple glow of a creature. They could choose when they wanted to turn that off, so the fact that the animal was currently showing its power meant it was preparing to attack or it wanted to be seen. I put two fingers to my eyes and then pointed to the fern. Our group all snapped their heads in that direction and the creature stepped out from behind the bush.

It was a beautiful white-tailed fox, not powerful enough for me, it was quite small and submissive by the looks of it. I could tell by how it had quickly dropped my gaze. I kept my voice low. "I know this feels quick, and we probably didn't expect this so soon, but this is a perfect creature for Meera or Tetra," I said.

"I agree." Anika flicked her gaze to Meera.

The small girl took a deep shaky breath but seemed ready to fight. I peered at Tetra and my stomach sank when I saw the raw fear coating her. She'd never fought anything. Asking her to do this would take time.

"Meera, it's all yours if you feel ready," I told her.

We'd been here barely an hour, so to have our first creature bonding fight already about to go down almost felt like bad luck. But Meera might not get a better chance. The next creature of mid power could be a bunny rabbit. A fox was reputable, and would land her a nice job in the Imperial Fleet. Anything lower was laughable and anything higher would kill her.

She took rapid breaths, before gripping her dagger in her right hand.

I was scared and excited all at once. Scared that Meera would die fighting this thing after I'd promised Kohen I'd keep her safe, and excited that I was about to witness a bonding firsthand.

"Give her room." I took four large steps backward and the group did the same, leaving only Meera, all five-foot one inch of her, to stand before the fox.

Anika rocked on her heels and I reached out and grasped her shoulder to steady her.

"You can't help her once first blood is drawn. You'll kill them both," I said.

"I know that," she snapped.

Once the bonding had started, if anyone intervened, it caused a magical rip in both the souls of the creature and human. Instant death.

Meera stared the fox down, beginning to walk a slow circle around it, and I was pleased to see that she had some training.

"Watch her. Learn," I coached Tetra. "The creature cannot tolerate a weak bond or it will cost them their life outside."

A bond too weak meant the creature wouldn't be able to breathe when they stepped outside. It had to be a strong connection.

My best friend was breathing rapidly, no doubt fending off a panic attack. I wished I could save her from this, sneak her out somehow, but her name had been pulled in the Lottery and her fate sealed. If you deserted, you went to the mines. Or worse: they just hanged you in the square. These lottery spots were opportunities others would kill for. So we didn't allow people to throw them away. Once the three days were over, they would send scouts for our bodies.

Just as Meera was about to lunge for the fox, it leapt into the air and went right for her throat.

"Meera!" Anika screamed, rushing forward. I reached out and yanked her back by the armpit.

The fox took a chunk of flesh from Meera's throat and I winced. A killing blow? I wondered, and then thought better as the tiny girl went absolutely feral. She slashed at the fox, one, two, three times, each blow drawing the mysterious blue blood that all creatures had. The fox then nipped her wrist, but she grabbed it by the back of its neck skin and yanked it up into the air.

Then it happened. The moment that I'd only read about and had never had the pleasure of witnessing.

A kaleidoscope of colorful arcs of magic flew from the fox's body. The bands wrapped around Meera, enveloping her as she held the fox firmly in her grip, never taking her eyes off of it. It was submitting to her. Bonding with her.

"Thank the stars," Anika breathed, shrugging out of my grasp.

We all released the breath we'd been holding, watching in awe as the colors wrapped around them both, blue, green, purple, pink. Now we couldn't tell where the fox began and Meera ended. It was like looking at an exploding star.

"It's beautiful," Tetra said, and I smiled.

It was.

After a moment, the colors died down and then Meera fell to her knees, dropping the fox as it curled up to her, snuggling on her lap, licking the wound on her wrist and throat.

"Meera? You okay?" As Anika moved towards her friend, a yellow snake shot from the ground and headed right for her arm.

I moved without thinking, a blur of motion. My sword cut the snake in half before I could even catalogue the threat.

Anika froze, staring down at the dead twitching creature and then up at me.

"Thanks," she managed with a shocked expression.

I nodded, eyeing the woods. "That bonding will bring more creatures. We need to move."

Bondings set off some kind of signal to others. Meera was safe now. She had her creature to protect her, and once you were bonded, the other creatures accepted you as one of their own. Meera could now come and go in The Wilds freely without fear of attack.

Meera looked up at us and I noticed the wound on her neck was superficial; the fox hadn't hit an artery. It was just a few layers of skin missing like you would get when you scraped a knee.

"I'm fine. Go!" Meera urged, stroking her fingers through the fox's fur. This was a special time when she and her creature would cement their bond.

Anika seemed as if she didn't like the idea of leaving her friend.

"She's more powerful than you now," I told the Imbrian. "Let's go."

It was true. Now that she was bonded, she had whatever power the fox had imbued her with, plus the fox's power.

"I'll see you on the outside!" Anika called after her as we ran to get away from where they'd bonded.

Tetra hobbled beside me, trying to break into a run but failing with her cane. We settled for a brisk walk with her wincing every ten steps. When I finally felt we were out of harm's way, we slowed.

"That was… violent," Tetra said, panting and rolling out her shoulder. I knew it caused her pain in her arm to walk on her cane for too long.

I glanced over at my bestie. "It will be. And you need to be ready. No flinching. No hesitating. You straight-up try to murder whatever creature you choose."

She frowned. "If I want to bond with it, why would I murder it?"

I shook my head. "That's the thing. If you are destined to bond, you won't be able to kill it. You will be equals."

She nodded. "Maybe I will find a creature with a gimpy leg too."

A few people in our group laughed but I didn't. Creatures were perfect. I'd never seen one with a deformity or weakness. But they would see hers, they would see it as a weakness, and her an easy kill.

The Imperial Fleet suffered no weakness, just as the creatures didn't. They were the same in that way. The more we walked, the more I wished I'd just convinced Tetra to take on that fox, though I had to admit I think it would have killed her. If a fox was too powerful, I'd have to try to urge her to a lower-class creature. She might be given grunt work when we graduated boot camp, but she'd be alive.

"I'm hungry." Dev reached for crackers from his pack and munched on them. We'd been walking several hours now and encountered no other creatures. It was relieving and depressing at the same time. It meant we were going to have to make camp. We did, however, each find a decent-size hunk of ember to bring back. Anika even got a smaller piece for Meera. I abstained from taking any home on account that it was not a good look for the richest girl in Amersea to be taking ember from The Wilds. Tetra found one the size of a walnut that would ensure her mother would no longer have to work.

"Don't you have any dried meats? Carbs will slow you down and make you sluggish," I told Dev as he brandished the crackers.

My brain already felt slow. I was tired, but I'd have some coffee and perk up.

"Can we camp for the night? I'm beat," Tetra said, basically dragging her leg behind her, limping with her good foot at this point. I knew all this walking was going to kill her arm that she leaned on.

"Yeah, let's camp," I announced for Tetra's benefit.

The sighs of relief made their way through our group and we started to gather wood for a fire. Everyone dug into their packs and pulled out tarps and rope to make tents. Tetra uncoiled a puffy sleeping bag and sighed as she slid into it.

"Who gave up their pack for me?" she asked me as Anika started the fire.

"Charline."

Tetra nodded. "I'll have to thank her." My bestie's eyes were already closing.

"Hey, stay awake and eat something." I pulled out some jerky but she waved me off.

"I'm exhausted. I couldn't care less for food right now." She rolled over and then she was out.

Time was hard to tell here. It was probably midnight but the sky was still a fiery glow above us. The canopy above the trees had some kind of shimmering coating to it, only allowing a pinkish light to filter in. It was kind of eerie and in no way refreshing like the regular sun.

I popped two caffeine satchels into my hot water thermos and chugged my water from the canteen while it brewed. I was gasping by the time I was done, not realizing how dehydrated I'd become. We'd have to refill in the morning by the creek that was about three hundred yards to the right.

I watched as Anika reached into her little gray bag and shoved something in her mouth, chewing as she glared at me.

"Candy?" I asked with a smirk.

So it wasn't tampons. *Interesting*. Whatever was in that bag she wanted to keep private.

"I wish," she snapped, making a disgusted face as she downed some water to seemingly wipe the taste of whatever she'd just eaten off her tongue.

Maybe it was caffeine as well. She didn't strike me as the type that would sleep in front of me or let her guard down at all.

Footsteps and low voices pulled my attention to the right. I grasped my throwing blade and pulled out my flashlight, beaming it right at a familiar pair of light blue eyes.

Kohen Badshah.

He walked about five yards from our camp and started to set up his tent with his group. He looked to be down about three people, and was sporting two cuts on his arm.

I stood, bringing my hot freshly brewed coffee over to where he was setting up. "Isn't that a little close to our camp?" I asked him as he instructed one of his teammates on how to make a fire.

He shot me a glare, wandering over to where I took a long and delightful sip of my coffee.

Now that he was closer, I could see that his lip was split and he had a black eye.

"I'll set up camp wherever I want," he spat, and my head reeled back in shock.

"What the hell's your problem?" I wanted to throw this hot liquid in his face, but wouldn't waste such a good drink.

His nostrils flared, and he reached down and pulled off his black shirt, exposing the most delicious set of abs I had ever seen. I wasn't prepared for the sudden undressing, so I just stood there staring like an idiot.

There was a giant gash across his left pec. It was bad, bleeding heavily, and so deep I could see the muscle underneath.

"Your crooked father and his stupid assassins are my problem. They tried to kill me and I wasn't able to protect my team. Lost two of them." He pointed to his group of rookies.

He said it like he cared about them or something, which was confusing. He just met them, and he admitted on the bus he knew my father was going to be after him.

I shifted uncomfortably, unsure what to say. To be honest, I wasn't sure I agreed with my father's decision to *take out* Kohen. He was a symbol of the future peace between Imbria and Amersea. His father died in the war but we'd let him live, schooled him, allowed him to enter the Lottery. It was a message to everyone that we were one nation now, united against Luska.

But my father couldn't have that. He couldn't have a possible future rebellion on his hands with Kohen as its leader.

Kohen was watching me keenly as he rummaged through his pack.

"If you were empress, what would you have done with me?" he asked suddenly when I didn't say anything.

I swallowed hard at the dangerous question, my fingers twitching over my knife on the off chance he was about to pull a weapon from his pack and try to gut me.

"I would allow you to live. If you became a problem later and started an uprising, I'd deal with you then."

He raised his eyebrows. "I'm surprised by your honesty, Aisling Everhart."

He yanked a small tool from his pack and pressed it to the laceration on his chest. He pushed down hard and flinched before pushing again and again. It took me a few seconds to realize he was stapling up his own cut.

"Jeez, why don't you get someone else to do that?" I waved at the rookies on his team.

It was an Imperial Fleet-issued medic device. I was willing to bet he'd stolen it.

He gritted his teeth as he stapled the last one. "I

deal with my own messes, princess," he snapped, and then glanced past me, his face suddenly falling.

"Where is Meera?" His voice shook, panic evident as his gaze darted around the firepit, no doubt counting everyone.

I took a long swig from my coffee. "Bonded to a fox creature. Both survived."

Relief washed over his face as he grinned at that, and stars help me he was beautiful. My stomach tightened, heat flushing over my entire body in response, and I hated myself a little for my reaction.

My body wanted what I couldn't have. It's like it knew that Kohen Badshah was the one man I couldn't touch and so I wanted to touch him. All over. *A lot.*

I cleared my throat. "If you are sleeping so close to us, then just try not to attract anything deadly," I shot as I strolled away.

"Impossible while your father is still breathing," he muttered under his breath.

I pulled my blade, spinning quickly and lashing out until the sharp end was pressed to his Adam's apple. He didn't move a muscle, just watched me like a cat who was curious about my behavior.

"Was that a threat to my father? *Your* emperor?" I warned. I wouldn't suffer treason, even if the words came from a beautiful mouth. I'd slice his throat right here if I thought he had plans to harm my father.

His gaze narrowed, and that's when I felt the tip of

something sharp at my back, right where my heart frantically beat behind my ribcage.

Anika spoke from behind me: "Having a nice little chat over here?"

Dammit.

I lowered my blade, keeping my glare focused on Kohen. "I'm sorry that your father was a terrorist and ruined your life, but don't threaten mine just because you have to live with the mistakes of yours."

His eyes widened, nostrils flared, jaw clenched—he looked absolutely livid. And the tip of that blade still hadn't been removed from my back.

I peered over my shoulder, sizing Anika up. "Do you have any idea the type of training I've had? I will have that blade and three of your severed fingers on the floor in ten seconds if you don't—"

"Stand down," Kohen ordered, and Anika dropped the blade, her face furious.

I peered back at Kohen to see that he was devoid of all emotion, as if the raging anger was never there. He'd caged it somehow, tucked it away for later most likely. No way was I sleeping tonight.

"Get some rest. Big day tomorrow," he said to me and gave me his back, a disarming move that let me know he wasn't scared of me.

I spun to Anika, narrowing my eyes at her. I was about to rip her a new one for coming at me like that when she shook her head, peering sadly at me. "You shouldn't have said that about his father. He was a great man."

It was like a punch to the gut. It shouldn't have been. King Ravi Badshah was an extremist. Brilliant in engineering but completely unrealistic with other things. He was obsessed with controlling ember distribution, saying that we should allow citizens to freely mine it from The Wilds. My father rightly didn't agree—they would strip it of ember in a day! Imbria had three times the population we did. No, the ember harvesting needed to be controlled, you couldn't collect it faster than it fell or you ran out. We were in peace talks one day and the next King Badshah just blacked out our whole city. His army bombed six of our busiest train stations. Killed thousands.

"He was a terrorist," I stated again.

She gritted her teeth. "Yeah, and you're brainwashed."

I frowned at that, about to retort, when Kian screamed like a girl.

We rushed back over to our camp and then Anika burst into laughter.

A small mouse creature had broken into his pack and was eating some dried fruit. Purple glowing ember swirls ran the length of its back.

Kian looked up at us, clearing his throat in embarrassment. "It scared me."

I grinned. "Quick, you better bond with it. You might not find anything more powerful."

He flipped me off and I glanced at Anika to see she was smiling again. It seemed our fragile truce was back.

I took a long swig of my coffee and Alek strode over to me and pulled me aside. Alek was cool, one of the most popular guys at our school. He had top grades and was on every sports team imaginable. We didn't run in the same clique but I respected him. Alek's family were all imperial soldiers. If they didn't get in the Lottery, they joined the human forces. He was loyal to the emperor through and through.

"You staying up?" He eyed the steaming mug in my hands.

I nodded. "Can't risk it."

I hoped it went without saying that as the emperor's daughter I couldn't allow my throat to be slit in the night.

"You wanna sleep in shifts? I can watch your back."

My heart pinched. I hadn't expected that, and I didn't want him to think I didn't trust him, but... I didn't trust anyone to look out for Tetra.

"Maybe the second night when I'm really dragging. I gotta look out for T." I inclined my head to her.

He dipped his head in understanding. "I'll get a couple hours, then. Yell if you hear so much as a twig snap. I'll be out of my sleeping bag with a knife in under five seconds."

I grinned. I'd never really spent much time talking to Alek. He was cooler and sweeter than I expected.

"You got it."

He slipped into his bag and zipped it up as I went to sit by the fireplace where Anika was drawing something in a notebook.

Everyone else was asleep. "Not gonna sleep?" I asked her.

She flicked her gaze at me. "Gotta look out for my people," was all she said.

I understood that. She didn't trust me fully. She would be stupid if she did.

She eyed the hot coffee in my hands. "Wish I had been able to afford that though."

A pang of pity went through me. Afford coffee? I mean, sure it was a luxury, but how poor was she that she couldn't afford three cups of coffee? I looked closer at her boots; they were scuffed and worn with seams popping. I hadn't noticed before. Her clothes were issued by the Imperial Fleet and looked freshly dyed black without a stitch out of place. I would readily admit I lived a life that only one percent of our population enjoyed, but I thought with all the travel I had done that I knew what it was like for the other ninety-nine percent of people. Though hearing Anika, who had a job in the ember mines, could not even afford coffee, I guessed not.

I handed her the mug. "Have some. Too much messes up my stomach anyway."

She looked at me warily and I rolled my eyes,

pulling the cup to my lips and taking a big swig. "It's not poison. I'm being nice."

She took the cup and drank some of the black liquid.

"Whoa, that's strong." Her lips puckered and I grinned.

It would be easier to pass the time if she wanted to talk a little.

"What's Imbria like?" I asked, hoping it was a neutral question that wouldn't start an argument.

She smiled. "Noisy, full of life, chaotic, beautiful, colorful—it's amazing. Better before the occupation I am told, but still amazing."

The occupation. That's what they called it?

I'd never been there, it wasn't exactly safe. Yes, we'd merged Imbria into Amersea, but not by choice. If I, the emperor's daughter, went there, I would probably be torn apart in the streets.

"Is it true you give babies red chilis to suck on?" I asked.

She grinned. "Gotta build up tolerance."

I wasn't sure if she was serious or not but it made me laugh. Imbrian food wasn't popular here as it was associated with our enemy of so many years, but I'd heard it was amazing and full of spice and had always wanted to try it.

"My turn," she said.

I nodded. "Shoot."

"Is it true you killed a man in training practice when you were five?"

Now I laughed. "Is that what they say? That's pretty cool. I don't know if I want to shoot that rumor down."

She smiled. "So never killed anyone?"

I shook my head, chuckling. "Have you?"

A shadow crossed over her face and she took a long swig from my coffee. "Thanks for the coffee. I'm going to walk the perimeter." Something dark had entered her features, a memory she didn't want to talk about, and I felt awful for asking. She was in the Avasan with Kohen—of course she had killed. Probably to survive.

She strode away and I sat there for a little while feeling bad, like maybe I didn't know the whole story there and shouldn't judge.

If I grew up unable to afford a simple cup of coffee and my family worked in the mines for next to nothing... what kind of lengths would I go to in order to survive? I didn't even know what we paid the ember-sorting workers, just that it was awful work.

The next several hours slogged past with me walking circles around the campfire, my fingers twitching over my sword, and Anika giving me the silent treatment. It was the dead of night and I was officially tired. Anika sat down on a rock and leaned against her pack, dagger gripped firmly in her hands. I watched as her eyes grew heavy and her lips went slack.

She was out.

I'd let her get some sleep.

I peered across the space to where Kohen sat behind his fire, whittling something with a small knife. As if sensing me, he looked up. We locked eyes and it felt like the world melted away. Even at this distance his presence had a tangible feel to it. In the darkness of this lonely night, I felt the emotions of the day rush up to greet me.

Jace cheated on me. I wasn't good enough and so he went elsewhere. It was like a hot knife to my heart, but I wouldn't allow myself to deal with it here. Not in The Wilds, not tonight. Shoving all of the emotions back down in the little black box I kept inside of my heart, I held Kohen's gaze. He wasn't looking away, and I hated to admit I would kill to know what he was thinking.

The Badshah family stories I heard growing up had caused me to form a picture of Kohen, the eldest of three brothers. I was told he was a heartless, rule-breaking, Amersea-hating monster who would slit your throat for a single coin. *But was he?*

A shadow moved in the bushes behind him and I jolted into action without thinking.

"Anika!" I shouted loudly to wake her as I sailed over Tetra's sleeping form.

Anika leapt into a standing position, knife in hand, as I ran for Kohen. He'd seen my alarm and spun just as three imperial soldiers dragged him into the woods by the throat, covering his mouth to muffle his scream.

I heard footsteps behind me and turned to see Anika there, gripping her dagger. "Protect our team, I've got this!" I snapped at her.

Her nostrils flared but I didn't give her time to respond. I sprinted past Kohen's sleeping team and through the woods, stepping into full-on mayhem. Kohen was bleeding heavily from the neck, staunching a wound with one hand while he fought off two attackers with the other.

One imperial soldier lay dead at his feet already. Kohen kicked out from where he sat on the ground, landing a boot squarely in the chest of one of his attackers, and at the same time slashed out with his sword in an effort to protect himself.

He was losing a lot of blood. What the hell was I doing here? What was I going to do, kill one of my father's men to protect my family's sworn enemy?

This is insane!

The imperial soldier he'd kicked to the ground stood, holding out a bolt shooter aimed at Kohen's head.

I never in a million years thought my first kill would be a soldier who had sworn allegiance to my family, but before I could stop myself I stepped forward, coming up behind the attacker and dragging my blade across his throat.

His bolt shooter dropped to the ground a second

before he did. The third and final attacker lunged for Kohen and I dropped him too with a sword through his chest.

Kohen stared up at me, eyes wide, as he grabbed the cut on his neck frantically to try to stop the bleeding.

We were locked in a stare. Again. This one all-consuming. It was like the wheels of fate had suddenly stopped and begun to spin in another direction.

My chest heaved as I backtracked through the woods and grabbed his pack. I returned a second later with the staplegun and some gauze from the medic-kit he had most definitely stolen.

My hands shook as I brought the stapler up to his neck. I'd been trained in basic medic triage; blood didn't scare me. Kohen Badshah did though. He watched me, silently, as I tended to his wound. I peeled his fingers away one by one, stapling his neck back together in such a crude way I was sure it would scar. He didn't seem like the kind of guy who would care about that though. My fingers touching his warm skin was sensual, though it shouldn't be. There was too much blood for that, and yet I kept stealing glances at his lips.

When I finished closing the wound, I was relieved to see it had stopped bleeding. He was so damn lucky it didn't hit an artery. I taped the gauze over it to hopefully ward off an infection and then set the stapler back into his pack. He stood and I glanced around, taking stock of the carnage. Three dead bodies. All imperial soldiers. Thank the stars I didn't know any of them personally.

What the hell did I just do? Was I insane? I needed to get out of here.

I turned to leave when Kohen's hand snaked out and his fingers deftly grasped mine. He tugged and forced me to look at him.

"Thank you." His voice was thick with emotion, eyes searching, fingers still holding mine as if I were made of glass.

"We never speak of this again," I told him. "It didn't happen."

Disappointment flashed across his face and he dropped my fingers, nodding.

I walked back over to our firepit where Anika was bopping on her heels. Alek was awake now with her.

"What happened? Is Kohen okay?" she asked, looking down at my blood-soaked hands.

"He's fine," I said, and then leaned over the fire and threw up the contents of my stomach.

I murdered two imperial soldiers. If anyone found out, I would not only lose my heir status, I could be tried for treason by my own father.

CHAPTER

SEVEN

The rest of the night was merciful. I didn't sleep and neither did Alek or Anika, though they graciously didn't ask why I had yakked into the fire or had blood on my hands which I'd wasted half a canteen of water removing. Kohen resumed his spot at his campsite, watching me like a bird watched prey.

By morning, we were all ready to get a move-on and start some actual creature tracking and hunting. Alek knelt on the ground and poked a piece of animal poop. "Cougar or lion up ahead. This scat is still warm."

"Gross," Tetra commented.

"I want it," Anika stated quickly.

Alek flicked his gaze at her. "A lion? That's... powerful."

She glared at him. "You don't think I can take it?"

Alek tipped his head to me. "Our future empress should have first choice."

A lion would be amazing and make my father proud, but if I fought with a creature right now, it would take me out of The Wilds and into a week's worth of healing. I'd be hobbling out of here with my newly bonded, not permitted to stay and keep an eye on Tetra. I needed to make sure she bonded first.

"I'll pass on the lion," was all I said.

Alek raised an eyebrow as if surprised by my response, but nodded.

We pressed on and I sidled up to Tetra, noticing her limp was worse today. "How you feeling?" I asked her.

She'd been quiet all morning, kept to herself, didn't eat much. She was more academic and had aspirations of becoming a physician for the Fleet or something along those lines. She'd never wanted to be a field-rated imperial soldier.

"I'm... adjusting," she lied.

I let the group go on ahead and pulled back to talk privately with her.

"I never should have invited you to the Lottery to support me," I confessed.

She chewed her lip, looking down at the ground in shame. "Aisling, about that... I... told the guard to put my name in."

It was like I'd been punched in the gut. "W-what

do you mean?" Maybe I wasn't understanding her correctly?

She swallowed hard, meeting my gaze. "At the Lottery, the guard said he had orders to throw my name out and... I saw everyone walking in, strong and able-bodied, and I suddenly felt like I was just as capable as them!" she snarled. "So I told the bastard to keep it in. But I never thought my name would be chosen."

"Oh, T." I pulled her in for a hug.

She squeezed me hard, sniffling a little, and when I moved away she wiped her eyes.

I grabbed her by the shoulders and forced her to meet my gaze. "You are *just* as capable as them! And that fiery spirit is what will bond you to a creature," I assured her.

It was true. Physically she was weak yes, but I'd seen her through so much. The death of her father, being bullied at school, daily pain. She was the strongest woman I knew.

She released a steady breath. "I should have taken the fox."

She should have, but she wasn't ready then. It would have killed her.

"Guys!" Dev snapped from up ahead, and we rushed to catch up.

There were sounds of snarling and grunting, and by the time I reached the group Anika was locked in battle with a medium-sized lioness.

Holy crap!

That took some serious balls, balls only Anika seemed to have.

The lioness swiped at Anika's face, dragging three lines across her cheek and causing her to cry out in pain.

"Go for its eyes or paws!" I shouted, trying to help her.

The lion would tear her face off before backing down. If it thought it was going to lose something valuable, it would submit.

At my advice, Anika pivoted, bringing her dagger down and sinking it right into the lion's paw. It screeched, but the bond started. Beautiful colors began to filter from its body and create a cocoon around them both.

We all whooped and cheered, and that's when Tetra released a bone-chilling scream from behind me.

I spun, my blade already pulled and ready to cut down whatever had scared her, but I froze when I saw the small black wolf, with green glowing ember marks, had batted at her bad foot.

Fresh streaks of blood filtered down her calf, and I moved to protect her, but Alek grabbed my arms and pinned them behind my back. "Blood has been drawn. You know the rules."

Don't make me watch her die! I wanted to scream as terror gripped me.

"Tetra, you have to fight it," I managed to get out

without falling into sobs. If one human in this world could make me cry, it was the little blonde right in front of me, gripping her cane like an axe. I hadn't even gotten her a bow and arrow. She had her cane and a hunting knife and a lot of sass. It would have to be enough.

The wolf was staring her in the eyes, and she right back. When I noticed she wasn't looking away and neither was the wolf, I started to feel slight hope.

"I'm good," I told Alek, who let go of my arms.

They were locked in a dominance stare, neither backing down.

"Tetra, this is a good match. Whatever strength you have inside of you, he sees that," I told her. The staring was a good sign. If she was able to hold this wolf's gaze for this long, it meant they were on even territory for a bonding.

"She," Tetra corrected me, pulling the twelve-inch hunting blade out from her pack slowly.

Holy crap, this was happening.

She already knew it was a she? I had heard that wolves sort of imprinted their name and gender on you before the bond while the rest of us had to wait until during or after.

With a warrior cry that would have made Elaine proud, Tetra burst from where she had been crouched, dragging her twisted foot behind her, and grappled with the wolf head-on. She was playing this smart, on her knees where she could move freely without her affected limb getting in the way. With her cane, she cracked the wolf in the jaw and it snarled, snapping at her wrist and taking it into its mouth, shaking it like a ragdoll.

Tetra wailed, but used the concealed knife she had in her other hand to swipe out at its ribcage. I noticed that she was holding back slightly, not wanting to kill the animal, which meant the bond was about to start. She had already felt something on a deeper level with it and didn't want to end its life, only prove her worth. The wolf went berserk then, snapping out rapidly, biting her anywhere it could.

"Tetra, fight! Show your strength!" I begged, feeling like I would go out of my mind if I had to watch my best friend be mauled to death by a wolf.

Tetra used the hilt of her blade to crack the wolf across the face, and then dropped the knife to the ground in a gesture that said she would fight it no more. She wanted the wolf to live.

This could be seen as a weakness. All I could do was hold my breath.

The wolf tumbled to its side from the blow, and with her bloody arms Tetra grasped the wolf's neck and yanked her upright, standing much like Meera had. The wolf dangled from her arms like a baby cub, and a starburst of color exploded from it and wrapped around my best friend.

I fell to my knees in relief, feeling like I might just

have to break my no tears streak right here and now, but I held it together.

Beside me, Alek and Roc began to chant Tetra's name, and laughter bubbled in my throat.

She did it. She was going to be okay. I'd gotten her through The Wilds just as I promised her mother I would.

I glanced behind me to see that Anika was alive as well, and bonded. She lay on the ground with her creature, stroking its honey-colored fur and tracing the red glowing marks that ran along her back. They were both panting, bloody but not broken.

I looked back to Tetra and she was back on the ground now with the wolf curled in her lap. She was stroking her fur and smiling down at it.

"You okay?" I took a step closer and the wolf snapped its head in my direction and growled, its hackles rising.

Tetra bopped her on the nose like a mother cub. "She would never hurt me," she taught the wolf.

With that, the wolf lay back in her lap and I sagged in relief.

Tetra peered up at me with tears in her eyes. "Aisling, nothing will prepare you for it. It's not like the books. It's so much... *more.*"

My heart beat wildly at her declaration. She looked like a changed woman. Was that possible?

"What's her name?" I reached out and gave the

wolf the back of my hand. She sniffed it, probably smelling Tetra, and licked it once.

Touching another person's creature without permission was frowned upon, unless in a fight or something like that. It was beyond rude.

Tetra smiled. "Ariyel."

"Hey." Roc tapped my arm. "This is great news for Tetra and Anika, but I just saw a crocodile heading this way, so unless you guys want to tangle with that, we gotta move."

I frowned. A crocodile was literally my worst nightmare of a creature to bond with, and if it drew blood I'd have no choice but to bond or kill it.

"You gonna be okay?" I asked Tetra, not prepared for just leaving her behind.

Tetra rolled her eyes at me. "I'm bonded now. I'm safe. Ariyel wants to go outside The Wilds. She's been waiting her whole life. I'm gonna leave now." With that, she picked up her cane and stood. "You don't have to worry about me anymore."

She leaned forward and pulled me into a hug. I inhaled her lemon and honey shampoo just in case it was for the last time, and nodded.

Tetra pulled back and peered into my eyes, her mouth pressed into a firm line. "Come back powerful, future empress." She mocked my father's voice and saluted me.

I smiled. "See you soon."

With that, she turned and limped out of The

Wilds, and it felt like she took a hundred-pound boulder from my shoulders with every step she took.

"Let's move!" Kian barked.

I spun around to find that Anika and her lioness were gone as well.

We were now an alliance of six.

OVER THE NEXT several hours we tracked three creatures. One was a rabbit so we let it go, but the others were decent, and Nikhil and Kian successfully bonded with a coyote and a rhesus monkey.

Alek, Roc, Dev, and I were all that remained and the sun was setting. We'd passed a few groups through the day, and sadly over two dozen dead bodies. We'd had to kill a handful of creatures that tried to attack us and were too weak or undesirable to bond. We were bruised, bloody, and battle weary. I felt the exhaustion of being awake the past few days pulling at me. At this point I wouldn't mind the risk of dying if it meant I could get a few hours of sleep. Going into a third day tomorrow was not ideal for bonding. I'd be tired and slow, and I was regretting not taking on the lioness that Anika had bonded.

As we were scouting for a place to make camp, we stumbled upon Kohen and some of his alliance. It looked like they'd been whittled down to about nine people. Each one of them was in rough shape, and

Kohen was favoring his left leg. I hadn't allowed myself to even think about what had happened in the woods last night, but seeing him and the bandage on his neck brought it all back to me.

I killed an imperial soldier. Not just one but two.

Kohen embraced Dev and they started trading stories. He inquired about Nikhil, Anika, and Kian, and grinned when he heard they were alive and successfully bonded.

I swayed a little on my feet and Alek reached out to catch me. "Whoa, you okay, Aisling?"

I widened my eyes, hoping the mere act would keep them open. "Just tired. I'll make coffee. Why don't you set up camp?"

Kohen cleared his throat. "You guys mind if we bunk together tonight? We could use the extra lookout. Sleep in shifts? A few from each team awake at a time?"

Alek and Roc flicked their gazes to me. Could this be an elaborate plot to get Kohen close to me while I was vulnerable and kill me? Maybe. But he had plenty of chances already and he hadn't. My mind was fuzzy. I wasn't thinking straight.

"I don't care," I said.

Alek nodded. "Just stick to your side of the fire," he said, and stepped in front of me protectively.

Whoa. Okay. Didn't expect that from him. It was kind of cute and funny at the same time. I could definitely take care of myself. I wished Tetra had been here to see it.

"Understood." Kohen had his team set up camp on the right side of the fire that Roc was currently building, and we set up on the left.

I started to brew some coffee when Alek walked over to me and took the thermos from my hands. "Let me take first watch, you need sleep." He stared me up and down as if telling me I looked like a sleep-deprived zombie.

I feared if I didn't get just a few hours of sleep, I wouldn't survive the bonding to a powerful creature. If there was anyone in this group I trusted to watch my back, it was him, though I knew Elaine would have counseled me to trust no one.

My gaze flicked to Kohen and Alek lowered his voice: "I don't trust him. I think he's been tracking us by day to meet up at night."

I'd considered that and I agreed with him. It was too coincidental he found us each night for camp. "Because he wants to keep an eye on his family." I flicked my gaze to Dev, who was speaking animatedly to Kohen about Anika's bonding.

"Maybe," Alek agreed, "or maybe he wants something else." He looked at me.

I sighed, too tired to care.

"I won't let him get within ten feet of you," Alek promised.

I nodded and rolled out my sleeping bag. I was in

the nauseated zone of sleep deprivation where I felt like if I didn't crash soon I was going to hurl.

"Wake me in four hours. I'll take next watch. Don't let me sleep longer than that, do you understand me?" It was an order.

"Yes, ma'am," he said with a grin, a *flirty* grin.

Interesting. I'd never considered Alek as a romantic partner before. The last year of my life had been consumed by Jace.

But I was too tired to care or even process that. The second I crawled in my sleeping bag, I was out.

EIGHT

Four hours later on the dot, dutiful Alek woke me up and then crawled into his sleeping bag for some rest. I brushed my teeth, ate some jerky, and drank some coffee by the fire with Dev and a few of Kohen's alliance.

I could see the sleeping form of Kohen in his bag just at the edge of the forest, and I wondered why he hadn't bonded with anything today. I wondered that for myself as well. The rhesus monkey would have been quite impressive, but impressive enough for my father? I wasn't sure, so I passed. Coyotes were known for being untrustworthy tricksters, and I wasn't sure what my people would think of that bonding, so I passed on that as well. I feared I was getting into the dangerous zone of day three with no bonding, when you were either forced out of The Wilds by the imperial soldier mop-up crew, and a total shame to society, or you bonded with a really lower-level creature out of desperation. This was the night that lottery winners started to turn on each other, worrying that there weren't enough creatures for all of us. Which I was starting to believe was true. We hadn't seen many out there today, unless we weren't good at tracking. But it seemed they were sparse. More so than I thought.

I repacked my bag, taking inventory of what I had left, trying to think up a gameplan for the next day, when I noticed Kohen rise slowly out of his sleeping bag, grab his pack, and look back at Dev.

Dev nodded once and then Kohen peered at me.

I frowned and he turned, slipping off into the woods.

What the hell was that? Where was he going?

I shouldered my own pack and started after him, but Dev reached out to stop me.

"Let him go," he warned.

"Don't touch me," I told him.

He removed his hand and I nudged Roc awake with my foot. He'd been sleeping a while by my count, but still looked bleary-eyed. I didn't trust Dev to protect a sleeping Alek.

"Look out for Alek. I'll be back in a bit," was all I said.

Roc nodded, rising out of his sleeping bag and asking zero questions. That's what I liked about the Imperial Fleet brats, we all knew how to take orders.

I had to run to catch up, but I chased Kohen

through the tree line and followed him into a deeper part of the woods. He was consulting a map with an ember-lit headlamp that looked Fleet-issued. Another thing he stole.

"Coming along for the ride, princess?" Kohen said without looking back.

I rolled my eyes, sidling up to him. "How did you know it was me?"

He flicked his gaze my way. "Your smell."

I scrunched my face up and sniffed my armpit. "I could use a shower," I agreed.

He grinned, and stars have mercy my thighs clenched with need when he did. "Not that. You smell like coconut, vanilla."

Oh. My shampoo?

I flicked my gaze to the map. "Where are you going?" We had been heading northwest for days and I feared we were dangerously close to the Luska border.

He swallowed hard and stopped walking. "Listen, I don't want to hurt you, but if you try to stop me I will."

I took a step backward. "What do you mean? Stop you doing what?"

He handed me the map and I peered down at it. I'd seen hundreds of maps of The Wilds. It was like a rite of passage to have one hanging in your house, but never had I seen one that looked this old, this detailed. The river cut through the center, the higher hilly regions, and the circled upper left corner that read Talanagi—the left corner that was in the Luska portion of The Wilds, beyond the wall we'd built to keep them out and lessen their attacks.

I gasped. "You're not..."

He yanked the map from me. "I am. It's clear to me now that if I don't do something like this, your father will never stop hunting me." He lifted his shirt to reveal his eight perfectly defined abs and two more large gashes that had been stapled.

"I've run out of staples, Aisling. I'm tired and out of options. I'd rather die at the foot of a Talanagi than by an assassination attempt because of your father."

I didn't have anything to say to that. In fact, I was questioning why I didn't kill him for my father right here.

Kohen kept walking and I had a moment of indecision.

Should I kill him and do the job I knew my father wanted done?

Should I just let him go?

Should I follow him?

He disappeared over the hill and I ran after him.

Damn my curiosity!

"The Talanagi are so powerful they will kill you just by staring at you," I said.

Kohen laughed. "I don't care. I'm going to find them and bond with one."

I had to admit his confidence was sexy.

There was an Amersean man a hundred years ago that we had record of who'd bonded with a griffin

Talanagi, but none had been seen or bonded with in Amersea since.

"Besides, what do you care what happens to me?" Kohen asked as he peered sidelong at me.

I shifted my pack a little. "I don't. I'm just curious."

We walked in silence for another half hour with Kohen consulting his map every few minutes. I was beginning to regret my decision when we reached The Wall.

I swallowed hard, staring up at the giant thirty-foot stone structure.

"What now?" I asked as Kohen walked towards the river that split Imbria and Amersea.

"Now I swim to the Luska side. The Talanagi are said to be just on the other side of this wall."

My eyes bugged and I reached out to grasp his arm, stopping him. "Dude, first of all, you could be eaten by a river shark... and secondly, you're going into *Luska*?" I widened my eyes.

If there was one thing Imbria and Amersea agreed on, it was our hatred of Luska. The war-hungry nation wanted our embers in their factories and our people in chains. Their strip of The Wilds, and therefore access to ember, was tiny compared to what Amersea and Imbria had. We were an unstoppable nation with that much ember.

His eyes practically glowed blue as he stepped closer to me and seemed to peer directly into the center of my soul. "If it means I have to swim through shark-infested waters and over into enemy territory to survive, I'll do it. I'll do just about anything to survive, Aisling. Something I don't think you know much about. So why don't you wait here for me where it's safe…"

He spun then, ripping his arm from my grasp, and waded into the river.

Bastard! Was he saying I didn't know how to survive hard things? Or that I'd never had to? Did he have any idea what being the emperor's daughter entailed? If we climbed The Wall we'd be killed by the guards up top. The only way over was in the river and around.

With a growl I took off after him, letting the cool water lap at my ankles as I held the pack over my head like he did.

He gave me a backward glance but said nothing. *I should turn back.* I could literally be killed if the Luskins found us in their territory. Or worse, kidnapped and tortured for days on end. But I did wonder, why did Kohen's map show the Talanagi on the Luska side? It kind of made sense… because over twenty percent of the creatures the Luskins bonded to were Talanagi. That's what made them such a formidable foe. Was it because the creatures bred there on the other side of the wall and we'd unknowingly blocked them out when we erected it? That would be very stupid if that was the case. My father would rip the wall down if he found it to be true.

I peered up at the top of the wall, looking for soldiers, but found none. Kohen reached the shore on the Luska side and scrambled up the steep embankment. Next it was my turn. I got one boot into the mud and slipped, swallowing a yelp as I sank into the river, drenching myself and my pack. When my head bobbed back up, Kohen was there, reaching down to haul me up out of the water as if I were made of air.

He steadied me, setting me on my feet, and I stared at him a little breathlessly as water rolled down my face and clothing. "Thanks," I muttered.

He just nodded and continued walking, consulting his map, and I followed because I was a curious idiot.

There was no turning back now. I was either following Kohen into a trap where he killed me, or we really did find the Talanagi and we both died. Either way I didn't see many options where we both made it out of enemy territory alive.

Suddenly his arm shot out and grasped my stomach, holding me back.

I'd been looking out into the tree line, but at his stopping me, I peered down to follow his gaze.

"What the *hell* is that?" I whisper-screamed.

The giant golden egg that lay at my feet was bigger than a small child.

Kohen's head snapped up, and then in one swift move he yanked me closer to him and tucked me behind him, shielding me from something.

I growled against his back. "I don't need you to protect m—"

The words died in my throat as I peered over his shoulder at the giant black, scaled... dragon.

Talanagi.

An ancient magical creature. It was... real.

Kohen and the dragon were in an epic stare down, and my heart hammered in my chest like a fragile bird. Kohen released the hand he'd been using to keep me behind him and pulled his broadsword.

"If I die, tell Anika to take care of my little brothers," he said calmly.

Holy crap. He was going for it.

I was no fool. I took three slow but large steps backward. I wasn't about to get in the middle of a fight with a Talanagi.

Part of me wanted to run back to the camp. Another part wanted to stay and watch even if it meant seeing Kohen die. This was a once-in-a-lifetime opportunity and I wasn't about to miss it.

I was wondering who would strike first when the dragon's tail flicked so fast and hard it sent Kohen flying into a nearby tree. He hit the trunk with a thud and slid to the ground. The second he hit the mossy forest floor, he popped up as if nothing had happened and he wasn't hurt. Then he ran right at the creature.

I barely blinked. I couldn't look away. Kohen had balls of steel and no fear. He leapt into the air, sword arm raised, and the dragon shot a stream of fire right in Kohen's direction. The Imbrian rolled midair and barely missed it, falling to the ground with a yelp.

He popped up a mere second later, his shirt bleeding from where I was guessing his staples had just opened up. Watching him fight was a thing of beauty. Technically, they hadn't started the bonding process yet; no one had drawn blood from the other. The blood from Kohen's old injury wouldn't count. If Kohen wasn't strong enough to make the beast bleed, the dragon would kill him.

Kohen needed a distraction. I didn't know why I did it, or why I wanted to help him, but I stepped out into the clearing.

"Is this your egg?" I yelled really loudly, pointing to the golden oblong sphere.

The dragon's gaze snapped to mine, and Kohen ran faster than my eyes could track, slashing out with his sword and dragging it clear across the dragon's chest.

Blue blood dripped onto the blade and the bonding began.

Yes!

'No, It's mine,' a female voice called into my mind, and I froze.

I slowly pivoted on my heel, turning around. When my gaze fell on the creature behind me, my heart stopped beating. I was sure I was going to drop dead right there as I stared into the eyes of the most magnificent creature I'd ever seen.

She stood over ten feet tall, with feathers that

looked like they danced with fire. They started gold at the base and moved to purple and even burnt orange. She stood erect on two large, taloned feet, and stared at me with glowing purple eyes.

A firebird.

They were real. All Talanagi were special, but fire-birds were said to be immortal, escaping even death itself.

I wanted to run, get the hell out of this place so fast and forget I'd ever found the Talanagi hideout, but I couldn't look away from those purple eyes. They peered right through me, challenging me to prove my worth.

Ignoring the sounds of Kohen fighting behind me, I thought of what Elaine said. That she'd specifically told me *not* to go for a Talanagi, that at times I was too cocky.

I held the beautiful bird's gaze, my fingers twitching over my sword, and then my father flashed into my mind.

If I bonded a firebird, there was no telling what he would do. I knew he loved me and was proud of me, but... he was also very career-driven. He took threats to his leadership seriously. I knew he would never hurt me, but the thought of doing something that he disapproved of made me... uncomfortable. He might very likely make Valor his heir instead. I relaxed my hand, and even though I hadn't felt the urge to look away, I did, and gave her my back, intending to leave this place and never think on it again.

A whoosh of air rushed over me, and a second later her talon ripped through my back. I screamed, falling to the ground, as panic washed over me.

Blood was drawn. That meant I had to fight.

Shit. Shit. Shit.

With a growl, I rolled on my back and lashed out just as the creature tried to bite a chunk out of my arm. My sword slashed across her face and she shrieked, reeling backward. I used the space between us to pop up onto my feet.

This was really happening. After all my years of training, I was now in a bonding fight with a freaking Talanagi!

If I survived this, which wasn't likely, Elaine was going to kill me.

The creature's nostrils flared and her beak opened to reveal a mouth full of sharp, serrated teeth.

Awesome.

Some candidates survived their bonding fight but were missing an arm or leg. I was really hoping this wasn't the case here. But I had to show her that I was strong enough to be her equal; otherwise she would continue to try to kill me.

She opened her mouth and a stream of fire shot from it. I yelped, ducking and rolling to the side. The blast of heat hit my back and was gone as I moved out of the way. By the time I popped back up, she was on me again, relentless. She flew up into the air, trying to dig her talons into my shoulders. I managed to nick her leg with my dagger and draw blood as I rolled out of the way, but it barely stopped her.

An explosion of colored lights pulled my attention about twenty feet to the right, and shock ripped through me.

Kohen? Was he actually alive and bonding the dragon?

Before I had time to focus on the thought, the firebird smacked me in the face with her wing and I went down, ears ringing.

My vision went double, and that's when something inside of me snapped. That feral need to survive bloomed in my chest like it did with every candidate when you reached a certain point in your fight that you thought you might be losing.

I needed to stop thinking so much. I needed to react on instinct.

With a warrior's cry, I charged forward, slashing out with my sword left and right as the firebird deftly flew zigzags out of the way, breathing fire at me once more.

I tucked into a ball and rolled at the last second, but felt the burn of singed skin along my back. The fresh cuts she'd made with her talons were raw, but I was running on adrenaline. She was fast, *too* fast, and at this rate I knew this fight wasn't going to last long.

I sheathed my dagger, keeping my broadsword out, and reached down to get a fistful of dirt. The next time she snapped her beak at me, I tossed the dirt into her face. She blinked, turning away, and I used the distraction to drag my blade along her wing, ripping some of those beautiful feathers out. It felt criminal to try to destroy an animal as stunning as she was, but I knew I had to get her to submit in order to start the bond or I was dead. The creatures of The Wilds lived in a kill-or-be-killed mentality. Their resources here were limited, and they were constantly fighting each other over them.

Her right leg shot out and swept my feet out from under me, knocking me flat on my back. Then her talon locked on to my leg with an iron grip. The razor-sharp claws cut into the meat of my calf, and before I even knew what was happening, I was being hauled into the air, upside-down.

My first thought was to tighten the grip on my broadsword.

I did, and even though she was flying up with my body hanging upside-down fifty feet over the jungle of The Wilds of Luska, I knew I had her. She had no idea that I'd done a hundred sit-ups a day hanging from a device that forced me to be upside-down in my father's gym.

I pulled myself up so that I could kiss my knees if I wanted, and pressed the tip of my sword against her throat.

She peered down at me with surprise, the intelligence in her gaze very apparent.

"I'll do it," I warned. If I killed her, it would kill me too. A drop from this height wasn't survivable, but I'd do it just to prove I won the fight.

I felt something knock against my chest, an invisible force boring its way into my heart.

The bond?

Then the colors burst from her back, raining down and curling under me. I had a wild thought that we must look like fireworks to anyone peering upward at that moment.

Everything they told you about the bonding in school, about the instant closeness you would feel for your creature in that moment, it paled against reality.

In a single second I knew almost everything there was to know about Liana. And she knew nearly everything about me. I knew her name, I knew that she'd had many children who were now gone, either passed on or... not here. It was hard to explain. I knew she was over a thousand years old and that she didn't like snow but longed to see it. I knew that her mate died a decade ago and she'd been empty ever since, a hollow shell waiting for her own end, but her end would never come. I knew she was immortal, the only type of Talanagi to achieve such a thing, and only because she was female. Male firebirds like her mate did not have such magic. I knew she longed to leave this place, that this enclosure called The Wilds was a prison for her and every other creature, but they could not survive outside without the bond of a human. Even her. Even an immortal. She needed me. She wanted me. She'd been biding her time, craving an end, and now I was her way out.

In that same instant, she knew I was the emperor of Amersea's daughter, an impossible role to fill. That Jace was the first guy I ever loved and trusted and he betrayed me. She knew that I hated broccoli and loved the rain. That Tetra was my best friend and I would do anything to protect her. It was hard to explain such a detailed sharing of instant information, telepathic in a way, but I felt when it started to fade and the bond began to seal itself.

Her name was Liana and she had found her equal, someone she would die for, protect with her life. And I felt the same.

I was so excited to have actually survived this that laughter bubbled in my chest as she began her descent and the colors around us began to fade.

We were about ten feet from the ground when she peered down at me with compassion. *'Be strong, Aisling. For the both of us.'* She spoke into my mind and I frowned just as she exploded into a ball of fire, encompassing my entire body in the flames. Pain like I'd never felt before consumed me, and then everything went black as I greeted death with surprise.

I was dead. Just a ball of awareness floating in the void. There was no pain, no light, no long-lost relatives to greet me. I was floating in a black sky with no stars and only the voices to keep me company.

"What happened to her hair?" It was my father's voice.

"We think she partially bonded before she died," a stranger said.

"Bless you, child. May you have your place among the stars with your mother." It was Elaine.

"I can't announce this yet. The city is still reeling about Kohen bonding with a Talanagi," my father said.

Shock laced through Elaine's voice: "What will you tell the people? They'll wonder where she is."

"That she's healing from extreme wounds. We can announce her death next week. I don't want to start a panic," my father said.

"What creature did this? Do we know?" Elaine asked.

"She was burned alive. And considering Kohen Badshah just bonded a dragon…" the stranger mused.

Elaine gasped. "You think Kohen killed her?"

They had it all wrong, but I was helpless to comment, floating in my black void.

"Or they fought for the same creature and he won," the stranger said.

My father sighed. "Dammit, Aisling." The words were angry, but his tone was not. His voice was broken. Like maybe the words *I love you* were burning a hole in his tongue just as they had on mine so many times. "Zip her up. I can't look at her like this anymore."

Zip.

Silence.

I floated in the darkness for hours, maybe even days, my mind subdued. I didn't have any entertainment yet I wasn't bored. It was like I was frozen in this moment and fully content with it. Only when a golden glowing sun appeared on the horizon did I feel my mind become fully alert. I began to get memories and thoughts. I remembered being in The Wilds and watching Kohen fight a dragon, I remembered the firebird.

Liana.

My heart hammered in my chest as if I were suddenly thawing from a long winter's sleep, like a bear about to leave hibernation. Panic rushed through me as my mental faculties became sharper.

Where was I?

I... died. My father and Elaine, I heard their voices but... the sun lifted higher in the sky and I began to grow warmer.

Be strong, Aisling. For the both of us. Liana's words came back to me as the sun suddenly wasn't a sun but a ball of fire. And I was no longer floating in darkness but on top of Liana's back. Her wings flapped madly as she turned in the opposite direction of the fire and tried to get us away from its flames. Was she there the whole time? Carrying me on her back?

The flames licked across the sky like lightning and I instinctively pulled my sword with one hand and gripped the feathers on her back with my other. Standing atop her shoulders, I turned around, rocking to keep my balance, and held the sword out to fight off any danger.

"What's happening?" I asked her. There were no mountains below us, only clouds, as if we were above the world I knew and loved, in a different place I couldn't explain.

'You have to be strong. I will survive but you might not. Others haven't. Fight, Aisling. Fight!' Liana said.

"Fight what?" I yelled, terrified as the now wall of fire rushed towards us.

Then, like magic, Liana disappeared, beneath me

one second and gone the next, and instead of falling I was consumed by the wall of fire.

With her wisdom in my head, I slashed out like mad as the fire tried to consume me. It was like a living beast with arms and tails of flame and eyes of smoke. It tried to suffocate me, but I hacked and cut as its fiery appendages were separated from it and then disappeared. I was sweating, burning; everything hurt and yet this bastard didn't know that I was too stubborn to die.

"Come on!" I screamed, continuing my slashing, blindingly fast and repetitive. My arms strained from the action, but each time I cut into the fire, it grew smaller. I wanted to give up, I wanted to drop this sword that weighed a thousand pounds and go back to floating in the darkness, but somehow I knew it would not be like that again, that if I died this time it was real. Every time I cut off one of its eyes, or tails, another popped up.

My arms were so heavy, so battle weary, and yet I dug deep down inside of myself for that place that every warrior has, that small pocket of reserve energy.

"You can't have me!" I screamed to the fire beast, spinning in a full circle with my blade, cutting more and more of it until the heat ceased, and I was suddenly staring at a four-foot ball of fire perched above a cloud.

It had only one eye left, and a few fiery feathers,

and I slashed through it with ease. "Just die already!" I commanded.

The fire monster dissolved to nothing then, and I collapsed backward onto the cloud, which somehow supported my weight.

I panted, looking up at the crystal-clear blue sky, and that's when the cloud ceased to exist and I fell.

I screamed, and the sudden weightlessness caused fresh hot fear to seize me.

Then everything went black.

MY EYES FLICKED OPEN and I gasped, panicked to find that I was still in darkness. I thrashed around, and then heard a strange male voice scream.

"Help me!" I shouted, and then rolled to my side. Bad idea. I was on top of something and fell down, hitting the floor and my right shoulder hard.

I was trapped inside of something, like a sleeping bag...

The sound of an opening zipper pulled my attention to the top of the bag as light splintered into the space and I stared into the horrified expression of an older man with wide eyes and shaky fingers.

He unzipped what I now saw was a body bag and I fell out of it, onto the tile floors of what I was pretty sure was the Riverine City Morgue.

And I was naked.

Awesome.

"M-m-miss Everhart?" the man mumbled. I recognized his voice from my dream, the one where my father and Elaine were talking about me like I'd died, except I now didn't think it was a dream.

"Can I have some clothes?" I covered my chest and the man snapped into action. He rushed across the room and grabbed me a lab coat. It was freezing in here, probably to keep the bodies from decomposing. A charming thought that made bile rise in my throat.

Then he gave me his back while I dressed in the long white coat that hung past my knees, and tightened the waistband.

"H-how is this possible?" the man asked, clearly trying to figure out how the chick from the body bag had just suddenly come to life.

I wasn't sure what to say. "I don't exactly know the answer to that myself," I told him honestly. "But thank you for your help."

There were dead bodies everywhere, some of which I recognized as my fellow candidates. I wanted to get the hell out of here.

"I'm gonna go now," I told him, a puff of mist coming from my mouth from the cold temperature in here.

He spun around. "No. Let me call your father."

"I don't think that's nec—"

"I'm calling your father," he warned.

Crap.

He walked over to a phone on the wall and spoke into the receiver. "Hello, operator, I need to be connected to the emperor immediately. This is coroner Davis."

He paused, flicking a nervous gaze over to me. I took this moment to step in front of a mirror he had hanging on the wall and check my appearance. No doubt my skin would be burned and bruised.

Shock ripped through me at my reflection. My skin wasn't burned or bruised. And not just that—my hair had changed.

I sucked in a breath as I reached up and fingered the new orangish red coloring that encompassed the left side of my hair. The right side was still black.

"Emperor..." The coroner's voice was high-pitched. "We... ahh... have a situation that I feel is very delicate. Can you come in person immediately?"

Pause.

"Sir, your daughter is alive." The man winced and then hung up the phone.

"He's coming to get you," the coroner told me.

Great.

"Can I use the bathroom?" I asked him, panic fully rising up inside of me. Was I scared of my own father? Unfortunately yes. He took his role as emperor and his legacy very seriously, and I'd gone and bonded to a potentially immortal creature that made me more powerful than him, which would embarrass him.

You didn't want to embarrass my father.

"Sure." The coroner pointed to a door in the back wall.

I rushed over to it and threw myself inside. Splashing warm water on my face, I sucked in deep lungfuls of air.

Where was my bonded? Was she okay?

Of course she was, she was a freaking firebird.

I splashed more water on my face, trying to regain control of my breathing. I needed to play this cool. Like I was excited to see my father and had no idea what powers I had now acquired.

No. That would scare him.

I needed to seem in control, like I knew exactly what was going on, and yes I'd just escaped death, but only this once. Only because of the bonding.

Yes. That was how I needed to play this.

I dried my face and smoothed my hair.

There was a bang at the bathroom door and I steeled myself.

"Aisling!" My father's shout was frantic, and I swung the door open only for him to stagger backward in shock.

He looked like he hadn't slept. His eyes were puffy, like maybe he'd even cried. Did I underestimate his love for me? Would he choose me over being emperor given the chance?

I'd never ask it. I didn't want the answer. He was the only parent I had left. I had to believe he'd choose me.

"Father." I stepped out of the bathroom, keeping a military posture as my gaze flicked to Zuri. His creature stared at me with an unreadable expression.

"You're alive." His voice was breathless.

He reached out and grasped my shoulders, squeezing as if to make sure I wasn't a ghost.

"I am," I said, reaching up to grasp his hands.

We didn't hug, but this was the closest thing.

My father said affection was a weakness, so he was sure not to show it, but this tender touch told me so much. He cared.

He released me, reaching up to rub the sides of his face.

The coroner was still in the room behind him and I knew my father would want to speak privately. "Go wait in the car," my father commanded, and then walked over to the coroner's desk.

"I would like to keep this private," he told the man as I walked to the door, Zuri following me.

"Of course, my liege," the coroner said, and I grabbed the handle of the door.

"I know that keeping secrets can be a burden. So what does a secret like this cost to you?" my father asked him and I left the room.

Zuri stepped in front of me, showing me the way out of the building and to the motorized car. My father was going to pay the coroner to keep my secret. That meant it was a big deal. Of course it was a big deal! I just woke up in a body bag! My mind raced with all of these thoughts.

Zuri stood by the door of the long black car, motor still running with my father's driver at the front. Was Zuri simply showing me the way as a kindness? Or making sure I didn't run?

I slipped into the backseat and saw that the partition had been raised so that our driver, Verik, could not listen to or see me.

My father came outside a few moments later and slid across from me, with Zuri leaping on the seat next to him as the driver took off.

My father peered at me with concern. "Tell me everything. Leave nothing out."

It was the worst thing he could ever ask of me. It made me wonder what he knew and how much to say. Had Kohen or anyone else seen my dead body? Had they seen me bond with the firebird? Had they told him? A lie could get me in trouble. When I was seven, my father told me that Zuri could smell a lie. I didn't know if he'd said it to scare his daughter into telling the truth or if it was in fact the truth. But I didn't want to find out.

"I was in The Wilds, nearly going on day three," I told him, "Then I happened upon an egg."

He frowned. "An egg?"

I nodded. "A large golden one. Then... I saw her... a Talanagi."

My father's sharp intake of breath confirmed my suspicion. He had no idea that's what I'd bonded with.

He leaned forward, as if to sharpen his hearing, and Zuri just stared at me, unmoving from where she'd perched.

I breathed the next two words in fear: "A firebird." Telling my father the truth was inevitable. Liana would show up and reveal it anyway.

My father's gaze narrowed slightly, but otherwise there was no way to tell how he was feeling.

"Go on," was all he said.

"I'm not stupid!" I told him animatedly. "I tried to run. I knew that there was no way I was going to survive a bonding with a Talanagi. So I gave her my back... intending to sprint away from her... and she drew my blood."

My father nodded. "But you did survive, didn't you?"

There was tension in the car. I wasn't sure what to say, or what he wanted me to say.

He smiled then, a rare emotion on him. "My daughter bonded to a Talanagi. We need to celebrate."

I released the breath I hadn't realized I was holding. "Yeah... holy crap, I can't believe it."

"Where is she?" He peered outside, eyeing the skies as if expecting Liana to be flying circles above us.

I cleared my throat. "I don't know... there was an explosion of fire and then I woke up in a body bag."

He nodded. "So you can escape death?"

"I don't think so. Just this once I think," I hedged.

He raised one eyebrow. "You bonded her, right? That means you should know things. Are you immortal, Aisling?"

My heart picked up a notch. I hated how I always felt like I was walking on ice with this man. My own father. He didn't know when to stop being emperor and just be Dad.

"My creature is," I said, my gaze flicking to Zuri. She probably *could* smell a lie and I didn't want to give my dad a reason not to trust me right now. "But I had to fight to be... reborn?" I used the word, unsure if it was the right one. "And she gave me the sense that I could have died and stayed dead had I not been strong and fought. I doubt I could do it again." Fighting the fire beast had been tiring, and I was speaking the truth. I wanted to tell him that the Talanagi we'd found had been just across the Luska border, but I feared it was an irresponsible act he'd never let me live down. So for now I kept it to myself.

My father relaxed a little then and nodded. "The Talanagi are very powerful. And now I have two at my command."

"Two?" I acted surprised.

His gaze narrowed. "Kohen Badshah? He carried your dead body out of the woods. He bonded to a dragon."

Kohen brought my body back? That was typically something left for the cleanup crew.

"Incredible." I tried to act surprised again.

"How did he know where to find your body? Were you both hunting Talanagi together?" my father asked.

My stomach clenched and I burst out in laughter. "Father, don't be ridiculous. But Alek and I did suspect that Kohen was tracking us in The Wilds the entire time." I hoped it sounded believable. It was half true.

He smiled, nodding. "I knew my daughter wouldn't do that to me." He reached out and grasped my hand. A rare show of affection. "She wouldn't align with my sworn enemy."

I cleared my throat. "Kohen is in your Imperial Fleet now though, right, Father?" *No longer an enemy* was what I was trying to drive home. Spending the last three days with Kohen had completely changed my mind towards him, towards all of the Imbrians if I was being honest.

My father sighed. "For now."

For now.

"I'm sure he will be loyal to his emperor," I said.

My father raised an eyebrow. "Are you? Then you have much more to learn before you are ready to take over for me."

I lowered my head. "Yes, Father."

We drove home the rest of the way in silence.

CHAPTER

TEN

The second we walked in the door, Elaine was there with wide eyes and pursed lips. Her eyes were red-rimmed like she'd been crying.

I smiled when I saw her, and she rushed over to me. "You stupid child! You took twenty years off my life." She pulled me into a quick hug and then all but shoved me away, looking angry.

I laughed. "I didn't mean to."

"Aisling!" three voices said in unison.

"They don't know," Elaine mouthed to me, and I spun to see the triplets descend on me.

My sisters all had identical black bob haircuts with bangs, and wore matching purple overalls with white tops. They were in a phase where they wanted to dress the same and try to trick people into knowing which was which.

"Oh my stars, her hair looks so cool," Victory said.

"We need to dye half of ours immediately," Virtue agreed.

"Yessss," Valor echoed.

"No one is dyeing their hair," my father said. "I'm going to get some work done. Celebration dinner is at eighteen hundred hours," he said, and then left the room.

Celebration dinner? That was unexpected and nice.

"Is it true you bonded with a Talanagi and almost died?" Valor asked.

"Yeah, Father said you were in the hospital hooked up to machines and weren't going to make it," Virtue said.

Victory simply walked over and fell into my arms. She was the sweet, affectionate one. The others had let the puberty hormones take control and had gone feral.

I met Elaine's gaze and she nodded as if saying to go along with the story.

"Yep. All better now though!" Which was weird. My entire body had been burned, my back clawed up, and now I looked like I didn't even have a scratch on me.

There was a knock at the door.

"That will be Tetra," Elaine told me. "I called her and told her you were... feeling better. Come on, girls. Let's finish your studies for the day."

They groaned but trailed after Elaine.

I answered the door timidly, unsure what to expect.

Tetra flew into me, pulling me in for a bone-crushing hug. "Holy stars, Ash," she sobbed into my ear as her wolf creature walked a circle around us, rubbing up affectionately against my leg. "I saw you... dead," she whimpered.

I squeezed her back, so damn glad she was alive, and then she pulled away from me, wiping at her eyes.

"I... was reborn?" I felt weird using the word, but I couldn't think of another one.

She peered behind me, as if looking for my father. They didn't like each other very much. "Let's walk the garden?" she said.

I nodded and followed her out. She leaned on her cane as her creature, Ariyel, trotted beside her.

"You bonded a wolf, Tetra! Is your mom proud?"

She grinned. "Very. But mostly just glad I'm alive."

We walked through the rose garden and to the bench we usually hung out at. My best friend sat down and faced me.

"Tell me everything. Because the last thing I saw, Kohen had you limp in his arms, half covered in burns, and he was screaming for a medic, with a *dragon* flying above him. Aisling, what in the hell happened out there?"

I took a deep breath and told her everything, holding nothing back. I told her how Kohen had snuck out to hunt for Talanagi and how I'd followed and then gotten into a fight with one myself. I told her about the bond, dying, and then floating in the blackness. Then how I had to fight the fire beast and woke up in a body bag.

"Holy crap, you're immortal," she whisper-screamed, looking over her shoulder as if one of our gardeners would kill her for saying such a thing.

I swallowed hard. "I don't know about that."

She peered at the sky. "Where is your creature?"

I followed her gaze, sighing. "I don't know." I felt her, barely, just sort of an awareness in my mind with no clear picture.

The first week after bonding, you never left your creature's side. It was the most important time to cement that bond.

"You're sure you bonded?" she asked.

"Yes!" I said defensively. "Maybe she's being reborn too. I don't know." I tapped my chest. "But I... feel her. We're definitely bonded."

I had half a mind to go back to The Wilds right now and look for her. Was she stuck in Luska? If Kohen's creature made it out, why not her?

Tetra nodded. "She'll show up. I heard that Talanagi are standoffish. Even Kohen's dragon isn't with him right now."

I raised an eyebrow. "You've been hanging out with Kohen?"

She snort-laughed. "Not like that. We got our itin-erary today. Boot camp starts tomorrow. I saw him."

My head reeled back. "Boot camp? We bond with our creatures and they give us a few days before—" my face fell. "How long was I gone?"

Tetra shifted in her seat. "Three days."

I stood, unable to sit with news like that. "Three days!" Holy crap. What if the coroner had incinerated me!

"Boot camp starts tomorrow?" I asked, feeling completely blindsided.

She nodded. "And tonight is a huge party at Sleuth. Everyone will be so happy to see you're okay."

I swallowed hard. "I dunno. I need to ask my dad. I mean, how many people know...?" *That I died*, was what I wasn't able to say.

"Just me, Anika, Kohen, and three imperial soldiers who your dad paid off and then threatened with death if we told. Aisling, you can't hide in your house forever. You need to start your training." She smiled.

Holy crap. Anika saw me dead? Kohen too. How would I explain this? Should I explain this? Maybe they would have mistakenly thought I was dead but I could say my father's medical team brought me back to life.

"Are Roc, Alek and Dev okay? I left them sleeping by the fire."

She nodded. "Roc bonded a lynx, Alek a hawk, and Dev a vulture."

A vulture? Yikes, I didn't even want to know what

kind of magic that creature had, but going on day three Dev was lucky to bond anything at all I guess.

"Club Sleuth?" I asked. My dad hated the dance club but would often let me go if it were in a group and I promised to be home by midnight.

She nodded. "Eight-thirty."

"Alright. I'll pick you up at yours before?"

She smiled, squeezing my shoulders. "A firebird. Aisling, you're my hero."

I grinned the entire walk back to my house.

THE FAMILY CELEBRATION WAS OKAY. We ate dinner in relative silence, and then when the chocolate cake came out, the triplets started fighting over whose piece was bigger and the kitchen turned into a warzone.

"I'm going to my office," said Father. "Congratulations, Aisling. I'll have Admiral Caruso send me your itinerary for tomorrow. I believe you are to report at oh seven hundred. You cannot begin boot camp without a creature, so hopefully she shows up, yes?"

That was a veiled insult. My father was a master at them.

I nodded. "Yes. I hope so too. Hey, Father? Can I go with Tetra to Club Sleuth and be home by midnight? Everyone is celebrating bonding with their creatures and I don't want to start the year off seeming like I'm not one of them."

My father's gaze narrowed. "You're *not* one of them. You're the future empress of this entire country," he said sternly.

"Yes, Father. I meant... it would help me to bond with them so that they would one day follow my commands when I am in a leadership role." My father needed things to be laid out for him practically.

"Okay, take the car and be home by curfew," he said curtly, and left.

I looked at Elaine, who had just reached out and smacked Valor's hand. "If you don't all shut your mouths and stop fighting, I'm eating all three of those slices and you get *nothing*."

The girls straightened, ceasing the argument immediately, and began shoveling their slices down before Elaine could take them.

Elaine never made a threat she didn't intend to back up. She'd eaten many of my desserts, and even though I hated it at the time, I respected her for it. She was a woman of her word. So when she said she had your back and would always look out for you, you could trust that too.

I met her gaze and we both smiled. Then she shook her head. "A Talanagi, Aisling?"

I grinned. "Too cocky?"

She pursed her lips and rolled her eyes, but then her gaze fell to the entryway of the kitchen where my father had returned to his study. "Just... lay low, follow the rules, and be good, okay?"

I nodded, reading her loud and clear. I wasn't going to press my luck.

"I want to meet your creature!" Victory whined.

"Yeah what's her name?" Valor begged.

"Liana," I told them.

"Will she let us pet her?" Virtue said.

I shrugged. "You can ask."

Where was she? Did she die and not get reborn like me? I knew spending the first week after bonding together was crucial, but I didn't know how crucial. What happened if she didn't show up by oh seven hundred tomorrow morning?

"Why don't you go get ready? And then these three need to bathe." Elaine gave Victory the stink eye.

Victory rolled her eyes. "Elaine, we are not children. You don't need to tell us when to bathe."

Elaine's hand snaked out lightning-quick and grabbed the last chunk of chocolate cake off of Victory's plate and shoved it into her mouth.

"What was that you were saying?" Elaine asked through the mouthful with a twinkle in her eye.

Victory crossed her arms and groaned. "Yes, ma'am."

I couldn't help but smile. It was nice to see the girls getting the same treatment I had growing up.

Elaine did not tolerate eye rolling or *any* level of sass, and there was a comfort in that.

VERIK PICKED up Tetra and then dropped us both off at Sleuth.

"I will be back at eleven forty-five to pick you up. Be outside and ready to go," Verik said.

I nodded.

I would normally have driven my motorbike, but the fact that my father told me to take the car meant he wasn't comfortable with that right now, and I was trying to do everything he said so that I didn't piss him off before I went to boot camp for a month.

The entrance to Sleuth had a line wrapped around the block, creatures standing by their humans waiting to get in. We walked right up to the front, bypassing the line. The bouncer took one look at me and his mouth opened in surprise.

"Miss Everhart, what a pleasure." He unhooked the red velvet rope that blocked the door and allowed Tetra, her creature, and me, to step inside.

I felt a little bit like a douchebag just cutting the line, but if you couldn't use your family status to get to the front line into clubs then what was the point?

The second we stepped inside, we were assaulted with loud music. Some live band was strumming away at their guitars and screaming into the mic. Not exactly my favorite type of tunes. I was into the more melodious lyrical stuff.

The thing that made Sleuth so cool was that the building was converted from an old warehouse. There was room for humans and creatures, which wasn't always the case. A few imperial soldiers stood at the edge of the room, eyes tracking me as I passed.

Great, my dad sent babysitters.

Tetra watched my gaze. "They could just be here to protect all of us, because of the war."

I shrugged. After the Blackout, we went to war with Imbria, and now that we'd merged with them, we stood united against our common enemy.

Luska.

The Luskins hated us and were constantly trying to inch into our borders and redraw maps, taking more and more of our land. They'd poisoned our reservoirs, set traps for our creatures, all because we had the most ember and they wanted it.

"Then why are they staring at me?" I asked Tetra.

She shrugged. "Because you are their boss' daughter. If anything happens to you, it's their head."

She was right, but I still didn't like it.

We finally met up with a group of people we recognized and I let my gaze scan over them to rest on Jace.

His arm was in a sling; he had a cut on his face which was sutured up, and standing beside him was a black puma, nearly identical to Zuri. Wow, I hadn't known how much like my father he was until now.

I swallowed hard as his gaze ran the length of my body, brows bunching together in confusion. I still hadn't processed the fact that he cheated on me, the ultimate betrayal. Our carefully-laid-out future was gone before I could see it realized. Maybe it was better that way.

"We heard you were clinging to life in the hospital?" Jace said.

And there wasn't a scratch on me now.

"I'm all better now," I stated.

One of his friends peered behind me. "Where is your creature? We heard it was a Talanagi, but no one knows what kind."

I understood their curiosity but it still made me uncomfortable to speak about. Before I had to answer, Anika's voice came from behind me.

"None of your business," she snapped to the boys. "You'll find out tomorrow with everyone else."

I spun with a smile and gave her lioness a nod. Anika had small scratches all up and down her arms that were healing, and she shook her head as she peered at me. Pulling me in for a hug, which surprised me, she pressed her lips to my ear. "Go to the bathroom alone. Kohen needs to talk to you."

She then pulled away from me. "Glad to see you're feeling better, princess," she said for all to hear.

My blood ran cold at the mention of Kohen needing to talk to me, but I gave her a fake smile.

"Thanks." Then I looked at Tetra. "Hey, I gotta pee. Be right back."

Tetra moved to follow me but Anika snaked out

and stopped her. "No, hang with me. I want to talk more about what you missed in The Wilds."

I gave Tetra a thumbs-up and a smile and made my way to the women's restroom at the back wall. Zigzagging between hundreds of candidates and creatures was a challenge, but I finally made it. As I headed for the women's bathroom, the door to the left opened and then I was yanked inside.

CHAPTER

ELEVEN

I was about to scream and put up a fight when I smelled cardamom and ginger. My favorite spiced-tea-drinking male had pulled me into a broom closet. The low light flickered above Kohen Badshah as he stared at me with wide, bugged eyes. Reaching out, he dragged the tips of his fingers across my temple and then down my jaw, causing a traitorous rush of emotions to wash over me.

"You're alive," he breathed.

His hand shook slightly as he pulled it back. "I... carried your dead, burned body out of The Wilds. But now... you live?"

My heart pinched at the thought of Kohen carrying my body out to the imperial soldiers so that I could be brought back to my father and given a proper burial.

"Yeah," I laughed nervously. "And you bonded the dragon?"

"Onyx," he corrected me.

"Where is he?" I asked, obviously noting he wasn't nearby.

"On the roof of this club, waiting for us to help him free your firebird."

The air whooshed out of me. "What?"

Kohen squared his shoulders. "I saw you bond. The sky glowed like the northern lights, but then you fell. Burned. Dead. And your firebird rained down in ashes. Gone." Kohen relived the memory and I felt bad that he had to see that. He thought I was dead this entire time.

"After I handed over your body, I thought that was it. Until thirty seconds ago when you walked in here and Onyx informed me that Li-ana..." He struggled with the name. "...was being held captive."

Anger like I'd never felt before rushed through me. "Tell me where!" My words were a growl. Who the hell was holding my creature captive? It explained why she hadn't shown up!

Kohen cocked his head to the side. "What are you going to do? Go and save her by yourself?"

"Don't mess with me, Kohen. Where is she?"

He sighed. "Onyx said that he just got word from her. They are old friends. She can't communicate with you because you haven't touched since the rebirth. The bonding needs to..." He paused as if trying to understand what Onyx had told him. "Cement itself in the first twenty-four hours after rebirth or it's broken. It's a firebird thing."

Panic seized me. Twenty-four hours? I'd already wasted nearly twelve of those since I'd woken up in the body bag.

I stepped closer to Kohen. "And Onyx knows where she is?" I pressed.

He gave me a halfcocked grin. "Sounds like you need me. A favor maybe?"

I let the murderous gaze that I had previously reserved for Jace in the Lottery slide over my face.

"Kohen, you don't want to know all the ways I have been taught to dismember a man."

His grin grew wider. "Fine, you don't have to beg, Aisling. But we need to lose the soldiers following you. Liana suspects the Imperial Fleet could have taken her."

No.

Pure shock coated my skin in that moment. "Why would she suspect that?"

Kohen rolled his eyes. "I don't know. But listen, can you meet me on the roof in a few minutes? We obviously can't be seen leaving together."

I snort-laughed. "Obviously."

A flash of hurt crossed his face, but then it was gone, replaced by a mask of indifference. "You have three minutes or we're leaving without you. I'm only helping because Onyx cares for your creature," he snapped and then slipped out of the closet, leaving me alone.

Jeez. Was he about to be on his period or something?

Stomping out of the broom closet, I turned the corner to look for the exit door and ran right into Jace.

His musky cologne hit me like a sack of bricks, and memories of us making out on his couch flashed through my mind. A deep ache formed in my chest and I had to push down the grief that tried to well up.

I thought Jace was my forever; his betrayal hurt me more than I would ever admit.

"Aisling." Jace put his hands on my shoulders.

"Don't. Touch. Me," I growled, and he immediately released me.

He stared at the floor and I moved to sidestep him when he spoke: "My parents are getting divorced," he said.

I froze, shock ripping through me for the second time in a few minutes. Aldric and Brianna were a perfect couple. He the leader of my father's fleet, she the doting housewife who'd raised two rowdy boys to be Imperial Fleet soldiers. She would cook scones from scratch and he would rub her shoulders and ask her if he could pour her a glass of wine. I used to watch them in awe, dreaming I could one day have a marriage like that.

"I don't believe you," I said.

He swallowed hard, his eyes suddenly swimming

with tears. "They told us two days before the Lottery and I... lost it. Went out and found the first girl I could and..."

Realizing where he was going with this, I reached up and grabbed his jaw firmly, forcing him to meet my gaze. "Jace Ledger, you will *not* make excuses for why you cheated on me. Nothing excuses that betrayal."

A tidal wave of emotions threatened to pull me under in that moment. I still hadn't processed the loss of him. These lips that I would kiss until bruised were no longer mine.

He blinked back the tears and nodded, but my heart broke at the sight of him vulnerable. Jace didn't cry. Jace didn't get emotional. Jace was made of steel like me.

"I'm sorry," was all he said. "I know you will never forgive me but... I miss my best friend." He whimpered the last part, and I wasn't sure if I wanted to punch him in the throat or hug him.

"Dammit, Jace, we were so good together," I breathed. My mind was suddenly flooded with memories of making pancakes with him and swimming at the cove and kissing for hours and naming our future children. I put all of my hopes and dreams in him and he crushed them without a second thought because he was having a bad day.

He nodded, picking at his nails and peered up at me with terror. "Tell me we can be friends. I don't deserve to ever have you as a girlfriend again but tell me we can still be friends?"

Dammit.

I had to get on the roof and go after my creature whom my bond would die out with if I didn't find her within the next twelve hours. And I had a curfew! I didn't have time for this soft, mushy stuff.

"I'll think about it," I told him honestly and he sighed, looking relieved. "And I'm sorry about your mom and dad," I added. Maybe his dad cheated too. It was an evil thought that I felt badly for the second it popped into my head.

He nodded. "Thanks."

I squeezed his shoulder and ran for the middle of the dance floor, scanning for my blonde-haired bestie.

I found her dancing her heart out, cane pumping up into the air as her wolf creature sat still at her back as if assessing threats.

"Aisling!" Tetra trilled as I neared. This woman loved to dance, and I never had the heart to tell her that she had zero rhythm. Her confidence was infectious and added to her appeal, making me just smile as I watched her awkwardly thrust her hips to a jerky beat, holding her bad leg up so it wouldn't get stepped on.

Stars, I adored this woman.

I grinned and she threw her arms around me, pulling me in to dance.

My gaze flicked around the room and to the soldiers stationed there. They were all watching me.

Damn.

I leaned into Tetra's ear and whispered: "My creature is being held captive and I have twelve hours to find her. I need to get to the roof and meet Kohen. His dragon is going to take us to her."

I pulled back to see that she was staring at me with wide eyes and an open mouth.

I gave her a fake smile. "I need a distraction," I mouthed, looking at the soldiers.

Her gaze flicked to the men standing against the walls of the club and she nodded.

"Be safe," she mouthed, concerned.

She then bent down and held her creatures gaze.

I had no idea what she was planning, but Tetra was cunning and would come up with something brilliant, I had no doubt. She suddenly dropped to the floor, convulsing as her creature tipped her head to the ceiling and let loose a spine-chilling howl.

Chaos exploded on the dance floor. People scattered, making room for the soldiers to rush towards Tetra as I ran for the exit.

Well, that was certainly a distraction!

I shook my head, slipping into the door that said *Stairwell.*

I took the stairs two at a time. That bastard better not have left me! I burst out the top of the steps to find Kohen mounted on Onyx's back. The Talanagi was a sight to behold. My heart increased its pounding as I neared the giant beast and he peered at me with curious green eyes. I bowed my head out of respect and Kohen quirked his lips.

"Why are you smiling?" I asked him, just now realizing we were probably going to fly to wherever we were going. Not smart then that I wore a black miniskirt and tights.

"Something Onyx said," Kohen mused.

"What did he say?" I asked as Kohen reached out a hand to me.

At least I was wearing underwear.

I grasped his hand and he hauled me up, tucking me behind him so that I was forced to straddle his backside and cling to his waist to stay seated on the beast.

"I'll never tell," he said, peering back at me.

"Hey, eyes forward. I'm wearing a skirt," I told him.

He scoffed as if my attempt at modesty was funny, but then his face darkened.

I frowned. "Onyx say something funny again?"

Kohen swallowed hard, his Adam's apple bobbing. "No. It's just that I carried you naked out of the woods for over a mile."

It was like all the air had been sucked from the area and I couldn't breathe.

Kohen Badshah saw me naked. For over a mile.

"Not that I was looking. I was too busy trying to

save your life and you were covered in burns," he added.

Silence descended over us and I nodded solemnly. "Thanks for that."

He faced forward, taking in a deep breath as I grasped his waist loosely, and he held on to two horns that protruded from Onyx's head.

"You're going to want to hold tighter than that," he stated.

I sighed, grasping his waist tighter and hating the way my body reacted to him being so close. I felt like I was betraying my father. "Can you get a saddle made or something?" I felt like I was going to fall off.

"Maybe if I were as rich as you." He chuckled. "I'm lucky to get three meals a day. I didn't have time to find any ember while I was fighting for my life in The Wilds."

He lightly clicked his heels and Onyx took off into the sky. My stomach dropped out and I clung to Kohen desperately as we climbed higher, pressing my chest into his back.

Lucky to get three meals a day? Was he joking? Maybe not. Shame washed over me and I wanted to change the subject.

This was crazy. I was flying on a dragon with the ex-prince of Imbria. If my father knew, he'd lose his mind.

We flew in silence northeast across the city

towards the farms and rolling hills of Cedar Creek for almost twenty minutes before Onyx began his descent.

There were so many things I wanted to ask Kohen—like did his dragon have special magic? Did Kohen? But I recognized we weren't friends and I didn't want to pry.

As we lowered over what looked like farmlands, I zeroed in on a huge red barn. Something knocked inside of my chest, an awareness of sorts.

"She's in there!" I pointed to the barn.

Kohen nodded.

I could feel her, and now that I could, anger raged within me. They were hurting her somehow.

My nails dug into Kohen's abdomen and he peered back at me. "Easy, tiger, I'm not the one hurting her."

I released my grip and focused on my breathing. Other than a small dagger stashed in my boot, I had no weapon. I wasn't prepared for some rescue mission when I went out clubbing. I should have told my father, let him bring a hundred imperial soldiers to this place and break Liana out... but I didn't. Which meant a small part of me questioned who could have done this. *It might be imperial soldiers...* That very thought made me sick.

"What's the plan? I didn't bring weapons," I told Kohen as Onyx landed in the thick forest near the barn.

Kohen looked back at me, grinning ear to ear.

"This type of thing is my specialty." He winked and my stomach bottomed out.

Why was he so dangerous and good looking? That combo was lethal. The one person my father wanted me to avoid was like a magnet to me. I ended up being around him whether I wanted to or not.

"Not to mention we have a dragon." He smoothed the scales on Onyx's back and hopped off of him and onto the ground. I went next, slamming onto my boots beside him and realizing I'd just ripped my black tights. Not very dragon rider friendly.

"So... we somehow sneak in and...?" I was hoping for a well-drafted plan, but Kohen just reached into his boot and pulled out a small hollow tube the size of a pencil, then a handful of darts from his pocket, and began uncapping the tips to reveal their razor-sharp points.

"Just follow my lead, princess. We will get your creature out, and then we can go back to not being seen together," he said, the last part with an extra layer of attitude.

I rolled my eyes. "You realize my father is the emperor, right? I can't just be... friends... with the son of his mortal enemy!"

His gaze flicked down at me and his eyes were practically burning. "Why not? I've done nothing to your family. And *you* took everything from me. My father, my mother, my home, my title."

His mother? I hadn't heard about that. "*I* took

nothing from you," I corrected. If he was saying that he personally did nothing to my family, then I was going to make the same distinction.

"Whatever. Let's just do this. I owe you for helping save my life with your father's goons, and after I help you get Liana back, we are even." His face was back to that mask of calm.

So that's why he was helping. He felt he owed me after what happened in The Wilds— something I couldn't believe I did and didn't want to think about ever again.

I shrugged. "Fine."

He loaded the mini darts into the small pipe and then crouched through the woods to the edge of the clearing that led to the barn.

I followed, keeping as silent as I could.

There were two soldiers in plain clothes leaning against the barn and scanning the woods. One held a bow in his hands, and the other a long broadsword. Neither had creatures with them, which meant they were either in the woods, or creatureless, which I doubted. I couldn't tell who these guys were. One looked like he could be Luskin, but without him speaking I wouldn't know.

Both men suddenly peered up to the sky, and I followed their gaze to see Onyx flying circles above, drawing their attention.

Kohen pulled the pipe to his lips and leapt from the cover of the trees, shooting darts and hitting both men in the neck before they even realized what was happening.

They both reached up and grabbed the darts at the same time, trying to yank them out, but then fell to the ground before they could.

"Holy crap, Kohen," I breathed. "Are they dead?"

He narrowed his gaze. "They should be. They stole your creature, Aisling."

I sighed. He was right. I glanced at the men to see they were still breathing, and I was reminded of Meera bragging about being able to make poisons and sleeping tinctures. Had Kohen gotten them from her?

My gaze fell to the men's boots. They could be Fleet-issued… it was hard to tell in the darkness and they were covered in dirt.

"Behind you," Kohen said suddenly and I spun, bending low to pull the dagger from my boot as I did. A wolf creature was already halfway in the air, pouncing at me. I reached up with my blade and met it, stabbing it right through the heart. Shock coursed through me as the animal twitched on the end of my blade and then slid off of it, dead, on the ground.

I turned to Kohen with wide eyes to see that he had just taken out a coyote creature. They'd attacked at the same time. They must belong to the two men. My heart raced, palms sweaty, as I looked down at the evidence of what we'd done. I'd never harmed another person's creature before.

"They were coming to kill us," Kohen told me.

I nodded numbly. One gift I had was the ability to compartmentalize trauma. I stuffed this event into my little black box inside and wiped my blade on the grass. The men would wake up and find their bonded dead…

"It's called self-defense, Aisling," Kohen said, and I cleared my throat, nodding again.

"Let's go inside. I feel her." I tapped my chest.

Kohen didn't seem fazed about gutting the coyote creature, and it made me wonder what he'd done in his life to survive. It reminded me of what he'd said in The Wilds, about doing anything to survive. It was both scary and commendable. He opened the door and slipped inside and I followed him.

"Hey! Who are you?" someone with a Marble Shores accent asked, and I looked up to see a man running at us with a sword in his hand.

Kohen froze, slipping his hand into mine. "Whoa, chill, bro. I was just trying to find some place to be alone with my girl."

The way he so easily slipped into character told me he'd lied often over the years to do things like this. But why was the man's accent from Marble Shores? Why would my own people be involved in this? My mind spun.

The man slowed, lowering his sword, and seeming less alarmed.

"Parker! Cane!" The man approached us, calling outside to his buddies.

When the man got close enough, Kohen dropped my hand and exploded forward, cracking the side of his temple with the butt of a dagger and knocking him out cold. He must be creatureless, because no animal jumped out to defend him.

I felt it then, a kick to the chest like my heart had just woken up after being asleep my entire life.

Liana.

I leapt over the fallen man's body, weaving in and out of crates and hay bales that were stacked up inside of the giant barn.

"Liana!" I screamed frantically. I could feel her now. She was in pain, weak. Kohen's footsteps sounded behind me, and then I turned the corner and found her. I gasped when I saw what had become of my creature. She was tiny, only about ten pounds if I were guessing, and twelve inches long, bare of feathers. A baby bird. They had her pinned to the ground with a glowing golden net. Some strong magic had been infused into the net and I reached out to grasp it and try to pry it off of her when Kohen yanked me backward.

"That looks protective in nature. It could kill you."

"We need to get it off her!" I growled. I wasn't mad at Kohen. I was mad at whoever did this to her. This was powerful creature magic.

"Stand back. Let me try something," Kohen said. I frowned, taking a step back, and he knelt before the net holding Liana. She stared up at him with wise purple eyes, unafraid but clearly in pain.

"Onyx, help me," Kohen whispered, and then opened his palms.

I gasped when an orange flame burst from each palm, coating his hands. He made no indication that it burned him, so I stood there in fascination as he grasped the golden ropes. His teeth clattered shut and he growled, his body convulsing.

"Kohen!" I rushed forward to try and help.

"Don't touch me," he groaned. His body shook and he snarled like an animal as he tore the net in two. The moment the net snapped, it turned black and then shriveled to ash in Kohen's fingers.

"Are you okay?" I asked him.

The flames died out on his palms and left nasty bubbled burns in their wake.

"I'm fine," he muttered.

Taking him at his word, I rushed to Liana, scooping her up into my arms and holding her like I would a newborn baby. The moment our skin touched, the bond burst to life inside of me, connecting us fully. I could feel her heart beat within my very own.

'Thank you, young one,' she told me.

With our mental link restored, I spoke back without moving my lips.

'Are you okay?'

'Put me in the moonlight. I was taken during my rebirth cycle and it needs to be complete.'

I stood, explaining to Kohen what needed to be done. He nodded, leading the way outside. By the time we got to the unconscious man near the front door, I peered down to see that Kohen's hands were completely healed.

I raised one eyebrow at him but he said nothing.

Talanagi powers were said to be incomparable to other creatures', sometimes giving their human multiple gifts. Fire... healing... it seemed Kohen had two. Maybe more.

We burst outside and I was relieved to see the two soldiers were still unconscious. Bending down, I lay Liana in the moonlight, then stood next to Kohen.

Almost immediately, a pearlescent glow engulfed her small form and she began to grow. Movement in the woods pulled my attention, and Kohen put out a hand to calm me. "It's Onyx."

I sighed, relieved. Onyx walked over to where Liana was growing, feathers sprouting from bare skin, and sat patiently with us. I was enraptured by the sight. Liana went from a two-day-old, bare-skinned bird, to a ten-foot-tall firebird with colored feathers and sharp talons in five minutes. When she was fully transformed, Onyx walked over and nestled her head with his.

'Are you lovers?' I asked bluntly. There was nothing too personal to ask my creature. I felt fully open and comfortable with her.

She chuffed, laughing. *'He is more like a son to me. His mother died in The Wilds and I raised him.'*

That was really sweet.

'How did she die?' I asked, curious.

'A rival dragon,' was all she said.

Yikes. It seemed in The Wilds they had the same issues as we had here.

'Do you know who took you? Kohen said you thought they might be imperial soldiers?'

She glanced at the two men on the ground. *'I do not know for sure, but these two had some kind of Amersean accent.'*

I nodded. *'Marble Shores.'* She spent her whole life in The Wilds. She wouldn't have known exactly where.

'And they somehow knew they had to trap me before I completed my rebirth. They were trying to keep us apart so that we wouldn't complete the bond. You are the first human in a thousand years to defeat the fire beast and survive.' She stood taller, proud.

Shock ripped through me. The fire beast? The thing I fought in the sky right before I awoke in the morgue? *'Others have tried?'*

She chuckled. *'Many. More try to bond with a Talanagi than you think. It just doesn't make it back to you since they all die or they are Luskin.'*

She appraised Kohen then, looking him up and down as he stood patiently beside me. *'I like him,'* she said randomly.

I bristled at that. *'That's complicated...'*

'I know. I've seen your memories. I still like him.'

Okay... noted.

"We should get out of here before they wake up," Kohen announced.

Liana peered down at the two men and I followed her gaze. These two men *stole* and *hurt* my creature. They tried to keep me from bonding her. I pulled the blade from my boot and walked over to them. I promised myself I would never be the stupid girl in the books who let the bad man live only to be shocked when he came back for her again and again.

I wasn't a stupid girl and I was going to make sure this was a one-time thing. I remembered when my father first took me hunting. My arrow wasn't a clean shot, so he made me slit the deer's throat to put it out of its misery. It's easier if you moved your face away and didn't look at them.

Dropping to one knee, I turned my head and slit their throats cleanly, tucking the trauma away in my little black box. Elaine and my father would approve of this. Let this send a message to whoever thought they could steal from Aisling Everhart, future empress. Because that's what this was, an attempt to steal my creature from me. They couldn't kill a firebird, but they could keep her and I from bonding. And they almost succeeded.

"Okay, that shouldn't have been sexy but it was," Kohen mused behind me, and I scoffed. He thought murder was sexy?

Ignoring him, I walked back inside. I finished off the man in the barn.

After stepping back outside, I wiped my knife on the ground, reholstering it.

Five people. I'd killed five people and I wasn't even enlisted in the Imperial Fleet yet.

"I don't relish killing anyone," I announced, because I didn't want Kohen or his creature to think any less of me for killing an unconscious man. "But I will not allow this kind of thing to ever happen again. Enemies must be dealt with quickly and fiercely." It was something my father taught me, and words to live by.

'Well done, young one, but the man who is in charge of all of this still walks free,' Liana said.

Chills raced up my arms. *'Who?'*

'I did not see him, as my eyes had not yet formed, but I would know his smell from anywhere. Cigars and whiskey, burnt ember, and cheap musk cologne.'

Relief rushed through me at her description of the smells. I hadn't realized until now that I had suspected my own father of possibly doing this in an effort to keep me from overshadowing him with my power. But my father didn't smoke, nor did he wear cologne; Zuri hated strong smells. I couldn't believe I'd gotten so paranoid as to suspect my own father of this!

Chill out, Aisling, I chastised myself.

"What time is it?" I asked Kohen.

He peered at his watch. "Half past eleven."

Crap. My curfew.

"I gotta get home or my dad will send the entire Imperial Fleet out looking for me," I told him.

He nodded, slipping his leg over the back of Onyx and hoisting himself up. I guess we both had our own rides now.

"Hey, thanks... for helping me find and free her." I stroked Liana and looked up at Kohen.

He nodded, his face expressionless. "Now we're even." Then Onyx kicked off the ground and took for the skies.

Man, he was hard to read. Calling me hot one second and then shutting down the next. Pretty on par for the men I seemed to attract.

'Can I ride on you?' I asked Liana, unsure if that would hurt her or not.

She bowed deeply in response. It took a few minutes for me to find a comfortable way to sit on her and not feel like I was going to fall off.

Once I was snugly seated, she kicked off into the sky and we sailed over the city on my way home. I just prayed my father was asleep when I got there.

TWELVE

As we flew over the farmlands and closer to Riverine, I stroked Liana's neck feathers.

'How should I give you directions?' I asked her. She'd never been out of The Wilds.

'Think in pictures and send them to me,' she responded.

Think in pictures... okay. Every human-creature bonded was different, and each pairing had to figure out how they would best work together and eventually fight together in battle. It was a huge part of what we would learn at boot camp.

I flashed pictures into my mind's eye about different parts of the city, and then finally stopped on the giant stone castle that we called home.

'Oh that's easy. I see it from here,' Liana said.

I reeled back. She did? I squinted, peering at the ground. There was no way she saw my house from here when we were still hovering over the north end of the city. I certainty couldn't see it.

'*I have special vision,*' she told me, and understanding dawned on me.

That made sense, and was super cool.

'*What other gifts do you have?*' I asked.

'*I can breathe fire, emit a poison from my talons if I want to, fly, see super far, fly super fast. I'm a good judge of character just by smelling someone, I am obviously immune to fire, and I regenerate and rebirth so that I never die.*'

Hah! That was all. '*You're amazing.*' I reached out and stroked her neck feathers.

She nuzzled into my hand. '*Oh, and I heal within minutes. I think you got that from me too.*' She peered back at me, noticing I had no burns on my body.

'*Thank you for that gift,*' I told her honestly. I couldn't imagine the pain of trying to heal from burns that bad.

'*Can I ask you more questions or is this annoying?*' I asked her. A creature and their human had to work out their personalities in the beginning. It could be a bit like having a new roommate. I didn't want to overwhelm her.

'*Not annoying,*' she told me, and I sensed a smile in her voice.

'*I saw that your mate passed and that you had children.*'

She nodded. '*But they are all gone now.*'

I frowned. *'How can they pass when you are immortal?'*

'They were males like my mate. Only females rebirth.'

Right, she had shown me that.

'I'm sorry.'

'I also consider Onyx as one of my children.'

I grinned at that. Thinking of Liana mothering Onyx made me smile for some reason.

'And that golden egg, you said it was yours but your mate is gone...' I was almost embarrassed to ask the question, but if a baby firebird was going to be born in The Wilds without a mother... *'Should we go back for it?'*

Her entire body rattled with what at first sounded like a cough and then turned into what I now recognized as a laugh.

'Aisling. You are a woman who bleeds, yes?'

My cheeks went red and I knew I never should have asked her.

'Yes,' I confirmed.

'But every time you bleed you are not pregnant?'

Oh my stars, if we were about to talk about sex I was going to die.

'Right.' I wanted to change the subject, but couldn't think of anything to say.

'I lay eggs that are not fertilized,' she confirmed, and I nodded, feeling like an idiot.

She was like the chickens we had in the barn. A giant magical chicken.

'*Sorry, let's never speak of that again,*' I told her, and her chest rumbled with a laugh again.

'*Hold on,*' she said, as she began to descend.

I dug my fingers into her colorful feathers and then we dropped. My stomach gave out and a thrill ran through me. She shot forward faster than I ever thought possible, and laughter bubbled out of me. I had to squeeze my thighs to stay on her and then she slowed in front of my house.

I scanned our large compound, then the smile was ripped from my face. My father was watching us with crossed arms and a curious expression, Zuri perched next to him and glaring up at me. I sat up straighter and leapt off of Liana the moment she landed.

"Father. I'm sorry if I'm late. There was—"

"Is this her?" He walked towards Liana, cocking his head to the side, making a slow circle around her. I could see the greed in his gaze, the jealousy. No matter how much he tried to hide it, his face dripped with it.

Could I blame him? I'd bonded a Talanagi. He was the emperor. It should have been him.

"Yes, Father, this is Liana. Liana, this is the emperor of Amersea, my father."

My father bowed slightly to her out of respect, Zuri doing the same beside him. "We are so pleased you have bonded with Aisling. You will make a great addition to my fleet."

Liana's nostrils flared slightly. I could tell something was off with her, a stirring within her that I couldn't explain.

But she bowed her large, feathered head out of respect, saying nothing to me.

"It seems we are all well met," I told my father, as he and Zuri relaxed after Liana's head bow, which was not only a sign of respect but submission. Something my father demanded of all of his subjects.

Meeting another person's creature for the first time was a bit unnerving. There had been attacks in the past if two creatures didn't get along well.

"I'm going to get her settled in the barn," I informed my father.

He nodded curtly. "Then right to bed. You start boot camp tomorrow."

I grinned at that. I never in a million years thought I'd bond a Talanagi and go off to boot camp with her. Every Imperial Fleet officer present would be staring at us no doubt. They'd be staring at Kohen and Onyx too.

I walked Liana across the large garden and to the huge barn my father had built just for this moment. There were four large stalls, enough for me and the triplets' creatures when they got them. I slid open the large double doors and then walked her into one of the open stalls. Fresh hay had been laid down and there was water and food.

Liana took one look at it and snorted. *'Oh, my precious child. I am not a pet. I will not be living in here.'*

My face fell and I immediately felt guilty. Of course she wasn't a pet!

'I've offended you? I'm so sorry.' This was the room-mate stuff we needed to work out. I reached for her and she nuzzled my hand.

'Not offended. Just educating you. I sleep among the trees and the stars. I hunt for my food. I drink from streams. I fly where I want and I will never be caged.'

I understood completely. She wasn't like other creatures and I needed to remember that. *'I'm sorry.'*

I walked her out of the barn to the back of our yard where the perfectly manicured lawn stopped and the thick wild jungle began.

She looked content. *'This is better.'*

I chewed on my lip, worried now that we might have to work some more things out. *'I start a month-long boot camp tomorrow. We are at war with Luska and boot camp is where we go to learn—'*

She nodded, cutting me off. *'I know how it works. I live near The Wall, I see the war firsthand every day. I will learn to fight beside you, Aisling, and protect you with my life. I will lead you into battle, and one day, when you are empress, I will carry you across the entire world in a victory parade.'*

I grinned. *'You know about that? The emperor's parade?'*

'I am well known in The Wilds. Other creatures tell me things and I offer protection or give them ancient knowl-

edge,' she mused. *'They told me about your customs and we had a similar parade where I'm from.'*

Where she was from? I didn't think she meant The Wilds... *'Where are you from?'* I asked, and felt nervousness run through her.

'Home. Above the fire sky, from before the rock fell and brought us here.'

I was stunned by her answer. Creatures considered The Wilds their home, a home they wanted to leave and explore the outside world. For her to say that above the fire sky was her home... well, she was much older than I had initially thought by thousands of years. The realization was mind-boggling. Incredible.

'I'm very grateful to have bonded you, Liana,' I told her.

'And I you,' she said, bowing deeply to me, deeper than she did to my father. *'I will follow every command you give me, and do everything in my power to serve and protect you. I only ask for one favor in return when the time comes.'*

A favor? My heart hammered in my chest. *'What favor?'*

'I will ask when the circumstances are ready, and you can decide if you want to grant my request.'

That felt heavy, an undefined favor. But she wasn't saying I had to grant it, only that she would ask.

'Okay, ask when you are ready, and if it's reasonable I will grant it.'

She opened her beak in what I could only describe as a grin. *'Goodnight, young one,'* she said.

'Goodnight, Liana,' I told her, and moved to leave when she stopped me with a feeling. It was like a pull on my chest, and then an uneasiness ran through my stomach.

I turned around to face her.

'Do you love him?' she asked.

I stood there in shock at her question for a wild second thinking she meant Kohen. *'Who?'*

'Your father.'

I sagged in relief, laughing. Did I love my father? What kind of question was that?

'I mean, yeah. He's my father,' I answered, unsure. I'd never said it to him, not even as a child. My mother said it all the time, too much probably, but my father never uttered the words and so we didn't either.

'Then I won't tell you what I think of him. Goodnight, Aisling.'

Her words carved their way through my heart as I wished her goodnight and walked back to my house in stunned silence.

She mentioned she was a good judge of character just by smelling someone. Was that what she meant? She smelled my father and she didn't like him?

I lay awake for an hour thinking about it before finally drifting off to sleep.

THIRTEEN

My first day of boot camp would not be fun. I had heard and seen firsthand how cadets were treated like the scum of the earth.

"You will not be given special treatment just because you are my successor," my father said at breakfast.

He normally poured a cup of black coffee and went to his office, but this morning he was sitting in front of me and the triplets with a muffin.

"I know," I told him.

He appraised me solidly for a few seconds and my heart picked up speed. Did he know Liana didn't like him? Could Zuri smell it?

I peered at my father's creature. She stood like a sentinel beside him, ready to devour any foe.

Finally a smile broke onto my father's face and he

shook his head. "My daughter bonded a Talanagi. I can't wait to see the drill instructors' faces when you walk in with her."

I sat up straighter, smiling a little myself. "You're coming to drop me off?"

I'd assumed he'd be too busy.

My father nodded. "I cleared my morning. But I need to be at Sky Reach by the afternoon. We've had a fresh attack there."

I grinned the entire way through my breakfast. My father, the emperor, was dropping *me* off at boot camp?

On the one hand, he never took time out to do that stuff. It was always Elaine, and so I was excited. But on the other hand, having your father, the leader of the free nation, drop you off at what was literally referred to as *hell month*, was bound to make a bigger target on my back. But I didn't care. If my father wanted to be a parent today instead of a leader, I was going to enjoy it.

I'd waited my entire life to make him proud, to do something that would make him notice me. But when I glanced at Elaine, she was giving me one of her warning looks. A look that said, *Be careful.* I frowned, unsure what to make of that, so I decided to ask her when we had some alone time.

But before I knew it, my father had packed all of my things into his car and I was saying goodbye to Elaine and the triplets on the front porch.

"Give them hell, big sis," Virtue told me, and reached out to fist bump me. I swatted her hand away and pulled her in for a hug.

"Mind Elaine. Pay attention in training," I advised her.

She pulled away, rolling her eyes, and nodded.

Valor, the eldest by three minutes, was next: "If anyone messes with you, remember a well-timed throat punch is effective," she informed me as she peered at Elaine, who smiled at the advice.

I hugged her and then went to Victory, who was already waiting with arms open. I pulled her in and just held her, the youngest of the three but with a mighty heart. She was submissive in nature, companionate, and my favorite. She would probably bond with a less-than-desirable creature and have a lame job in the Imperial Fleet, but she'd be the most well-adjusted and happiest of the Everhart clan.

"I love you, Aisling," she whispered in my ear and I froze, shocked by the three words. My brain short-circuited as if it didn't know what to do. She never said it—no one in this family did, and that was normal.

Did she think I was going to die or something?

"You too," I mumbled, as she pulled away from me and reached out to touch my now half-black, half-red hair.

"So cool," she muttered.

My father stepped up next to me and Elaine caught my eye, giving me a salute. "Remember what I taught you. Be respectful to your drill instructors and your fellow cadets. Head down. Follow orders."

"Yes, ma'am." I saluted her back but there was so much more I wanted to say. This woman had raised me for this moment. All the training and advice she'd given me was so that I would bond with a creature and make it to boot camp.

My father tugged my arm and I followed him, hoping that Elaine knew me well enough to know the unspoken words that were lodged in my throat.

I love you.

When we got to my father's car, something caught my eye in the garden. I turned to the source and saw Liana, with her vibrant purple, red and orange feathers.

'Let's make an entrance,' Liana told me.

I grinned. "Dad, I'll follow you there?"

My father raised one eyebrow but I didn't wait for him to comment. I was totally flying to my first day.

MY FATHER'S car pulled in the parking lot and already I could see hundreds of cadets gathered around the huge gates of the Imperial Fleet Training Center. The gates of the training center had a giant puma on the front standing in a ring of fire, my father's creature, in a portal. An homage to him.

When my father stepped out of the car, the crowd

gasped. Parents, students, creatures, they all formed a circle around him until each and every one pulled up their right hand and saluted him.

Liana began her descent, and one by one the crowd turned from my father and looked up at the sky. Whispers became shouts, then there was pointing and gasping until Liana landed right in front of the closed school gates.

"That's my bestie!" Tetra stepped out from the crowd, her black wolf creature trailing behind her as she limped her way over to me.

I grinned, jumping off of Liana and hugging Tetra.

"Dude, what happened last night?" she started.

"My dad is here to see me off, did you see him?" I asked her with a warning tone in my voice.

I did *not* want my father finding out about last night and the three men I'd killed.

Tetra nodded in understanding and she spun. The crowd parted and my father walked right up to her, with three of his personal guard on either side of him.

She bowed her head. "Mr. Everhart."

His mouth ticked. He hated when she called him that and not emperor, but she'd been doing it since she was seven so there was no changing her ways.

"I'm pleased to see you survived The Wilds," my father told her, and then peered at her creature. "And made a decent bonding."

Decent. She was a wolf! That was more than *decent.*

My father and Tetra always found ways to subtly insult each other.

"Oh yes, sir. Thank you. All I can hope for now is to serve the Imperial Fleet as best I can." She was laying it on thick and my father knew it.

He rolled his eyes, about to retort, when the puma-adorned gates opened. People stepped back, no one wanting to be in the front as the half-dozen drill instructors, equally male and female, walked out to greet us, marching in lockstep.

They stood erect but I noticed one of their gazes flick to my father. It was one of the females. She had a blonde pixie cut that was slicked back, and a hawk tattoo on her neck. I noticed six creatures waiting just inside the gates, one of them a hawk. Oftentimes humans got a tattoo of their creature to display for all to see. I was betting that hawk was hers.

"Emperor Everhart on deck!" the hawk drill instructor screamed and they all dropped to one knee and bowed their heads.

My father smiled, clearly loving the attention.

"Dismissed," my father said, and they stood as one.

I released the nervous breath I had been holding and the drill instructors went at ease, breaking apart their little display of unity and standing three on each side of the entrance to the school.

"Please say goodbye to the cadets," a drill instructor with a black buzzcut said. "After they cross this threshold, they are no longer your children. They are mine." The others grinned.

My father was smiling too. Elaine told me that most of the drill instructors were a fan of theatrics, but a few were serious and would push you to the limit, inflicting pain both physical and emotional to see how well you could submit to orders.

Everyone turned to their parents then and I moved to say goodbye to my father, but he was talking to the lieutenants.

"Aisling, honey," a familiar female voice called over my shoulder.

I spun and Tetra's mom pulled me in for a bone-crushing hug. "Thank you for protecting her," she said into my ear.

I relished Bethel's mama hugs. They were the kind I imagined my own mother would give me if she were still alive—all-encompassing, vulnerable, and filled with unspoken love. I pulled back and her eyes were wet.

"Of course," I told her. "And I will continue to."

Not that Tetra needed it much, she had a creature now. A powerful one.

Bethel nodded, holding out something wrapped in cloth. "My banana bread. I know it's your favorite."

It was.

I took it, sure it would be confiscated but unable to tell her no.

Tetra was beside her mother, looking like she was

on the verge of tears. I worried for my friend when the drill instructors would start screaming in her face. I hadn't prepared her for any of this.

Her mother waved goodbye to us one last time and then moved to the street to wait with the other parents.

I turned to my bestie. "Hey, T, you gotta do what they say. No sass. No jokes. No rolling eyes. Don't even think it. They will know."

She rolled her eyes in response. "They can read minds?"

My eyes widened. "T, no eye rolling. I'm serious. You have to show that you can be respectful and take orders without any questions."

Her brow furrowed. She was the queen of questions. "What if—?"

"T, I'm warning you. They will shave your head and parade you around in your underwear at 2 a.m. in the freezing cold if you cause problems. Do as I say," I snapped.

She swallowed hard, looking scared for the first time. "Okay, jeez."

She reached up to touch her long blonde hair as if horrified by the thought of it being shaved off. Maybe I was being a touch overdramatic, but I'd heard of it happening.

A shadow fell overhead and I looked up, instinctively knowing who it would be.

When I saw the black dragon, I sighed.

Onyx landed right next to Liana and Kohen dismounted, carrying a backpack filled with his things.

My gaze flicked to my father. I could practically see the hatred fuming off of him as he stared at Kohen. My father leaned into one of the lieutenants, the oldest one, with silver hair and a take-no-prisoners look on his face. My father said a few things into the lieutenant's ear and then walked away. I followed after him, his guards allowing me through as he reached his car.

"Thanks for coming to see me off!" I told him.

He spun, like he'd forgotten I was here. "Oh yes. Be good, Aisling. Don't embarrass me."

Ahh, there was the warm and cuddly man I knew.

"Yes, sir," I saluted him, and he mirrored the move back to me and then he drove off. One of his guards handed me my duffle bag and I ran to meet up with the others, who were now going through the open gates with their creatures. Ours were too big to fit side by side, so Kohen and I waited until the last cadet had entered the gate.

"You first, princess," Kohen said, but the words held no harsh tone. They even sounded respectful. If that were possible. Had he given me a pet name?

I peered at Liana, who nodded and stepped up beside me. Swallowing hard, I walked through the gates, watching as every eye at boot camp turned to look my way, even the drill instructors.

I found a place at the end of the line, placed my bag at my feet, and stood tall next to Anika of all people. Liana wandered to the field behind us and stood with the other creatures. The drill instructors knew better than to try to train the creatures. That was something we would each do ourselves. They might guide us but they wouldn't be screaming in the faces of a wolf or lion. They weren't stupid. We had to submit to the instructor so that our creatures would submit to them through our bond.

The hawk lieutenant stepped up to the front line with her hands behind her back. "If you think you are special because you survived The Wilds and bonded, THINK AGAIN!" She roared the last two words in Tetra's face and my bestie squeaked.

"I am Lieutenant Ashendell, your lead lieutenant. It is my job to make sure you can survive in a war and I take my job VERY SERIOUSLY!" She screamed into Anika's face but the Imbrian didn't move.

She then walked right up to me and stared me up and down. "If ANY OF YOU think you are special because of how much money you have, or who you parents are, YOU ARE WRONG and I WILL PROVE YOU WRONG," she shouted in my face, so close that I felt spittle fly onto my cheeks.

I didn't move a muscle, just stared ahead as if nothing had happened.

Lieutenant Ashendell walked up to Kohen. "And if you have a weakness, and the creatures chose wrong."

She stared Kohen up and down. "I will pull that weakness out of you and display it for all to see."

She paused, just glaring at him. I peered at him without moving my head since he was right next to me. He appeared to be glaring her down, not looking at the space in front of him like he should be.

Oh stars. He was an idiot.

"DO YOU UNDERSTAND ME?" she shouted suddenly, making half the cadets jump, and probably hoping to jostle Kohen, but he didn't move.

"Yes, ma'am!" Kohen replied with the rest of us.

I had a feeling this was going to be an interesting month.

Over the next twenty minutes, we stood there as they tore open our bags, displaying our stuff for all to see. They took heavily padded bras, makeup, curling irons, and threw them all in the trash. One of the male cadets had brought cookies and letters from his mother pre-written for each week he was here. She read a few out loud, got everyone laughing, and tossed the rest.

"WEAK!" one of the lieutenants said.

They took my banana bread but that was it. Elaine was no fool. She didn't pack anything that would have been confiscated. When Lieutenant Ashendell's gaze fell to my necklace, my stomach dropped.

How could I be so stupid? No jewelry. She could see the panic in my gaze as I was unable to contain my fear that she would destroy the locket.

"Give it." She held out her hand.

My heart pounded in my chest, and simultaneously another lieutenant took Tetra's cane.

"I need that to walk, you asshat," she snapped.

Oh crap.

Lieutenant Ashendell tore away from me and ran up to Tetra. "WHAT DID YOU JUST SAY?"

Suddenly there were fingers on my neck and I froze, peering over at Kohen in shock when he pulled my necklace off and popped it into his mouth!

What the hell?

Lieutenant Ashendell made Tetra do one hundred push-ups and then came back over to me. Her gaze fell on my neck and her eyes narrowed.

"Turn out your pockets," she ordered.

I did without question.

"Open your mouth," she said next.

I did.

"Where is it?" she growled.

"Where is what, ma'am?" I said in the rhythmic answering tone they preferred.

She reached out and grasped the sides of my cheeks, hard.

I felt movement behind me but I dared not turn around to look, and Lieutenant Ashendell's hand fell away from me almost as soon as she'd touched me. I was about to wonder why when I felt her. Liana.

My creature walked out from her line where she had been standing with the others and strode over to

Lieutenant Ashendell, pausing a mere six feet from her.

The lieutenant narrowed her gaze at me. "You will not get special treatment."

"Yes, ma'am," I answered, staring straight ahead and ignoring the fact that my creature was threatening her.

'Go back in line,' I told Liana.

Liana reached her head forward and sniffed Lieutenant Ashendell's leg, causing the lieutenant's eyebrows to raise.

"*Control* her," she said to me through a clenched jaw, but I could hear a slight shake to her voice.

'She won't hurt you. She was bluffing. I like her,' Liana decided, and then strode back over to the line with the others.

Bless the stars! This firebird was going to give me a heart attack.

"Sorry, ma'am," I said, and Ashendell rolled her eyes, stomping off to make fun of the fact that Tetra could only do twenty push-ups.

I wanted to tell Tetra that they would give her a Fleet-issued cane. It wouldn't be cute like the crystal one she had now; it would be rubber and safe for her and others. But I couldn't say a word. And I couldn't stop thinking about how Kohen had my special locket inside his mouth.

FOURTEEN

An hour later we were waltzed into the building as some older soldiers grinned and tossed immature comments our way. The training facility housed boot camp cadets, and then also higher-level soldiers doing advanced officer training.

When we turned a corner we had to bunch together and I felt Kohen's hand slip in mine, depositing the locket into my fist. I slipped it into my pocket before anyone could see and flicked my gaze to his, but he faced forward, ignoring me.

Why did he do that? Risked getting his butt chewed out for a stupid necklace. There was only one answer I could come up with.

Psychological warfare. From day one, he'd moved out of the way so that Tetra could take his place; he had his team of Imbrians protect her in The Wilds; he helped me save Liana—he did these nice things so that I would grow soft towards him and then he would betray me.

I was not going to let that happen.

"Choose a bunkmate of the same sex!" one of the drill instructors screamed, and I scrambled to get next to Tetra. We formed an orderly line of two by two and the instructor pointed down the hallway of open rooms. "Find a room. This is a co-ed dorm, not a brothel. You are here to learn. We are *not* your parents, you are grown-ass adults, so we expect you to behave like it. Remember that," she said, and then all the instructors flattened their backs against the wall as we walked briskly to the first open room we could find. My stomach sank when Kohen and Dev slipped into the room directly next to mine, but I shook it off.

We were given ten minutes to unpack and make our beds. Perfectly folded sheets were set at the end of each bunk. I instinctively started making the top bunk bed up because I knew with Tetra's foot she wouldn't be able to get up here. When I was done folding the corners exactly like Elaine had taught me, I slipped my locket under the mattress between the boards and then jumped down to look at Tetra's bed.

It was awful.

"Tuck them tightly," I whispered, yanking the sheet and bedspread down and showing her how. She nodded, doing the next one.

"Tighter, crease it with your hand," I told her.

She did, and struggled without her cane, falling over a few times.

"They will give you a Fleet-issued cane made of rubber," I whispered. "I forgot to tell you that."

She looked relived at that.

"Inspection!" an instructor screamed, and I stood, creasing the last part and then standing at attention, back ramrod straight, hands clasped behind me and chin up.

Tetra mimicked my position and I worried less about her. She was smart and a quick learner—she would catch on. Boots sounded down the hall and then I heard the sound of sheets being torn off a bed.

"This is the Imperial Fleet! Not your mother's basement!" an instructor bellowed down the hall.

"Yes, sir!" a female yelled back.

In the next room the same thing happened.

And then it was our turn. Instructor Ashendell stood in the doorway of our room and peered at me.

"If the emperor's own daughter doesn't know how to make a bed, you all have to run a mile," she said from the doorway, and there was a collective groan down the hallway.

My heart burst to life inside my chest as her gaze ran over my top bed with a critical eye. She even stepped up on the first rung of the attached ladder to get a closer look. When she jumped down, she held my gaze.

"Congratulations, Miss Everhart, you are the new official cadet bed-making instructor."

"Yes, ma'am!" I said.

It was a compliment. I would need to train anyone who had their bed torn up and it would fall on me to be punished if they couldn't learn. Elaine told me things like this happened. It was a test of my leadership skills.

The instructors fanned out and tore apart nearly all of the bedrooms.

"Pathetic!" the older instructor my father had spoken to outside screamed. "You have twenty minutes to remake them or you all have to run a mile. You may ask Miss Everhart for a tutorial."

Great.

My room was suddenly flooded with worried-looking cadets. My ex-boyfriend Jace was among them. Tetra stepped to the side and I tore her lower bunk apart for the tutorial. My nervousness ramped up a notch when I noticed Kohen in the crowd, and then went even higher when I saw that three of the instructors were watching me.

I separated the blanket and sheet and then shook the sheet flat, draping it over the bed.

"The trick is constant creasing with your hands, every step of the way." I tucked the sides, lifting up the mattress and creasing as I went. "Think of your hand as an iron, and crease tight. If you think it's tight enough, it's not," I said.

"Got it," a girl with long brown hair said and spun to leave the room. I recognized her from the academy; we went to school together. She dated Alek in eleventh grade and was super stuck-up. Her name was Summer and she was a know-it-all. I'd seen her come in with a beautiful male lion creature. We didn't run in the same social circles, so I normally did my best to ignore her.

"I'm not done!" I snapped at her back, and Kohen stepped out from where he'd been and barred her way.

Why did he keep doing that stuff?

The girl turned to me with a narrowed gaze. "An idiot can make a bed. I've learned enough. I'd rather have more time to work on it."

I saw the instructors' eyebrows raise but they said nothing, as if they were watching me to see how I would deal with this confrontation.

I nodded. "Then when everyone else passes and you fail, you will know that your pride and impatience are the reason we will likely have to run a mile."

She rolled her eyes, spun and bumped Kohen out of the way.

A nearly all-consuming rage washed over me as she left. I wanted to tear after her and drag her back here to finish the tutorial, but I'd learned from my father that some people only learned from their mistakes. I was betting she was one of those.

I faced my fellow cadets: "The corners must be folded at a forty-five-degree angle." I demonstrated. "And even if you crease and tuck everything tightly, where you will fail inspection is not folding the sheet *over* the blanket and *then* folding both down together." I showed what I meant, pinning my knee onto the blanket and sheet to keep it taut. When I stood, there was a knee imprint on the bed so I reached out and creased that. "Try to pull the blanket up with two fingers," I asked Tetra.

She stepped forward and pinched the blanket with two fingers and lifted up. It snapped from her fingers, unable to be pulled up because it was so tight.

"Good luck," I told everyone with a smile.

I was their future empress, and the odds were that my fellow peers in this very room would one day guard me. I wanted loyalty that I'd earned, not ordered.

Everyone burst from the room and scattered down the hallways, running to fix their beds.

Instructor Ashendell stepped inside and pointed to Tetra. "You are needed in medical."

Her eyes widened and she looked frightened for a second.

"For your cane," I whispered, and she relaxed.

Instructor Ashendell shot me a glare as if she didn't appreciate my chatter. Well, I didn't appreciate her freaking my friend out.

Sure enough, fifteen minutes later, just as they were inspecting the newly made beds, Tetra waltzed in with a new black rubber cane. It was ugly compared to her crystal one, but functional, and I was just grateful they'd given her one at all.

"Pass," one instructor said, and then moved down the hall. Pass, pass, pass, pass.

With each passing bed inspection I felt pride swell in my chest. This meant I was a good leader, or at the very least that I gave a mean tutorial on how to be a good bed maker.

"FAIL!" I heard a scream. "Get out in the hall and lead your cadets in their one mile run punishment."

I shook my head. I knew who it was going to be before I saw Summer step to the front of the hall and pass my room with her head down. Hopefully, she learned from this. We all stepped out into the hallway and I saw the panic in Tetra's gaze.

She couldn't run, not for long. It was more of a frantic hop, and only when being chased by a feral dog or something.

"I can't run," Tetra said in a low voice to Instructor Ashendell.

"WHAT IS THAT, CADET? I CAN'T HEAR YOU," she shouted on purpose.

"I CAN'T RUN!" Tetra screamed in anger.

I wanted to come to her aid and defend her, but I knew that would only make things worse.

Instructor Ashendell glared at Tetra. "How can you expect to protect this great country if you can't even run?"

Tetra matched her glare. "Oh I don't know. Maybe with my badass wolf creature?"

Over a dozen snickers burst from the lips of the

cadets present, and I wanted to smack Tetra in the back of the head.

Was her comment funny? *Hell yes*. But was it also stupid? Yes again.

A shadow crossed Instructor Ashendell's face. "Because of your fellow cadet's attitude, you all now have to run two miles while she sits on a blanket and paints her nails like a princess."

I could see the retort building in Tetra's throat, so I stepped forward.

"Yes, ma'am, let's move out!" I nudged two people in front of me and we began to march.

As far as first days went, this could have gone worse.

BY THE NEXT morning at breakfast, everyone was over the two-mile run. Everyone but Tetra.

"She's awful. I *hate* her," Tetra growled, shoving potatoes into her mouth angrily.

I chuckled, half asleep still as Jace pulled into the seat next to me.

"Hey," he said shyly.

"Nope." Tetra pointed her fork at him. "Not happening."

I had to hide my grin as I glanced at him.

Jace looked offended. "Tetra, Aisling and I talked. We're cool now. Friends. Right, Ash?"

I hated that he still used his pet name for me.

I remembered him telling me at Club Sleuth about his parents' divorce, and I pitied him.

Turning fully to him, I met his gaze, a gaze I had once gotten lost in for hours. "We are cool, but I need time before we just sit next to each other and act like nothing happened."

Because he still cheated on me. I wouldn't soon forget that, if ever.

His face fell and he nodded, getting up and moving to another table.

"Don't worry. I still have a revenge plot in place," Tetra said.

A new tray plopped next to mine and I looked up to see Alek and smiled genuinely. He was followed by Roc, Anika, Dev, and Meera. The Wilds alliance was all at one table.

"How are you feeling after that two-mile run, Tetra? My legs are sore," Anika asked my bestie sarcastically, but there was a smile on her lips.

Tetra hadn't run at all. She'd sat in the middle on a blanket with a bottle of Instructor Ashendell's nail polish, painting her nails as ordered.

"Mine too." Tetra matched Anika's sarcasm.

I felt at ease with this group. Maybe it was because we'd bonded during our time in The Wilds. Meera was the quiet introspective and smart one. Anika was clearly one of the leaders, with a chip on her shoulder. Nikhil was the ladies' man, who even now was flirting with Tetra and asking to touch her new cane. Dev was more like Kohen, quiet and always calculating. A man of few words.

Speaking of Kohen... the Avasan gang leader had arrived. If it weren't for Roc and Alek sitting next to me, I might have had to switch tables for fear of people thinking I was aligning with him or something. I couldn't let that kind of word get back to my father.

"Aisling." Kohen said my name so delicately it made heat bloom in my core.

I looked up at him. He was holding his tray and eyeing the empty seat at the end of the table, farthest from me.

"Do you mind if I sit with you guys?"

Why in the stars was he asking? And so politely? Had he gotten hit over the head?

"Sure, dude." I tried to be casual. "Why would I care?"

He plopped down next to Dev and across from Meera and peered at me. "I know you have to be careful about your reputation. I don't want to cause you trouble."

My gut clenched at the thoughtful statement, and for some reason I was getting really pissed off by his hospitality. Was this his plan? Lure me in, chew me up, then spit me out?

I turned to Alek, giving Kohen my back. I couldn't deal with this right now. He was playing games. I knew it. My father murdered his. There was no way his kind gestures were authentic.

"Do you think we will get put into wing training soon?" I asked Alek. "I bet Instructor Ashendell will be our trainer." He was hawk bonded, like her. All those who bonded with a beast of the air had special "wing training." Just as those who bonded with a water animal had water training.

He nodded. "That's exactly what I think," he agreed and popped a piece of bacon in his mouth. We all chatted casually for the next ten minutes until the lights went off in the room, plunging us into darkness.

"This is a drill, get ready," I told everyone. Elaine warned me about this. Random attack drills. A mean thing to do on day two.

The mess hall door was kicked open and low emergency lights flicked on as a dozen instructors wearing gas masks walked inside. One had a bullhorn. "This is a drill to assess your readiness for battle! Prepare to be tested!" It was Ashendell. I recognized her voice.

I pulled off my shirt, sitting in just my sports bra, and wrapped the shirt around my nose and mouth.

Everyone at my table looked at me like I'd grown two heads, everyone but Kohen. He stared at me with eyes that felt like they were on fire, blazing right through my soul.

"They are wearing masks for a reason, you idiots!" I told everyone at my table.

Tetra and everyone else followed my lead, pulling

off their shirts and wrapping them around their mouths. I then grabbed my plastic knife and crawled under the table. Everyone else followed my lead.

That's when the smoke grenades went off.

"You've just been fired on," Ashendell screamed through the bullhorn. "In the middle of breakfast while you are still barely awake. Your weapons are back in the armory, your creatures are outside, and the enemy is about to attack. What do you do?"

Coughing rang throughout the space as our fellow students gagged and choked, their eyes burning and running with tears. Still, there were fifty of us and twelve of them.

I had an idea.

Leaping up onto the table top, I pointed at the instructors. "Even without weapons, there are more of us than there are of them!" I shouted. "We rush them on three!" And my entire table stood at the ready as the rest of our fellow cadets began to fall in line.

"One." Even though my fellow cadets were coughing and throwing up, they stood and grabbed a plastic utensil, food tray, whatever they could. The instructors fanned out, anticipating the attack.

"Two!" We spread out as well, forming two lines of twenty-five people each.

"Thr—"

"Congratulations. You passed." Instructor Ashendell pulled the bullhorn to her lips. The lights came on, the doors behind the instructors opened, and the smoke stopped.

My eyes burned. Tears streaked down my face, but when Instructor Ashendell yanked off her mask, she was grinning at me.

"Lesson of the day," she screamed into the bullhorn. "Have a weapon on you at all times."

Then they left, like nothing had just happened.

"Holy hell," Tetra said, standing in her hot pink sports bra with her shirt still bunched over her mouth and her rubber cane raised like a bat.

"I need fresh air," I called out. My eyes were burning. I ran for the back door that the instructors had just left out of. There were no windows in here. What a stupid design. It was like being in a sarcophagus.

I stepped out of the mess hall and into the hallway, but stopped when I heard voices around the corner.

"We've never had a drill solved that early," a male instructor was saying. "That's a record." I didn't recognize his voice.

"Well, yeah, she's the future empress. What did you expect?" Another male voice I couldn't recognize through the mask they wore. But I didn't want to eavesdrop and get in trouble, so I backed up only to stop at what I heard next.

"Not if we take care of her in here she's not," an older male said. This one seemed like it might be familiar, but the damn gas mask was making it hard to hear.

Take care of her?

My chest heaved at the threat, and I was about to march over there and demand he remove his mask and show himself when a hand came around my mouth and dragged me backward. I was going to fight when I smelled that it was Kohen. His fingers permanently smelled of fragrant spices, which I had grown to love.

Damn.

He dragged me into an alcove and then released my mouth. I spun, with my shirt still bunched at my neck and glared him down. "You need to mind your own business," I growled.

He frowned. "You looked like you were about to get yourself killed. I'm just trying to help you."

Help me?

"I'm going to report them." I moved to leave the alcove and Kohen yanked me back.

Oh this bastard was begging for a throat punch.

"Hear me out," Kohen spoke softly, his body inches from mine, causing a delicious wave of heat to move through me, catching me off guard. "If you rat out these guys, it will stop them, but it won't stop who hired them."

His words stole my breath. Someone hired them?

"How do you know someone else is involved? It could just be them," I told him, knowing that these precious seconds were costing me. I would soon lose my ability to identify these perpetrators.

He looked at me like I was stupid. "You think three

well-paid drill instructors would risk their careers trying to take out the emperor's daughter of their own accord? Why? Because of some vengeance against the country? No. They are being paid, probably four times their salary to turn on you, by someone in a much higher position."

His words struck fear into my heart because I knew they must be true. It made sense.

'Everything okay?' Liana's voice shot through my mind.

'Fine,' I lied. It wasn't like I was in mortal danger right this second, but she must have felt that I was off.

"Like who?" I breathed to Kohen. "And why the hell do you care?"

His face clouded over. "I assume it's whoever trapped Liana and tried to keep you from bonding with her. And I wish I didn't care. Do whatever you want," he snapped, walking away, back into the mess hall.

I stood there for a moment, processing what had just happened, and decided Kohen's advice was good, but I still wanted these men arrested. I walked out of the alcove and into the hallway where the lieutenants had just been talking... but they were gone.

Not if we take care of her? I had no idea if they were talking about killing me, and now I had no idea who it was.

The second day of school was truly outshining the first.

CHAPTER

FIFTEEN

I barely slept. I woke up every hour, peering at the door and wondering if someone was going to come in and slit my throat in my sleep. I slept with a small dagger Elaine gave me, that the Fleet approved of, under my pillow with my fingers clutched tightly around it. I was still processing what I'd heard and hadn't yet told Tetra about the possible plot to kill me. I had bigger things to worry about. Like the power display we were about to be forced to go through. Every cadet would have to stand before the Imperial Fleet admirals and give a display of power to be recorded in their file for future job assignments. This would also match you with which base you would be stationed at, and I was gunning for Sky Reach. It was the most notorious for attacks, but you learned the most there as well. The most powerful

217

soldiers in my father's fleet served at Sky Reach, and I wanted to be one of them.

It was barely light out, but I couldn't sleep so I snuck out of our room and went down the hall to the girls' bathroom to shower and get ready for the day. I showered with my dagger. The solid gold one-piece had an engraving along the entire blade that was reminiscent of the Cedar Creek countryside where Elaine was from. It was very special to me and it was very sharp, so I was keeping it with me at all times.

After lacing up my boots and tucking my cotton shirt into my Fleet-issued belt, I slicked my hair into a bun, still shocked at the red and black contrasting sides. Sometimes the bond between creature and human left a physical mark like a birthmark or scar, but I'd never seen hair change color.

I headed outside to look for Liana and found her in the woods behind a practice field. Something within me just guided me to look there. I assumed it was our bond. Some soldiers were out jogging, but otherwise the campus was pretty dead.

"Hey," I greeted her, stepping over some fallen logs to walk up and stroke her neck. She leaned into my touch, using my fingers almost as a scratching post.

"Where's Onyx?" I asked. She and the dragon were pretty inseparable.

She looked up at me with her purple eyes and I felt nervousness rush through me. As if she was preparing to tell me something I wouldn't like.

'I sent him away for the day,' she said.

Sent him away? Did Kohen know?

"Why? Today is really important. We need to show the admirals our powers so that we will be given important jobs within the Fleet and be stationed at good bases," I told her.

She nodded. *'I know what today is. I overheard the lieutenants talking about it yesterday.'*

I sighed. "If you know it's important, why would you send Onyx away? Kohen is going to look like a fool."

Not that I cared. Okay, I sort of did.

She nuzzled her head into my stomach, *'If they know the power that Onyx has given Kohen, they will likely kill him where he stands.'*

Chills ran the length of my entire back. *'What power?'* I asked into her mind.

She was silent.

My eyebrows arched. *'The fire and healing? Or something else? What power did he give him?'*

'That's not my information to share, Aisling. I'm sorry.' She sounded genuinely sad, and I respected her for keeping a close friend's secret, but damn I wanted to know. Clearly Kohen had manifested another power besides the healing from burns and conjuring flames into his hand, which he'd shown me in the barn.

I nodded.

'I am leaving too,' she said and my gut sank. *'But only because it is in your best interest. If they learn you*

could escape death and whatever other powers may manifest through our bond, it may bring negative attention. There are some things humans are not ready to know, and the full extent of a Talanagi's powers is one of them.'

I didn't like it one bit. I was going to look like a total asshat up there with no powers to display, but her warning scared me. Especially since Kohen seemed to have manifested some big dark power.

I stroked her neck feathers. *'So you're leaving?'*

She nodded, *'I'll be back tonight, after Sahiri is gone.'*

My eyes widened. *'You know about Sahiri?'*

Sahiri was one of the admiral's creatures, a giant silverback gorilla who had the power to force another creature or human to display their power.

Liana dipped her head up and down. *'Sahiri was well known in The Wilds, a formidable creature with a rare talent. Do not allow her to cast her power over either you or Kohen.'*

I frowned. *'I know you and Onyx are like family, but Kohen is my family's sworn enemy. I can't be doing favors for him.'*

She sighed. *'Understood. Do not allow Sahiri to reveal your power. Kohen is on his own I guess.'* She shrugged her winged shoulders nonchalantly, but I felt bad. What the hell was I supposed to do if some three-hundred-pound gorilla came up to me and tried to use her power on me? Knock her out?

I actually burst out laughing at the thought, and Liana cocked her head to the side in interest.

This was a good time to shift the conversation to what happened yesterday when the three soldiers said I wouldn't be their future empress if they *took me out*.

I told Liana what had happened, and when I was done telling her the story, a fine tendril of smoke came off of her skin. Her eyes flashed orange; she looked ready to burst into flames.

'Aisling, if that ever happens again, you run up to them and slit their throats. Do you understand me?'

Whoa. That was hardcore. *'Umm, you can't exactly kill a superior officer in boot camp for making a veiled verbal threat.'*

She huffed, smoke leaving her nostrils. *'Then send them outside where I can take care of them.'*

Okay... she was not going to see reason. Most creatures were very protective, and Liana was no different.

'I guess. I'll see you tomorrow, then?' I asked her.

She nodded and then took off like a rocket, shooting up from the forest floor and into the tree line.

A twig snapped behind me. I yanked my dagger from my waistband and spun, ready to throw. The blade nearly left my fingertips until I recognized Kohen.

"I almost took your eye! Don't sneak up on me," I snapped.

He held up his hands, peering up to where Liana had just flown off. "I'm just looking for Onyx. Everyone is lining up with their creatures for the revealing."

Crap.

"He's not coming. Neither is Liana. They don't want the admirals—or any other humans for that matter—knowing the extent of their powers. Or ours," I told him plainly.

He looked relieved, actually exhaling and slumping.

My gaze narrowed. "Why, what power are you hiding?"

He looked up at me then and there was a vulnerability in his gaze. He seemed like he wanted to tell me, to confide in whatever gift his bonding had brought about. "A horrible burden," he said instead, and then walked away, giving me his back.

A horrible burden?

I walked five paces behind him, my mind spinning with how to handle this situation. I was the emperor's daughter, yes, but I couldn't pull rank during an official ceremony like this—*could I?* Tell the admirals that our powers were secret?

No way, we'd be court-martialed.

Liana had no idea the bind she'd put me in by doing this.

TWELVE ADMIRALS SAT at the back of the auditorium. Eight men and four women. All of whom I'd seen on occasion with my father but had barely exchanged more than a few words with. I only knew half by name. All the lieutenants were fanned out along the walls of the arena with their creatures in tow, and we, the cadets, stood in the middle with our creatures behind.

The arena was giant, four times a normal human sized one, so that it could fit our creatures comfortably.

Drill Instructor Ashendell walked over to me, and with every footstep I dreaded the conversation we were about to have.

"Where is your creature, Cadet?" she shouted.

"Gone, ma'am!" I shouted back.

Murmurs rose up around the hall and another instructor asked Kohen the same thing. We were the only two who had arrived creatureless. He was a few paces away from me.

"Gone as well, sir!"

"Have you informed them that they needed to be here?" Instructor Ashendell asked.

"Yes, ma'am." My heart felt like it might burst out of my chest at any moment.

"Then go *get* her!" Ashendell grabbed the hem of my collar and lowered her voice. "You will not embarrass me in front of the admirals," she growled.

I gave her a pleading look, lowering my voice as well. "You don't force a Talanagi to do anything. She left. I cannot make her be here."

Her eyes widened. "If you can't control your creature, you're not bonded."

It was true. I could have taken over Liana's will—well, in theory, she was a Talanagi so I wasn't one hundred percent sure on that, but I would never do that. Most humans wouldn't.

"I won't," I told her.

She let go of my shirt just as one of the admirals stood from his chair on the platform.

Admiral Blade.

Bonded to Sahiri.

I was so screwed.

The admiral walked down the long empty space between us, his silverback gorilla creature following closely beside him. The gorilla was huge, with glowing green ember marks along her back.

Kill me now.

Lieutenant Ashendell stood at attention, looking away from me, and I flicked a panicked expression towards Kohen. He looked cool as a cucumber.

Awesome.

"At ease. What's the problem, Lieutenant?" the admiral asked.

Lieutenant Ashendell relaxed a little. "Two of the cadets' creatures didn't show up, sir."

She answered just as Sahiri dropped on all fours and walked over to me, sniffing my boot. A wave of dizziness washed over me. I felt so exposed, so fragile. Her magic was terrifying.

"And why is that, Aisling Everhart?" He directed

his next question to me and I felt the color leach from my cheeks.

"I informed her she needed to be here, sir. She chose not to," I told him, looking straight ahead. No way would I look him in the eye if I didn't have to. This man was in my father's monthly war council meetings and he scared the life out of me.

"Your creature suggested it but you had to have agreed with her. Otherwise, you would have just forced her to be here."

I felt physically nauseated from being interrogated like this. Maybe if I threw up they would send me to the infirmary. I said nothing, hoping he would drop it and just test everyone else here.

"What are you hiding?" he then asked.

Don't embarrass me. My father's words flushed through me and I knew whatever I did now would get back to him.

No human should know what the Talanagi can do. Liana's words rushed over me as well.

I said nothing. I had nothing to say.

"Sahiri, reveal her power," Admiral Blade ordered his creature.

Panic rose up inside of me. Would I burst into flames and wake up in a body bag again? Or worse, not at all? Or did I have some other power yet to be uncovered? Something like what Kohen was hiding.

"No," I said as sharp intakes of breath came from all around me.

"Excuse me, Cadet?" The admiral got up in my face, and this time I did look at him, regretting it instantly. He was in his late forties with a black buzzcut and an absolutely feral gaze. There was something inherently evil about him and it gave me the chills.

"No," I repeated. "I do not consent to having my powers forced on display, SIR!" I screamed in his face. He reached up then, lightning-quick, and grabbed my lower jaw, *hard*, surprising me, and that's when chaos erupted. I hissed at the pain his forceful grip had caused, and then Tetra stepped forward, holding her cane up in the air like she was going to strike the admiral. He looked over at her and burst out laughing. That's when there was a blur of tan skin and black hair. Kohen came out of nowhere and cracked the admiral in the side of the temple, knocking him out cold.

Holy crap.

Just when I thought I had a moment to process what the hell was going on... Sahiri attacked. She stood on her hind legs and barreled over to Kohen, taking him down to the ground with one yank of her meaty hands. She was pummeling him, her fists smashing into his face and arms as he brought them up to protect himself.

It felt like time had stopped. My breathing came out in ragged waves as I reacted without thinking.

Grabbing my dagger from my boot, I threw myself onto Sahiri's back, holding the blade to her throat.

She froze.

"I will bleed you out right here and now if you don't get off of him," I told her.

The whole room was in an uproar.

Lieutenant Ashendell was trying to rouse the admiral. The soldiers flanking the walls stepped closer but were waiting for commands. The other admirals who had been sitting on the dais were now rushing towards us with angry strides.

This entire thing had gone to crap.

'You have no idea how bad this is.' I reached for Liana with my mental communication and felt her close by.

'Not as bad as it would be if they knew what you both were capable of. Some people are too powerful to be kept alive.'

Her words sent chills down my arms. What was Kohen hiding? What did she know about me?

'What do I do?' I asked Liana.

'You are the future empress. Handle it.'

I wasn't empress here though. I was a cadet like everyone else.

"Stand down, Cadet!" an admiral barked from behind me, and realizing I still had my blade to Sahiri's throat, I slid off her back.

Kohen was covered in blood, his nose having exploded onto his lip and chest, but he looked alive and conscious, which was miraculous considering a giant gorilla had just pounded him in his beautiful face.

Sahiri spun, glaring at me with a menacing gaze, and all I could think was that my father was going to kill me when he heard of this.

One of the admirals, a female, walked right up to me, jaw set and eyes blazing. Her tawny wolf creature stalked around us in a slow circle, and I prepared for her to do her worst.

This was Admiral Caruso. Her gift was being able to tell if you lied.

Some said she smelled it, others that she heard the lie, but either way I was so screwed if she was about to interrogate me in front of everyone.

"Throw them both in the brig!" she snapped, and I sagged in relief.

The next thing I knew, Kohen and I were being hauled by the armpits and dragged out of the room. The last thing I saw was the terrified look on Tetra's face.

CHAPTER

SIXTEEN

They put Kohen and I in different cells but we were right next to each other. I could see him through the bars, lying on the bench with a rag pressed to his nose.

The soldier had just left and we were all alone in the dimly lit room with four cells, two currently empty.

"You okay?" I finally asked.

He sat up slowly, pulling the rag away to reveal puffy eyes and a purple cheek, but the bleeding had stopped.

"I'll live," he muttered.

I frowned. "Why did you attack the admiral like that?"

His eyes practically glowed. "He hurt you."

Heat rushed through my entire body then, and I couldn't get my heart to stop pounding.

"So? That's none of your business," I snapped.

I watched as he swallowed hard, his Adam's apple bobbing.

"You're welcome," Kohen finally said, and I sighed. Point taken.

"Thanks. Now, don't do anything stupid like that again. I had this handled."

Sort of.

Kohen laughed. "Really? He was about two seconds from forcing you to one knee and revealing your powers in front of everyone, which would probably have gotten us both killed because I would have been next."

I frowned. That was oddly specific. "So that's why you took him down."

Kohen's eyes blazed across the space, searching for me, and I felt them like a physical caress when they landed on mine. "He *hurt* you. That's why I knocked him out. And I would do it again."

"Why?" I pressed. "Why do you care if someone hurts me?"

Kohen's jaw pinched and he stood, beginning to pace the cell. "I hate this," he said, causing me to frown in confusion.

"Hate what?"

"Nothing," he snapped, and I decided to leave him alone. He'd probably gotten a head injury and needed some space.

We were quiet for a while, then the door on the

back wall opened. Kohen returned to the bench and took a seat as Admiral Caruso strode towards us, her tawny wolf right at her side. Caruso had brown skin, brown hair, and brown eyes. Her face was perfectly carved, plump lips, sharp nose, high eyebrow arch. She could have been a model in another life, a life without war. She was in her early forties; her hands were littered with little battle scars that told me she'd earned her title. My father counted her as one of his closest advisors.

She walked right up to me and pinned me with a blank look. "Elaine told me to keep an eye on you, and here you are attacking an admiral's creature to save a Badshah." She flicked a disgusted gaze in Kohen's direction.

I sighed in relief at the mention of Elaine. If she was friends with Elaine, she was an ally.

"I didn't plan on doing that, ma'am." I stood and walked closer to her so that she could use her truth telling power to know that I was not lying. "I woke up this morning with every intention of going through the power revealing process like everyone else."

She raised one eyebrow and nodded, apparently pleased with my answer. "Then why stick up for him?" She jerked her head in Kohen's direction.

My heart beat frantically in my chest. I had just reacted without thinking, but I couldn't say that. And I couldn't lie.

"My creature is a mother figure to his. They are

bonded in a way and... I just reacted, doing what I knew my creature would want."

Truth.

I didn't look over at Kohen but I could feel his eyes burning into me.

Caruso stepped closer to me. "And why did your creature want to hide whatever your powers are?"

Crap.

Be smart, Aisling.

"What I want to know," Kohen interrupted, giving me some time to think of an answer, "is why an admiral nearly broke the jaw of the future empress."

Caruso snapped her head in Kohen's direction. "You will speak only when spoken to, Cadet. Do you understand?"

Kohen swallowed hard. "Yes, ma'am," he growled.

His outburst had bought me time I needed to gather my thoughts.

Caruso peered back at me. "The entire admiralty cabinet is telling me to march you both back in there and reveal your powers. Give me *one* reason not to."

"They will be revealed in due time," I told her. Because if they weren't, we weren't getting good postings. "But right now it's a matter of national security that both of our powers stay hidden."

She frowned, concern pulling at her features. "National security?"

She must have sensed the truth. I was the heir, the next empress, my father's successor, and if I died it would be a matter of national security, as keeping the line of succession alive was of utmost importance. And right now there was a current plot on my life, as I had heard yesterday morning outside the mess hall. Liana said that revealing my powers right now would get me killed and I believed her.

"That's all I can say for now, ma'am. That to force me or Kohen to reveal our powers would put my life in danger."

Her frown deepened. "Why him?" She jerked her head towards the cell next to mine.

Why him? I'd been asking myself that since the day I laid eyes on him.

"I don't know."

Truth.

My fate was intertwined with Kohen's in some way. That was something I just felt deeply in my soul, and it filled me with equal amounts of excitement and fear.

"YOU ARE ONE UNIT! When one of you fails, you all fail!" Instructor Ashendell shouted into my face as I ran past her for the seventeenth lap. Rain pelted down on me as sleep pulled at my limbs. It was 3 a.m. and we'd just been woken for punishment for Kohen's and my outburst. On the lawn in front of us, sitting under some floodlights and an umbrella, was Admiral Blade.

He grinned as our entire unit jogged in the rain around him. Sahiri stood next to him, soaking wet and tracking me with her gaze like a predator.

Tetra had been doing sit-ups this entire time. I flicked a gaze her way to see that she had just vomited from overexertion.

Everyone was going to hate us come morning, but we'd gotten away without having to show our powers. Kohen ran well ahead of me. We were trying to keep distance from each other. The last thing I needed was for word to get back to my father that we were some item or alliance or something.

We'd totally missed the power reveal, but Tetra told me that she and her creature had discovered she had the power to shield people, and eventually with practice, buildings, from harm. It was an incredible power that would make her useful to the Fleet. Jace had apparently revealed he had the power to project illusions, which could confuse someone or lead them astray. His father would be thrilled. It was an amazing power to use in time of war.

My muscles burned, my lungs felt like they were on fire, and I had mud up to my knees, but I kept running. Someone beside me fell and I slowed, reaching down to pick them up before the instructor could yell at them. It was Anika.

"Thanks," she muttered, looking miserable.

Tetra told me that Anika had the power to manipulate the wind. With practice, it would be an amazing gift on the battlefield.

"I don't know but I've been told!" I shouted, trying to boost morale.

"I don't know but I've been told!" half of the cadets around me echoed.

"It's cold as hell and I feel old!" I yelled, and was rewarded with chuckles from my fellow cadets.

"It's cold as hell and I feel old!" they said.

"I don't know but I've been told!" Tetra yelled between push-ups in the middle of the field.

We echoed her.

"Punching an admiral is pretty bold," she said, and I couldn't help the grin that slipped over my mouth. My gaze flicked to the admiral, who was now glaring at Tetra.

"I don't know but I have heard!" Kohen said and we echoed him. I was curious what he might say.

"I have regrets about punching the admiral. I should have just flipped him the bird!"

More laughs echoed around the field, including my own, and I noticed the admiral glare at Kohen, but the corner of his lips twitched as if he was fighting a smile.

Sahiri beat her chest in response to that and we all shut up and ran for another hour until most of us were puking our guts out, or had fallen so many times we couldn't get up. Me included.

Stick a fork in me. I was done.

THE NEXT DAY, everyone walked into the mess hall on three hours of sleep wincing with pain—everyone but Kohen and I. It seemed the Imbrian and I shared the same gift of rapid healing. My muscles should be killing me right now after all the running, but I didn't feel a thing. Kohen's face, previously bruised and swollen, was looking as normal as ever.

"Aisling!" Alek strode up to me as I placed food onto my plate from the self-serve bar. I was starving from the middle-of-the-night workout.

"Hey, what's up?" I peered at him.

Alek's power had been revealed as the ability to control metal. A huge help in the war when the enemy used swords and other metallic weapons. He'd need to practice it though.

"Are you going to the karaoke thing tonight at Club Sleuth?" he asked.

I frowned. "The what?"

"Yep, we will be there," Tetra peeped beside me, and Alek broke into a handsome grin as we walked over to the table we had taken to sitting at every day. Our little Wilds alliance crew, plus Kohen.

As Alek took a seat on my left, Tetra dropped her cane to the ground and kicked it under the bench, folding her bad leg in first and then sitting on my right.

"You were in the brig when we planned a karaoke night at Sleuth to celebrate revealing our powers," Tetra said.

I nodded, popping a French fry in my mouth.

Alek reached out and grabbed one of my fries. "For those of us that did reveal our powers." He winked at me and I smirked.

"Too soon for jokes about that," I told him.

Suddenly a hand reached over my shoulder and grabbed another fry. I followed the hand to see Jace casually smiling down at me. "Hey, Aisling." But when Jace's gaze flicked to Alek, he glared.

What Jace didn't see was Kohen looming behind him. I opened my mouth to say something just as Kohen's hand snaked out and wrapped around Jace's wrist, shaking the fry loose of his grasp.

Jace dropped it on the floor and yanked his hand free, spinning around and getting right up in Kohen's face.

"What the hell, Badshah?"

One by one, the Imbrians from our table rose. Anika, Dev, Nikhil, even little unassuming Meera. They didn't make a move on Jace but their message was clear. They had Kohen's back.

"Where I'm from, if you take food from a woman, it means you are a coward," Kohen spat.

Jace moved blindingly fast then, coming up with a right uppercut, intending to connect with Kohen's jaw. But Kohen was ready for it. He blocked the move and took Jace to the ground quickly, kicking his legs out from under him.

As I watched the boys fight, anger boiled within me. What the hell did Kohen think he was doing? Last night with the admiral and now this? Over a French fry?

I got up from the table, picked up my French fry tray, and chucked it at the boys on the floor, letting my food spill all over them. They stopped their fighting when the fries pelted their face and looked up at me.

"Grow up!" I snapped, and stalked off, hungry and pissed.

I stormed outside and headed for the woods, toward where I knew Liana would be waiting. I could feel her, like a gentle nudge in my heart, beckoning me closer.

'*What's wrong?*' she asked.

'*Men suck,*' I told her, and trudged through the thick trees.

I found her and Onyx together in a field with a few other creatures. It took me a moment to recognize Lieutenant Ashendell's hawk and Alek's. They all stood in a circle like they were having some kind of bird chat.

"Am I interrupting something?" I asked.

Liana stepped over to me and bowed, '*We are wing training in the air today. Let's go for a flight before class starts.*'

I needed that. I needed to get the hell out of here

and away from Kohen's possessiveness. I happily crawled onto her back, surprised when I saw that she was wearing a small harness that had two handles.

'They outfitted us this morning,' she told me, and kicked off the ground.

I screamed in excitement as my stomach dropped and the wind rushed through my hair. *'You let them?'* I was impressed. She didn't seem the type to allow any kind of restraint.

'Yes, so that we can do this. Hold on,' she said, and I grasped the handles and clenched my thighs, thinking she was going to do some evasive sharp left turn. Instead, she did a full flip. A scream of terror ripped from my throat as my heart beat frantically. She righted herself and I could almost swear she was smiling.

'What the hell? I could have fallen!'

'You're not thinking of stupid men anymore though, are you?'

That got a smirk out of me. I was not.

'Touché.'

'Do you want to talk about it?' Liana asked.

She had this mother energy, an energy I had been missing most of my life. I felt like I could come to her with anything and she wouldn't judge me and might even give sound advice.

'Kohen is being...' I fought for the words. *'We're not friends, okay. He's my family's sworn enemy and yet he's being nice and possessive over me. Like he's protecting me.'*

It felt good to tell another person what I was thinking. *'Maybe it's because Onyx and you are close and he is feeling some need to protect me because of that?'*

'That's not why,' she answered, and I frowned.

'Then why? Why is he so... why won't he just leave me alone?' I asked. *'Is he playing some kind of game? Trying to draw me in so he can get revenge for his father's death?'*

She was quiet for a long time, so long I thought she might not answer me. *'Let me be clear, Aisling. My allegiance is with you and you alone. I will put your safety above anyone else I may care about, including Onyx and by extension Kohen. But, as this does not concern your safety, I will not answer you. Kohen can tell you when he's ready.'*

I felt like I'd been slapped. She knew the answer and wouldn't tell me. *'Is it related to his power?'* I questioned.

'Yes,' she replied.

What the hell? I hadn't even discovered my power yet, assuming I had one beyond rapid healing and seemingly escaping death, and Kohen's was apparently messing with him so much he was punching out admirals and Jace?

'Okay.' I was quiet the whole rest of our flight, lost in my thoughts. When we landed, Kohen, Alek, and Ashendell were in the field, waiting. Dev was walking through the trees with his giant vulture creature on his shoulder. Tetra told me his power had been revealed to be so intense that the admirals didn't know what to do

with him. Sahiri revealed that one day he would kill with a single touch.

"Getting a head start, cadet?" Instructor Ashendell asked me.

My gaze flicked to Kohen, but he was staring straight ahead, ignoring me.

Great.

"Just a light flying practice, ma'am," I told her, dismounting.

She nodded and then pointed to Kohen. "The fact that you can both fly on your creatures is an incredible asset to the Fleet."

Onyx craned his black scaly head in Ashendell's hawk's direction and sniffed him. They both froze.

Kohen grinned. I was guessing Onyx said something funny in his head.

"What's he doing?" Ashendell asked Kohen as her hawk flew from the ground to her shoulder. She was a badass, but she definitely seemed terrified, and had been avoiding looking at our creatures the entire time.

Kohen straightened his back and stood erect. "Nothing, ma'am. Sorry, ma'am."

Ashendell brushed it off, but Liana used one of her long tailfeathers to smack Onyx in the side of the head. I wondered how old he was, because he behaved like a cocky teenager. Kohen and Onyx were perfect for each other in that way.

"Today we will be practicing using our powers

with our creatures. This will prepare us for the mock attack we will have at the end of the week," she said.

My powers. I didn't know what they were yet. Other than possibly being immortal, which made me want to vomit just thinking about it, and healing.

Ashendell peered at Alek. "Since we don't yet know what these two can do…" She cast a glare at Kohen and I. "We will start with Alek."

She pulled some throwing knives from behind her back and handed them to him.

"Cool." He picked one up.

Ashendell whistled and her hawk took flight. She closed her eyes, concentrating, and I realized she had the power to see what he saw, a very cool if somewhat common power. He could fly ten miles away and she would see through his eyes.

"Send out your hawk," she told Alek, keeping her eyes closed.

Alek's hawk, who I'd learned was named Iniki, burst from his shoulders and took off to the skies.

Alek closed his eyes and mimicked what Lieutenant Ashendell was doing.

I gasped. "You have two powers?"

Alek grinned, making himself look even more handsome than usual. "I do."

For some reason I felt like Kohen was watching me. I glanced his way to find him glaring. I rolled my eyes and focused on Alek again. He was seeing through his hawk's sight, which I imagined was such an amazing experience second to flying.

"Now throw the knife, but use your metal-moving power to guide the sword through the woods using Iniki's sight," Ashendell ordered.

He winced. "That sounds hard. I can barely move a quarter across the room."

Ashendell nodded, her eyes still closed. "It will take a lot of practice, but eventually you could kill an enemy from a mile away—slitting their throat in their sleep."

Badass. But she was right. His power was amazing when you thought about it like that. We stood there for twenty minutes while Alek tried to move the thin blade through the woods using his hawk's sight, but it fell about ten feet from him.

"Alright, good try. Take a break," she told him, opening her eyes and calling her creature back.

Then she peered at me. "Are you going to tell us what your power is yet? Otherwise I don't know how to train you."

'Don't tell her that you don't know yet what your power is. That will make you sound weak,' Liana coached, and then stood beside me, bending so that I could ride her.

"I have a little something I can show you," I told her, processing Liana's advice.

Was sounding weak in front of Ashendell danger-ous? She sort of made it seem that way. And wasn't being impervious to flame, and possibly immortal, power enough?

'You have more abilities. They just haven't shown yet,' Liana told me.

She seemed so sure... maybe she felt it. I certainly didn't.

I climbed onto Liana's back. She leapt into the air as I held onto the handles of her new holster and squeezed her back with my thighs. She went really high.

'Hold on,' she instructed.

She dove at that moment and my stomach dropped. Halfway down, she did a barrel roll and let loose a twenty-foot stream of fire that nearly shaved the top off of the trees near us.

"Showoff!" Alek taunted from the ground, and I grinned.

It wasn't a power display from me, but it showed what I could do with Liana.

When I landed, Ashendell marked something on her clipboard and nodded.

"Okay. That will do for now. Kohen, you're up."

She didn't seem very impressed. Maybe she was hoping for me to display something.

Kohen leapt onto Onyx, staying upright, and I noticed his feet slipped into the hand straps sewn onto a harness Onyx had that was nearly identical to Liana's. Onyx flew around like a teenager who had drank way too much caffeine and Kohen stayed standing the entire time. They ended their little display with Onyx breathing a ring of fire and flying Kohen through it.

"Talk about a showoff," I muttered to Alek, who chuckled.

But Ashendell was smiling at the display and I saw her write, *battle ready* on the top of Kohen's paper before pulling the clipboard out of view.

Battle ready. In his first few days of training? Did she mark that on mine?

We all had to be battle ready by the end of this month, but seeing him get the nod of approval so quickly made jealousy flare to life in my chest.

WHEN I GOT BACK to our room, I found Tetra lying in bed with her bad foot elevated and an icepack on top. Her creature was lying on the bed next to her with her head in her lap.

"You okay?" I rushed inside and knelt before her.

She nodded, but I could tell she wasn't.

"What happened?" I asked, lifting the icepack to see that her normally pink and crooked foot was black and blue.

"Jace, we were training and—"

I stood angrily, ready to rip that bastard's head off.

She yanked my arm, forcing me down on the bed beside her. "And he accidently jumped on it. He apologized profusely and even carried me here."

I growled. "That's going to put you out of commission for a few days."

She laughed. "Are you serious? He hurt my already mangled foot. I'll be fine. It's nothing I'm not already accustomed to. Pain and uselessness."

Her words hit my chest like a bomb and my heart fissured. Pain and uselessness, that's what my best friend was accustomed to?

"You're not useless," I told her, but she turned away from me and I saw her wipe at her eyes.

"Tetra, look at me. You are *not* useless!" I forced her to face me and my heart broke when I saw the unshed tears in her eyes. Her mouth was set into a grim line. "What's gotten into you? Did Jace say something? I'll nut punch him right now if he did," I promised her.

She shook her head. "I overheard one of the instructors saying my power was really valuable but that my leg would get me killed in combat. They are going to bench me, Aisling. I'm going to be a drill instructor after we graduate, right here at the training center. I was so stupid to think I could do this, that I could make a difference in this war."

She turned back away from me, and this time I let her. Becoming an instructor without any combat experience was frowned upon. It was a known demotion that signaled the Imperial Fleet thought you couldn't handle real battle. I wanted to argue with her and tell her to show them she could do better, but I also selfishly wanted her to stay here after graduation.

I wanted her to be an instructor and live out life in the city and see her mom every day. I wanted her to be safe.

Imagining Tetra in a warzone or sleeping in tents while moving through enemy territory would keep me up at night.

"It will be okay," I said instead. Because it would. If Tetra was safe, then everything would be okay.

A FEW HOURS LATER, we got ready for our first off base night since we'd gotten here. Tetra assured me her foot would be fine with the cane and she'd ice it later. We were not permitted to wear civilian clothes, so that all of the people we encountered tonight would know we were cadets in training. Tetra and I had, however, found a way around the dress code. We both tied our black Fleet-issued t-shirt into a knot just above our bellybuttons and I cuffed my black pants to just mid-calf, pairing it with my imperial boots and some light makeup that was allowed. For the first time since I'd entered the Fleet, I wore my hair down and free around my shoulders.

"This is so cool." Tetra smiled as she stroked both sides of my hair.

I grinned. "The triplets loved it."

Tetra laughed. "I'll bet they've all dyed their hair to match yours by now."

She knew them well. I missed their feral little hormonal asses very much. Elaine too.

"Elaine would never allow it," I told her.

"True," Tetra agreed, wincing as she hobbled.

I lowered my voice. "What about those pain pills I got you?"

I'd had to pull some strings with my father last year but I'd gotten Tetra some pain pills for days when her foot discomfort really flared. The war had put a strain on supplies, and pain medicines were the first to go scarce.

She'd be fine for months and then bam, she'd wake up with her twisted foot hot to the touch and swollen. She was born this way, a deformity that the doctors said was so rare they didn't really know what to do about it. But the pills were the good stuff that made you feel woozy and forget about everything.

She shook her head. "It's not that bad yet. I'm saving those for a flare."

I nodded. "You brought them though?"

She bopped her chin up and down. "Medical cleared me to have them, but I have to tell my drill instructor if I take one."

I just hoped she would before it got unmanageable. My bestie was known for hiding her pain and not complaining about it until it was really bad.

We exited our room, and I skittered to a stop to keep myself from slamming into Jace.

His fist was poised to knock over our door.

"Oh, sorry." He pushed himself back to allow us to leave, his gaze running the length of my body. Jace checking me out before would have delighted me, now it just made me pissed-off and sad. He'd ruined such a good thing.

"I'm so sorry about your foot, Tetra. I wanted to offer my family's driver to take us to the club together," he said.

The bar was within walking distance normally, but with Tetra's injured foot, a hired car would be better.

"Thank you," Tetra said simply.

"Excuse us." Kohen's voice came from behind and I spun.

He was standing behind me, looking hot as all hell in all-black Fleet-issued fatigues and glaring at Jace. His hair was slicked back and I spotted a blade tucked into his belt.

Why did I want things I shouldn't have?

Jace narrowed his gaze on Kohen, unmoving, and I couldn't take this anymore.

"We can get our own car," I told Jace, and started to walk away with Tetra hobbling behind me. I slowed, letting her catch up, and then threw the door wide for her, leading us both outside.

I was done with this male pissing match.

SEVENTEEN

When we got to the bar, Tetra hopped on stage and started singing one of my favorite songs about late nights and not caring what others thought. She even flipped me off during the best parts and I grinned. She was my ride or die. Even with a bashed-up foot, nothing would stop her from singing and having fun.

The song ended and then the DJ picked up for a bit, playing mostly high vibe dance music.

"Dance with me?" Alek's voice washed over my neck and I turned to find him leaning forward, inches from my cheek.

Oh. I swallowed hard.

He looked handsome in his black fatigues with rolled-up sleeves showing his bulging bicep.

Was this like a friendly dance? Or something more?

I didn't see this coming, so I just accepted his hand

and allowed him to lead me onto the dance floor, where others were moving to the beat.

I peered back at my bestie and she waggled her eyebrows, causing me to grin.

I hooked my arms behind Alek's neck, and he placed his hands on my hips as I moved against him.

"Crazy week," I said into his ear.

He nodded. "But we're surviving."

We were.

"Your powers are super cool. I can't believe you got two," I said.

He pulled back and cast me a sexy smile. "Says the girl who bonded a Talanagi!"

I tipped my head back and laughed and he pulled me closer to him.

"Stars, I love your laugh." His voice was husky now, and I swallowed hard.

Alek? I mean... he was hot and I'd known him since we were twelve, but I'd never considered him as—

"Can I step in?" Kohen growled, suddenly looming next to us.

My fingers dug into the back of Alek's neck, and I could see the muscle in his jaw tic.

"Well, I don't speak for Aisling, but no. I do not want you to step in," Alek told him respectfully but point blank.

It was kinda hot that he wasn't speaking for me, but one look at Kohen told me something was up. He looked pissed and ready to explode. This must have to do with his power, but for the life of me I couldn't figure out what power would cause this aggro male behavior.

Which was also kind of hot if I was being honest. I hated myself for loving the alpha male fight over me thing, but dammit, Kohen looked ready to rip Alek's fingers off of my waist one by one... and I liked it.

But I couldn't dance with the Imbrian prince. Was he serious?

"Kohen, I can't dance with you." I flicked my gaze to the soldiers lining the walls, and watched as pain crossed over his features for a split second before being replaced by a stone-cold wall.

"Understood," he said, and then stormed off.

"Dude, he's got it bad for you," Alek said, and I shook my head.

"No, it's something else. Our creatures are bonded in a way. He's been acting like this since then." Kohen didn't like me. *Right?*

Alek gave me a look. "You can't believe that, right? The way he knocked out an admiral, then taking out Jace for stealing a single French fry. Now trying to break up our dance. He's claiming you."

I chuckled. "Claiming me?"

Alek's face grew serious. "Aisling, I'm not kidding. He wants you. The questions is, what do you want?" He peered at me with a vulnerability I wasn't prepared for, and I took a closer look at Alek. He was handsome, there was no denying that, and a complete opposite looks-wise from Kohen: blond hair and blue eyes, fair skin. But there was no spark there. No ember to light the fires of passion that I'd experienced with Jace. And if I was being honest, Kohen too. But was there spark potential? Given different circumstances? I was confused.

He was a great guy, someone my dad would like well enough. Someone the country would approve of. But the spark... wasn't there.

I pulled my hands from behind his neck. "I don't know what I want. I'm sorry, Alek," I said, and then bolted for the bathroom.

I hadn't expected the night to go like this and for Alek to confront me like that. As I passed the bathroom, I heard banging in the storage closet to the left, the same one I'd met Kohen in before. It sounded like someone was punching holes in a wall.

I yanked the door open and found Kohen doing just that. Until his knuckles bled.

"Kohen, stop it!" I slammed the door behind me and yanked him back by the shoulders.

He spun to face me, eyes filled with a mixture of rage and agony. His hands shook as he looked down at me in the soft light.

"I can't do this, Aisling. I'm not strong enough," he admitted.

His emotional display scared me. "Do what? What's wrong?"

He reached up and cupped my face, staring into

my eyes and taking the breath from my lungs. Just one touch from him and my entire body was buzzing. There was more than a spark, there was an entire forest fire.

"You're mine, Aisling. And I can't watch other men throw themselves at you when I *know* that you will be mine."

His words knocked my heart from my chest, and dizziness washed over me.

He *knew* that I would be his? What the hell did that even m—?

It hit me then. His power. It was unheard of. Not permitted. A power so hard to handle that the few people in history who carried it killed themselves or went insane. If my father didn't kill them first.

"You can see the future," I breathed.

He whimpered in relief that I had figured it out and then released my face. "Yes, and it's a curse because no one around me understands what is coming, or what we will do."

He shook his head and tapped the side of it with a fist. "I can't sleep. I just want it to stop. I just want to transport myself to the future when it's over."

Holy effing shit. Kohen could see the future? No wonder Liana kept this from Sahiri. He would have been torn apart on the spot. It was a forbidden power to carry. Outlawed by my great-grandfather.

"Kohen..." My voice shook. "My father will kill you if he finds out you can do this," I said.

He looked at me and swallowed hard. "I know."

Did he know or did he *know?*

I couldn't handle this right now. It was too much. I came here to blow off some steam with Tetra and now I knew too much to go back to my relaxed state of mind.

He reached up and grasped the back of his neck. "Please don't flirt with Alek or I'll have to kill him."

I barked out in laughter at the ridiculous comment, and then stopped when I saw that he was serious.

He stepped forward, locking his gaze with mine, and then leaned into my ear, bringing the heat of his body with him and sending an inferno through my veins that settled between my legs. "Aisling, I've seen myself make love to you under a bed of stars, and I've heard you cry out my name begging for more. Anything with Alek or Jace would be fleeting. You are mine, and I am yours."

I stumbled backward, emotion clogging my throat.

His words were crazy. It was too much. I couldn't make love to the prince of Imbria. My father would kill me. It would be the ultimate betrayal.

"I've freaked you out." He took three giant steps backward and then gave me his back, squatting on his heels and hanging his head in his hands.

"Kohen, it's just... a lot."

"Just go," he ordered.

"Kohen..." I searched for a kind thing to say, but

telling me that I was his and that he already owned my heart in some future where he had yet to romance me was *definitely* freaking me out.

"Just go," he said again, and so I did. I stumbled out into the hallway and went right for the bathroom, where I stared at myself in the mirror for ten whole minutes in shock.

'*Kohen can see the future,*' I told Liana.

'*Yes.*' Her reply was filled with sadness.

This changed everything.

OVER THE NEXT WEEK, all I thought about was *making love under a bed of stars and crying out his name.* He'd implanted that into my head and now I was going insane with it. He was avoiding me. He ate lunch at our table in under two minutes and then went outside to run. He ran all the time now, as if he trying to run away from his problems. We trained daily as a group with my fellow wing mates. We did flying drills and combat drills, and all I thought about was Kohen and I having sex.

It was driving me crazy. I wished he'd never told me. The only way I would have sex with him were if we married. I was a responsible successor to my father's throne, held to the highest standard, albeit an old law that was outdated. But I wasn't about to go sleep around and ruin all my prospects just because

Kohen whispered something in my ear. One check from the doctors telling my future husband that I was impure and I'd be a spinster for the rest of my life, collecting cats. But there was literally no world in which I would marry Kohen Badshah, which led me to believe that he was either mistaken about his visions of the future or he was deliberately lying to mess with me. My mind was a wreck, and there was no one I could tell, because on the off-chance Kohen wasn't lying, or making this up... revealing his secret could get him killed.

I WAS FUNCTIONING on such little sleep that my movements were sluggish when we were dragged out of bed at 2 a.m. Another week had passed and the instructors were torturing us with nighttime drills.

"This is a drill!" Instructor Ashendell announced through her bullhorn as she walked down the hall. "Pretend that we've just been attacked by Luskins—who will be wearing red vests. Go find your creature and defend the training center, detaining as many red vests as you can."

Tetra limped over to the dresser in her underwear, half falling over until I caught her midair and helped her into her pants.

"There's no time for lacing boots, ladies and gentlemen!" Ashendell barked, and I released Tetra as we both stumbled into the hallway still dressing as we ran.

My gaze flicked to Kohen, shirtless and not even bothering to put one on as he strode into the hallway in low slung pants and a long sword in each hand.

Stars help me.

You're mine, Aisling. His words reverberated around my head and I had to push them out of my brain. It wasn't the time to think of such things. The second we stepped outside, we were hit with an onslaught of mock weapons. Blunt rubber tipped arrows, water balloons filled with paint, and wood throwing "knives" rained down on us. We scattered like bees, running in every direction, and I tucked myself flat to the building and moved to the woods that way.

"Cadet Everhart!" a male whisper-screamed from a nearby bush. "You are with me." He stepped out and waved me over. It was one of my instructors, and he wasn't wearing a red vest, so I followed him, keeping my head low.

"What's the plan?" I whispered-screamed to him as we walked in a crouch farther away from the noise and chaos.

He peered back at me. "We are going to make a jail of sorts and hold the red prisoners there securely."

Okay, not my ideal position in battle because it sounded more like babysitting, but I wasn't going to complain if this was what the lieutenants had come up with for me.

I followed him across the back field of the school to an abandoned building. The windows had been blown out and it was missing a roof. It looked like they had tested bombs in here or something. It was basically four brick walls and nothing else, but would make a decent jail if we bound everyone's hands together.

"Alright, come in and check out the space first," the instructor said to me as we entered. The second I stepped through the threshold I felt air whoosh at my back and I ducked just in time to avoid a blow to the head. Dropping to one knee, I rolled out of the way, and that's when both men came at me.

Their creatures joined in.

The two men grasped me by the arms and hauled me up as a small fox creature stalked towards me, the electric blue ember lines on her back glowing as a wind stirred around the room. Her power.

"Quickly, kill her before her creature shows up!" the one instructor barked.

I didn't know if I was tired or what, but this entire time I thought this was a part of the drill. It wasn't until he yelled about killing me that I realized this was an ambush. They'd lured me away from my friends and now I was going to die. Ice cold dread settled in my stomach as I realized these were the men wearing the gasmasks who had spoken of "taking me out."

A wolf creature then stepped out from behind a stack of bricks and my stomach sank. His power was poisoned teeth if I remembered correctly. These two instructors weren't our main ones. They popped in to help from time to time, but I think they were normally on the officer side. I didn't even remember their names. But I was keenly aware that there were only two of them and three had spoken of offing me on that day.

The fox creature suddenly dove for me but I kicked out and connected with her belly, sending her flying across the room. She hit one of the walls, knocked out cold, falling to the ground with a thud.

Four on one were not great odds, but there was no way I was going out like this.

'*I need help. I'm under attack,*' I told Liana, my brain finally awake enough to make smart decisions.

'*I'm coming,*' she said just as the wolf creature lunged for my throat.

I jerked my head to the right, cracking skulls with the instructor on that side, and he let go of my arm, which allowed me to block the wolf's attack. I punched the wolf in the side of the head before he could bite me, and he fell to the ground but got up quickly. I was just about to try to run when the other instructor wrapped his hands around my throat.

My dagger was in my boot, the stupidest place it could be if you were standing and currently being strangled. Trying to fight him off, while also keeping my eye on that wolf was proving too much. So I did what Elaine called panic mode. I went berserk and thrashed every which way, throwing knees and elbows, hoping to catch my opponent off guard. It worked, until it didn't.

I was able to wrestle out of his grasp, but then his partner cracked me over the skull and I went down, ears ringing and darkness dancing at the edges of my vision.

These bastards were really starting to piss me off. Smoke filled the room and I wasn't sure where it was coming from, until I realized it was me. Curls of gray puffed off of my skin as if I were a hot coal doused in water. I was smoking like a damn steak on a grill.

"Quick! Her powers are manifesting," one guy said, and then his wolf lunged for me again.

In the midst of the chaos, it happened. A surge of energy pulsed through me like an unexpected force that seemed to saturate my entire being.

I focused my thoughts on the advancing wolf and threw my arm out.

"Stop!" I flung the word as if it was a physical force, and a thin, silver, glowing string flew from my mouth and wrapped around the wolf's head. The wolf dropped to the ground before me, head bowed with a whimper in his throat.

What the hell?

"No," the man beside me breathed, and that's when I noticed a shadow overhead.

I peered up, just in time to see Liana dip from the sky and take one of the instructors into her mouth, biting his midsection like a snack.

He screamed and she shot into the air with him in her mouth, carrying him away.

The other instructor stood there in shock, watching me in fear.

"Y-you can control minds," he stuttered. "That's forbidden, even for you."

What? No. I didn't control anyone. Did I? But I replayed the scene in my head and fear washed over me. *Maybe I did.* I told the wolf to stop and he did. Was that what the silver cord was? A manifestation of my control?

The instructor slowly stepped closer to me. "You might as well just let my wolf end it here, because they will never let you live. No one will follow a leader that can't even give them free will." He spat and lunged for me with a dagger in his hands.

Another dark shadow dropped from above and I thought it was Liana, returning to finish off this second guy. But suddenly Kohen landed behind the instructor, wearing a feral expression. The ex-prince grabbed the instructor by the head and snapped his neck cleanly, causing his body to fall dead to the ground in front of me.

The wolf was still kneeling, as if stuck in a trance, and I realized that I still had my power over him, thick like a blanket I could almost feel. The silver cord I had somehow attached to his head was still there, connected to the center of my palm. I pulled it back and the cord snapped. The wolf tipped his head back and howled before dropping dead beside his bonded.

When we died outside The Wilds, our creatures died as well.

I heaved deep breaths as I processed that two instructors from the Imperial Fleet that my dad ruled over had just tried to kill me.

Kohen was watching me like you would watch a caged bird flit around wildly looking for an exit. Which was exactly what I was doing, but I couldn't move. I was in shock. What the instructor said... what I did to the wolf...

My power.

Kohen heard, he must have. The guy said it right before he dropped down.

Kohen knelt before me and I realized I was hyper-ventilating.

"I don't want this," I told him. I didn't want to control people. It was a dark power, forbidden. I couldn't help but think that Kohen and I were the same. Both carrying a terrifying power neither of us wanted.

Kohen reached for my hand and took it into his, stroking my palm with his thumb in such a tender way it made my heart ache.

"You *will* be empress, Aisling. And if you want to live, you will never tell another soul that you can do this one thing. I will take it to my grave, you have my word." So he did hear, or maybe he had known this whole time.

The confident way in which he spoke of me being empress made me wonder if he was just being nice—the instructor had said no one would follow me—or if he *knew* something.

I didn't want to know either way. I felt insane. The wolf had been about to attack me and I'd basically frozen him in a trance mid-attack. That wasn't normal. That was...

Liana returned with a blood-soaked beak and two instructors, one being Ashendell.

Ashendell took in the scene and her eyes flew wide.

Kohen dropped my hand, storming over to the lead instructor angrily. "Is this how you protect your future empress? By having two of your own instructors try to kill her?"

Ashendell's mouth flew open as her gaze went to the dead man's body and then to my neck, which I was guessing had marks from where he choked me.

"Call the emperor and tell him there has been an attack on his daughter. I'm sure he will want to know how this training facility is being run," Kohen growled.

My father? *No way.* I could be on my death bed, and if I thought it would piss him off I wouldn't want him called.

I stood, holding out my hands. "That's not necessary." My voice was raspy and painful.

'*Let Kohen lead,*' Liana told me, and I shot her a glare.

"If the emperor finds out his daughter was almost killed and you did nothing..." Kohen shook his head. "You're done for."

Ashendell swallowed hard and nodded. "Of course. Come with me, Miss Everhart. I'm not letting you out of my sight."

I allowed Ashendell to pull me away as a whistle was blown and the drill was called off. When I peered back at Kohen, he was mounting Onyx and flying off into the night, away from campus.

What the hell just happened? And why did it feel like Kohen had orchestrated something?

EIGHTEEN

I sat inside of medical and through the giant glass window watched my dad rip every single admiral a new asshole. They stood erect, against the far wall as my father and Zuri stalked before them, threatening to close the school, pull funding, and fire them all.

"She's your future *empress*! If you cannot protect her, you certainly cannot protect our borders," he shouted to the stony-faced men and women. They did nothing. Just stood there and took it, only speaking when directed a question.

Liana insisted on not leaving my side, so we had to open the double doors at the end of the hallway to get her inside, and then she had to duck low with her wings tucked in to enter the room I was in. She stood alert beside my bed, watching my father with her head cocked to the side.

He was pissed.

I needed to confide in someone about what happened, but I took to heart what Kohen said about me not telling a soul. Still, I didn't think that meant Liana too. I was pretty sure she already knew through our bond, but I wanted to make sure.

'Do you know what I did?' I asked her.

She looked at me. *'Yes. We call it the thrall where I am from. It's a form of mind control.'*

That sounded scary. *'What is it? Are there limits? Can I control ten people at once? Could it hurt me if I use it too much?'* I had a thousand questions.

'I don't know. I only know one other person who had the gift, my grandmother. A firebird of great power who was not weakened by a human body.'

I knew she wasn't being mean, just factual. The creatures of The Wilds were filled with magic, magic our human bodies could only hold so much of.

'Did you know I had it?' I asked her. She seemed so confident.

'I suspected you had the power to control another since we bonded.'

I peered at her in shock. *'You did? How?'*

She glanced at me, *'When you fought the fire beast. It was only fully defeated after you shouted at it to just die already and it did. I thought I sensed the power in you then.'*

I cocked my head to the side, remembering the

scary fire beast that tried to consume me. I'd used the mind control then?

'*Were you there with me and the fire beast?*' I asked. I barely remembered her flying underneath me at one point and then gone the next.

She was quiet a second. '*I am the fire beast, Aisling. It's part of me, a part of me I cannot control. The dominant part of me you had to subdue in order to bond.*'

I sat there in shock for a full minute, absorbing what she had just said.

'*I would never want to hurt you,*' she told me, nuzzling my neck. '*If I could choose, I would have allowed you to live without a fight. But my magic is bigger than that.*'

That was heavy. The fire beast that was trying to consume and kill me while I was in stasis was her? The same Liana that protected me now. And yet I understood. She could not allow a weak bonding to be reborn.

"It's okay. Thank you for telling me." I stroked the feathers on her neck and she peered up at me. '*Does that mean if I were to die again, I would enter that void again and have to fight before being reborn?*'

'*I wish I knew. But if it's any consolation, each time I die I have to fight the fire beast as well.*'

My mouth popped open in surprise at that. She did?

'*Did you notice the other power that manifested before*

you enthralled the instructor's creature?' she asked, changing the subject, which I was grateful for.

I frowned. *'No.'*

'The smoke that was coming off of your body. Not only are you impervious to harm from fire, but you can produce and direct fire at will. Like me.'

My eyebrows rose at that. *'That's something I can share with the Imperial Fleet, right?'* That would be an amazing power to have in battle.

I could almost see a smile in her eyes. *'It is. Along with your ability to rapidly heal. But the rest... let's keep to ourselves.'*

Like the fact that I could possibly come back from the dead again, and the very secret fact that I could control minds. *Yes, let's never tell a soul about those.*

"Aisling," my father snapped, and I jerked my head to the door. He must have already called my name once and he didn't like to repeat himself.

"Yes, Father?" I sat up straighter.

He stepped inside the room, Zuri trailing behind him; both their gazes went to Liana. There was a flash of trepidation there which I wasn't sure was a good thing.

"I have dealt with this matter, but if anything else happens I want you to send for me right away," he said. A spinning wheel of fire began to open at his back. I'd seen him create portals a hundred times and it never ceased to amaze me when I saw another place come into view behind him—his office at our home, the place where he spent most of his time.

What I wasn't prepared to see, however, was Kohen closing my father's desk and peering at me before running out.

I gasped and my father frowned.

"What is it?" He stepped closer, concern etched onto his features.

I grabbed my side, pretending I had a pain there. "Nothing. I'm fine."

My father nodded and then turned around, following Zuri back into his office, and the portal snapped shut. Was that why Kohen made such a big deal about calling my father to the school? So that he could sneak into his office while he was away? I knew it. I knew he was just using me!

That bastard.

I peered at Liana in anger. *'Did you know he was going to break into my father's office?'*

She looked surprised and hurt by that. *'Of course not.'*

I yanked the IV out of my arm and stepped out of bed, struggling to get my clothes on and not flash all of the admirals who were still talking outside in front of my window.

My father had insisted on a full checkup and I was checked up. Time to get the hell out of here and find Kohen. Why had I stayed silent and protected him?

Because if my father had seen him, he'd have killed him on the spot without question.

I was going to handle this my way.

After getting dressed, I tossed the medical gown on the bed and flung the door wide. I threw it so hard that it hit the back wall. Every single admiral turned and faced me, all wearing stony expressions.

I saluted them and then passed them down the hallway as Liana struggled to make it through the doorframe. She stopped to glare at the admirals and they all took a few steps back to give her a wide berth. Outside, I hopped on her back. "Take me to Kohen. I know you can find Onyx."

She didn't argue, she just kicked off and took to the skies. I was fuming mad by the time we saw the black dragon in the sky flying over the park near my house. How dare he! With my sisters home. Would he have hurt them?

'Tell Onyx to land,' I told Liana.

I knew she had a mental connection with the dragon, and seconds after I'd made my request both Onyx and Kohen looked up to see us looming over them.

Onyx lowered immediately into a dark and deserted portion of the park. The second Onyx landed, I didn't wait for Liana to get me to the ground. I pulled my dagger from my boot and leapt off of her. I crashed into Kohen's back, forcing him to sprawl out on his stomach before I shoved my knee in his back and pulled the blade to his throat.

"What the hell were you doing in my father's study? With my sisters home. If you hurt them—"

"I would never hurt your sisters!" he said, aghast, turning his head to look up at me in shock.

His shock made regret flush through me.

You're mine, Aisling. I've made love to you under a bed of stars.

His previous words were so far from the current place we found ourselves I couldn't help but shake my head. He was a liar. He was playing me!

"Answer me or I'll bleed you right here," I growled.

Onyx chuffed behind me as if he wouldn't allow that to happen, but Liana stepped in front of him, blocking his view and clearly telling him to back off.

Good. I'd wondered what she would do if it was ever us against them. Now I knew. My creature was loyal to me alone, as promised.

"Left pocket," Kohen said sadly.

I frowned, pulling one of my knees off of his back, and reached into his left pocket, fully ready to slice him if this was some trick. When my fingers wrapped around a cold, flat, metal disk, I pulled it out.

Bringing the item up to my face, I frowned.

"A pocket watch?" I stepped off of Kohen and allowed him to stand.

The watch was heavy, solid gold, and it had a

beautiful etched tiger on the front. I clicked the button to open the face and peered at the inside.

The inscription engraved under the lid had my throat closing with emotion.

To my beloved son, Kohen. Rule with justice and compassion in equal measure.

"My father had it made for me when I was born. Your father stole it from him the night he killed him. I was just getting it back. It's mine."

My heart sank into my stomach like a stone. I reached out to hand him the watch, which he took gingerly from my outstretched palm. Here was the man who helped me keep my locket the first day of boot camp, and all he was doing was getting back a similar object from my father.

I felt like a jerk.

"You could have just asked me. I would have gotten it for you," I told him, though the thought of sneaking into my father's office terrified me.

He frowned. "Would you have? I don't know anymore. I don't know anything anymore."

Then he walked past me, got on Onyx, and flew away.

'He should not have broken into your home where your sisters sleep. You were right to confront him,' Liana told me.

I nodded. *'I know.'*

But then why did I feel like such crap?

THE NEXT MORNING AT BREAKFAST, there were two drill instructors standing ten paces behind me as I ate, seemingly guarding me. Kohen sat at a table in the corner and Anika and the rest of his crew moved with him. It was painfully apparent that there was a separation there, and I couldn't help but feel like I'd screwed up.

"He broke into my freaking home!" I whispered-screamed to Tetra. "And I'm the jerk for calling him out on it?"

Everyone had heard about the attack on my life and the fact that two drill instructors were now dead over it, so all my fellow candidates stared at me as they passed.

"I mean, did you call him out on it or did you hold a knife to his throat and almost kill him over it?" Tetra asked seriously.

Damn. She had the tongue of a viper when she wanted to.

"The triplets were home. He could have—"

Tetra rolled her eyes. "He could have tried to kill you plenty of times but he hasn't. In fact, he seems to have the hots for you. He flipped out over Jace taking a fry off your plate. That's not normal."

I wanted to tell her what he said about me being his at karaoke night so badly that I had to physically squeeze my lips to keep quiet. Doing that would reveal his gift, and although I was pissed at him, I wasn't that pissed. I trusted Tetra, but even knowing this could put her in danger.

"So you're saying if he broke into your mom's house you would be cool with it?" I asked her.

She gave me a look, a look that I had grown to know meant she was about to say something I didn't like.

Alek and Roc were just checking out at the lunch counter; they would be here any second. For now we were alone.

Tetra leaned into me and lowered her voice. "Have you stopped even once to ask yourself why your father would steal a sentimental pocket watch off of a dead man and keep it in his office all these years?"

I gasped. When she said it like that, it made my father sound like a lunatic hell-bent on revenge.

I met her gaze. "Ravi Badshah was a terrorist who killed over—"

"I know." She held out her hands to stop me, and then flicked her gaze to where Anika was sitting next to Kohen, chatting happily. "Unless... we don't have the whole story there."

I frowned, and she swallowed hard.

"I'm just saying... what if we don't know everything?"

So Anika had been talking to her too. I opened my mouth to argue when Alek dropped next to me, concern etched all over his face. "I heard about the attack. Are you okay?" His gaze frantically ran over my body as if looking for injuries and I nodded, giving him a tight smile.

"My father has enemies even in his own backyard it seems. Luckily, the perpetrators have been taken care of and all is well now." The coined answer Lucinda Lark, my father's personal secretary, had written me this morning, informing me that I was supposed to tell anyone that asked.

Alek frowned. "But the instructors—"

"All is well now," I assured him, placing a hand on his and giving him a look that said *Let it go*.

"Damn, I regret not getting tater tots," Roc said, peering at his plate. "I would take one of yours, Aisling, but I'm afraid Kohen will rip my ear off for it."

Everyone at the table burst out laughing, everyone except me.

I peered across the room at the same time Kohen did and our gazes caught. Even from here I could see those piercing blue eyes locked with mine. It was like he was peeling back my protective layers one by one and trying to stare straight into my soul.

I had so many questions. Why did I see heartbreak in his eyes? Who broke it? Me?

He finally looked away and it felt like I was suddenly all alone. Confused and alone.

"Aisling and Kohen finally have powers to show us!" Lieutenant Ashendell told our squad. I'd gone to her and told her that the night I was attacked I had acquired the ability to conjure fire. Though it was really smoke, Liana had assured me I could conjure fire when needed.

Everyone cheered and I swallowed hard. Hopefully, Kohen had something else to display, because everyone finding out he could see the future would sign his death warrant.

"Kohen, will you please do the honors of going first? I think we've waited in anticipation long enough." Ashendell looked bored, and I perked up as I watched the former Imbrian prince walk across the field and stand in the middle.

He looked so calm. Like he'd been practicing, or just wasn't scared. I envied that. I was terrified as hell to turn into a fireball for the first time, and in front of my peers.

Onyx and Liana stood off to the side with the other creatures and watched.

"Lieutenant Ashendell, would you please direct your attention to that bush over there?" Kohen pointed to a shrub that stood at the edge of the tree line over forty feet away.

The lieutenant's brows pinched together in confusion but she did as he asked. We all did. I turned to face the plant, my gaze flicking back to Kohen and then the bush, and back to Kohen. Kohen looked to be in deep concentration, arms at his side as he stared at the shrub and then...

We all gave a collective gasp as the bush burst into flames.

Wow, to be able to direct flames to something from so far away... without shooting the flames across the lawn. It was pretty incredible.

My fellow cadets burst into applause, myself included, and Kohen gave a slight grin of pride.

"Wow, okay, that's very impressive, Mr. Badshah." Ashendell had her clipboard with her and marked something in it.

Then she turned to me. "Miss Everhart?"

'I'm going to vomit,' I told Liana.

'Well, then vomit and get it over with, because they expect great things from you, and that's what you need to give them right now,' Liana said.

Oh great. That was *not* helping with the pressure.

I stepped forward, sweat beading my brow as I stood in the center of the practice field with my fellow cadets all around me. A few higher-level soldiers who were here for officer training stopped what they were doing and walked over to watch me.

I was Aisling Everhart, future empress. If I couldn't handle pressure now, I couldn't run this country.

'How do I make the fire come?' I asked Liana.

'Tell everyone to step back,' Liana advised.

I raised one eyebrow at my creature. "Take a step back!" I told everyone.

They exchanged curious glances but took a giant step back.

'More,' Liana said.

Oh stars, this was embarrassing.

"Farther," I told the surrounding crowd, and they stepped three paces back.

I took a deep breath.

'Now crouch down, make yourself like a ball.'

If this didn't work I was going to look like such an idiot.

I did as she asked and lowered my head to my knees, tucking myself into a ball.

'Now go inside your mind. Remember the fire beast? Remember what it felt like to fight her? That all-consuming heat, the way she grew when you cut her down and didn't let up...'

'Yes,' I said, because I did remember. I would not

soon forget that experience. Even more now that Liana had told me the fire beast was a part of her.

'Reach for her, and let her out,' she coached.

I was keenly aware of the fact that I likely looked like an idiot curled into a ball on the practice field while I had a conversation in my head with my creature and everyone stared at me. But I didn't focus on that. I focused instead on the heat in my core, the fire beast who was wild and terrifying and glorious and impossible to control. She was there, inside of me, like a second creature almost, Liana's alter ego, this one slightly terrifying. I reached out and touched that power and then opened the invisible cage she'd been resting in all this time.

One second I was just sitting on the ground concentrating on this power, and the next there was a flash of heat and dozens of screams. A blast exploded from my skin and I looked up just in time to see a wall of fire rushing outward from me towards my fellow candidates. People ran farther back, screaming, including Instructor Ashendell, and then the fire dissipated as its pressure was released.

My skin, hair, and clothing were untouched, though I was sweating and felt slightly warmer than usual. With a hard swallow, I stood and surveyed the giant circle of scorched grass I was standing in the center of.

Ashendell just stared at me for a full thirty seconds before marking something on her clipboard and then smiling. "Our future empress is a human bomb."

The class erupted into cheers and I smiled, rubbing my sweaty palms on my pants. I'd finally given them something to be excited over without revealing my dark hidden power—the power I'd already put in my little black box and would never think about again. I hoped word got back to Admiral Blade about this, because if Sahiri had forced such a power, it would have burned her and whoever stood nearest me alive. This would explain my behavior that day, and the admirals would trust me again. Most of all, my father would be pleased.

AFTER KOHEN'S and my power display, we had sword practice with our fellow cadets. We were just finishing up when I got in line behind Kohen to turn my practice blade back in to the instructor. Kohen turned to Anika and asked for her practice blade, and when their hands touched, he sucked in a breath.

She cocked her head to the side. "You okay?"

He just stared at her for a second as if lost in a trance, then he seemed to snap out of it. His hand shook, but he slipped it into his pocket to cover it. Did he just see the future? Even now he still had a far-off look in his eyes.

"I'm fine. I'm gonna go for a walk, clear my head,"

Kohen said to Anika after setting the practice blades at the instructor's feet, and then stormed off into the woods. The guilt that had slowly been rising up inside of me reached a level I could no longer tolerate. Kohen should not have broken into my house, but I couldn't let him go through this alone.

I didn't hate him. I should but I couldn't.

I turned in my blade and then went after him, stepping into the thick woods to find that Kohen was… running. His legs pumped fast as he bolted full-speed through the trees, leaping over fallen logs and dry brush. I didn't think, I just acted. I ran after him, pumping my legs hard as I streaked across the dense forest.

"Kohen!" I screamed, and he slowed.

His back heaved as he fought for breath, and when I reached him he fell to the ground on all fours, hands splayed out, breath coming out in rapid gasps.

He was having a panic attack.

Victory had had one once when she shot her first deer with a bow. It had looked like this.

"Hey, deep breaths." I rubbed small circles on his back, like I had for Victory, and he stilled, calming.

He looked up at me for the first time since I'd gotten here and I was shocked to see the anguish in his eyes.

"So much death," he whimpered.

Chills broke out onto my arms and I staggered backward a little, falling onto my butt.

"What? What did you see?"

He reached up and ran his fingers through his hair before slipping into the Imbrian language, a string of incoherent rambling that was both beautiful and terrifying because I couldn't understand any of it.

"Kohen, what did you see?"

He quieted, looking at his hands as if there were something on them. He brushed them on his pants and then shook his head. "I don't think I can live like this," he said, and my heart tore in half. It was such a vulnerable thing to say, and to say it to someone who'd held a knife to your throat just a short time ago probably made it so much worse.

"Yes you can," I told him.

He shook his head. "I see an attack. Here. On this very campus. I see my friends near death... I don't know if they make it. And the worst of it all is that I'm falling in love with someone who hates me." He held my gaze, staring at my lips in a reverent way and my mouth popped open in shock.

Me. He was talking about me.

That was *a lot* to process, but strangely the L word scared me less than the attack he spoke of.

"Attack? Here? We need to tell my father." I stood, ignoring the *falling in love with me* part.

He glared at me. "And how do we tell him that without getting me killed? My stars, Aisling, you're my best friend and you don't even know it yet. I can't do this."

Best friends. Lovers. My heart yearned for that with him and I knew it shouldn't. I hated that he told me these things. It made me wonder if I would desire him on my own or only because he planted the thoughts in my head. It didn't matter either way. He was a Badshah.

He stood and started to walk away, leaving me to sit there in shock.

"Hey!" I snapped, storming after him. "That's not fair!" I reached him and yanked his shoulder so that he spun to face me.

Best friend. Love. *This is insane!*

"How do you know your visions or whatever are even real?" I hated to ask but I did.

He didn't look hurt, he just sighed. "The night you were attacked by the drill instructors, I saw it in a vision. That's how I got there so quickly. Then I had a vision of your father coming to chew out the admirals, and a flash of his office desk drawer with my father's pocket watch inside."

My mouth popped open again. I had wondered how he'd been the one to find me and so fast. I'd assumed Liana told Onyx, who in turn told him, but there wouldn't have been that much time. I'd have been dead without his help. So that's why he fought to get my father there, so that he could sneak into his office and get the pocket watch back just like he'd seen in his vision. I still wasn't convinced that his visions and seeing the future were real. He was a Badshah—

cunning and ruthless—this could all be an elaborate ruse.

"I also know that if you don't braid your hair before bed, you wake up with it all tangled." He reached out and fingered the strands hanging over my shoulder. My breath caught as he then trailed his fingers down my neck. Red hot need pulsed throughout my body but I fought it. This was too much. What he was saying was crazy. But I also wanted it to be true, all of it. I leaned into him, licking my lips to wet them, warring with my own desire. "I know that under this shirt you have a group of freckles that look like a constellation." He pulled his hand back and sadness filled his gaze. "And I know that no matter how much I want to kiss you right now, this isn't where we have our first kiss because you freak out and—"

I ran. I couldn't hear another word. I bolted out of there as my heart pounded like it was in a cage begging to be freed.

'Liana, I need to get out of here,' I called for her, and then followed the nudging in my chest that told me where she was. Kohen had scared the crap out of me. All those things he said were true. My braid... the freckles... I felt sick. It was overwhelming. Not because the thought of kissing him or doing any of those things made me sick, but doing them meant I would betray my father, my family. Kohen Badshah was the son of the man who'd brought great pain to my coun-

try. If I did these things in his vision, if I gave into these fleshly desires, then I was a traitor to everything I ever knew and loved.

Liana appeared, dipped her head, and I leapt onto her back. Without a word she shot up to the sky and took off for the clouds, higher and higher than we'd ever flown before.

So high that my ears popped, and when I was all alone in the sky, just me, Liana, and the clouds, I let loose with a gut-wrenching scream from the depths of my soul.

This was impossible. Kohen was the one man in the entire world that I couldn't have. My father would kill me.

So why did I want him so badly? And why did I believe that everything he said was true?

CHAPTER

TWENTY

The days passed quickly, and before I knew it we were in the final stretch of boot camp. We knew there was a final test that would be pressed upon us at any moment before we could be cleared to graduate. That night we were woken in the early morning hours by sirens.

My heart jackknifed in my chest at the loud noise blaring into my sleep, waking me with a start.

The attack. The death Kohen had spoken of. It had plagued me all week and now it was happening.

"Take cover!" I screamed to Tetra, but then I heard Instructor Ashendell on the bullhorn.

"This is a drill!" she said, and Tetra peered up at me like I'd sprouted a second head. Relief crashed through me. *Not the attack Kohen spoke about.*

"In this simulation, you will be protecting a shipment. Your task is to safely get it from point A to point

B. Along the way there might be some trouble, so make contingency plans. This is a twenty-four-hour simulation, and we leave in one hour. Get ready!"

Twenty-four-hour simulation!

I immediately started to get dressed.

"Pack some MREs," I told Tetra. We couldn't count on the Fleet to feed us during a simulation. Elaine had told me that there would be simulations. Some would last a few hours and would even take you off campus into the woods. But protecting a shipment for twenty-four hours was new. If I was being honest, it was exciting. I'd trained my whole life for this, to be thrust into the action. I really hoped they put me in a leadership position, but if not I would defer to whoever my leader was.

Ten minutes later, I walked into the mess hall with Tetra hobbling beside me. She winced as we moved quickly and I peered over at her.

"You okay?"

She gave me a look of alarm. "Flare."

No. No. No. Panic rose up inside of me.

"Did you pack your meds?" I asked her, eyeing the pack on her back that we'd just thrown together in minutes.

She nodded once, lips pursed. "I'll be fine."

I was worried about her going out there like this but I couldn't voice it. The drill instructors had pushed three lunch tables together and had spread a bunch of maps out on it. We had to join the others. Tetra had dealt with this her whole life. I had to trust that she'd speak up if she wasn't okay.

"I will be announcing our team leaders!" Instructor Ashendell said, and Tetra and I moved closer. "These leaders will take turns picking one of you for their team. If you are last to be picked, you owe me a hundred push-ups because you are PATHETIC!" she shouted and I wanted to laugh. Elaine told me that boot camp was all about psychological warfare, and that most of these instructors were nothing like this on the outside. They just thought of mean and demeaning things to say to try to break you down. It wasn't working. My entire cohort of cadets had been pretty badass so far. No one had given up or been kicked out.

"The leaders for this simulation are..."

I wiggled my toes inside of my boots in an effort to expel the nervous energy from my body without making it look like I was anxious.

"Jace!" she called and everyone cheered. There was a small "Booo" that came from Tetra's direction, and I had to contain my smile.

Jace walked up to the front, grinning and proud. We'd been so busy with training and drills I hadn't really had much time to think of him and his betrayal. But when I looked at him now, I could honestly say there was no attraction left for me. He was dead to me emotionally and physically.

"Kohen Badshah!" Ashendell announced, and

there were fewer claps as he strode across the room to stand next to Jace, his face emotionless. The boys' muscles twitched at being in close proximity to each other.

"Alek!" Ashendell said, and my stomach sank a little. I was happy for Alek, but... was Ashendell going to pick me? Was this because I was the emperor's daughter? Maybe they thought if I was a leader I would get hurt. But as the future empress, shouldn't my leadership skills be tested?

"Summer," she called, and I was no longer nervous—I was pissed. They thought *she* had leadership skills and I didn't? That was such BS.

"And finally..." Ashendell's gaze flicked to mine and I nearly vomited in anticipation. Was she messing with me? *Say my name already, woman!* I wanted to scream.

"Roc!" she called, and I felt disappointment bloom in my stomach.

I wasn't chosen. Was this a direct reflection of my service thus far? I wanted to cry, but I was an Everhart, so instead I just glared at Instructor Ashendell.

She met my gaze and tipped her chin high as if she stood by her decision. I clenched my teeth so hard they nearly snapped in half.

"Each leader will pick one person for their team until there is no one left. All teams will work together as a single unit, but each team will be given a separate task. Navigation, security, scouting, medical, and a battle unit, in case of attack."

I knew right away I wanted to be in the battle unit, but I also knew that choice was not up to me either. This was what being a part of the Imperial Fleet was. It forced you to be obedient and take orders without complaint, and I was no exception.

"Jace, you can start. Pick your first teammate," Ashendell said, and stood back.

Jace's gaze flicked to mine and I shook my head slightly. There was no way in hell I was taking orders from him. He rolled his eyes as if I were being overly dramatic. Was he serious? Like I was going to just get over him screwing some rando after promising a future to me?

"Tucker," he said, and his best friend walked up and stood behind him with a grin.

"Aisling," Kohen said without skipping a beat, catching me off guard.

Jace shot Kohen a glare and I swallowed hard, stepping up behind him.

Was this complicated? Yes.

Was I going to make a big deal out of it in front of everyone? No.

I didn't want to overthink it.

As more names got called, my gaze flicked to Tetra. I wondered if I could somehow communicate to Kohen to pick her on his next round—

"Tetra," Kohen said when it came time for his second pick, and my heart nearly stopped.

He did that for me, there was no doubt about it. Kohen turned slightly and flicked his gaze back at me, and I wanted to thank him, but thought better of it with everyone so close and listening.

Tetra was slow to make it up to us, wincing as she leaned on her cane and dragging her bad foot more than she usually did.

"You okay?" I breathed.

She nodded, saying nothing, and stood behind me. Tetra was the toughest chick I knew. She lived with daily pain and never complained. I wished then that I'd been given healing powers and could take the pain away from her foot forever.

When it was Kohen's third pick, I thought for sure he would pick Dev, Nikhil, or another strong male, but he chose little Meera. It wasn't until he made his next choice, Anika, that I realized what he'd done, who he was. At his core, Kohen was a protector. He'd chosen all of the women in his life that he cared about and wanted to keep safe. Not because he thought we were weak but probably because he couldn't stand not being able to keep an eye on us.

And he chose me first.

It caused a mixture of feelings to bloom in my chest. Warmth, adoration, desire—confusion.

His last two picks were Nikhil and Dev. And Roc chose the remaining person, a scrawny guy named

Sven who was bonded to a racoon and indeed did have to do a hundred push-ups.

Instructor Ashendell then walked over to each team leader and gave them a folded note. "This is your team assignment. It is not a secret. You may share it with the others, but no trading. Now you have twenty minutes to strategize. Dismissed."

Kohen flipped over our card and I read it: *Battle Unit.*

"Yes!" I pumped my fist and Kohen gave me a grin. It seemed we'd finally moved past all of our weirdness and were both just set on passing this final test so that we could graduate.

"Let's go look at the maps," Kohen said. "See if there are weak spots that would be vulnerable to an attack."

He moved with our team over to the table scattered with maps. I went to follow, then Ashendell hooked her hand gently under my arm and pulled me to the side.

"Are you wondering why I didn't choose you as team leader?" she said. Her face was calm and introspective.

I swallowed hard. "Because my father or the admirals asked you not to?" I assumed.

She shook her head. "On the contrary, they advised me to test your leadership skills on this final mission."

I couldn't help the hurt that crossed my face, and Ashendell saw it too, because her expression softened.

"*But*, as your instructor, I want you to learn a lesson from this," she said. "As your father's successor, you are assured a leadership position in the future, and I have no doubt you will go on to do great things for our country. But this is your one chance to see what it's like to take orders, even when you don't agree with them, so that when it's your turn to do the ordering, you know how big of an ask it will be."

Her wise words shocked me into silence. Elaine would approve of this lesson. It sounded like something she might say.

"Yes, ma'am," I said, and she clapped me on the back and walked away.

But taking orders from Kohen Badshah? My father better not find out about that.

WE REVIEWED the maps and the travel plan. The assignment was to travel with a special shipment, something secret that would be kept in the backmost train car, to Thunder Cliff base six hundred miles north near the Luksa border at The Wall. Kohen had suggested that we both fly over the train on our creatures and I agreed. We found two passes through the mountains near Golden Hills that looked like weak ambush points, so we were going to strengthen our battle unit over those two areas, being fully at the ready for attack.

As we hiked with the five groups out to the train station, Kohen let the others go ahead and he pulled me back. Tetra was wincing with every step and I was nervous for her. Even her creature Ariyel looked up at her sadly as they walked side by side.

Onyx and Liana flew above us until we got to the train. I peered at Kohen, wondering what he was going to tell me.

"Tetra rides into battle on her wolf in the future. It takes the weight off of her bad foot," he whispered to me.

I stopped walking, eyes wide. Had I just heard him correctly?

"I'm sorry. What?" I said.

He looked impatient. "I've seen Tetra ride her wolf in my visions. I wonder if you should suggest it. It will sound weird coming from me."

It sounded weird already and I knew about his gift, which had yet to be proven to me. He could be lying. Everything could be a lie. But in my heart I knew it probably wasn't... and that scared me.

I frowned. "Her wolf is too small." But even as I said it, I wondered if that was true. Tetra herself was barely five-foot-one and had a petite frame. She couldn't weigh more than a hundred and five pounds. Her wolf wasn't a normal wolf. She was a magical creature. Maybe she had super strength...

Kohen stared at me like I was a child. "Aisling, I've

seen it. Small or not, her wolf is strong and she can handle her weight."

I looked up at his arresting blue eyes and then to his lips, thinking about when he said he wanted to kiss me but it wasn't where we'd have our first kiss. Now I wondered where that was. It drove me insane, knowing that I would one day kiss those lips. My brain said that could never happen, but my body ached for it.

I cleared my throat.

"Do you know how this simulation goes? Do we pass and go on to graduate?" I asked him. I needed some of his predictions to come true so that I could learn to trust them. Even so, he could be lying to mess with my head. But would he do that? He didn't seem the vindictive type that my father made him out to be. I was trying to be loyal to my family but also listen to my heart. My heart told me that Kohen Badshah was a good man, and my body told me that it wanted that good man to do all the things he said happened in his vision.

He shrugged. "I assume we pass since I've seen us all graduate."

Hmm, that was handy knowledge, but not detailed enough for me to use as an indicator that he did indeed see the future. "And the attack you spoke about... on the training campus?"

He swallowed hard. "I don't know when that happens. It could be tomorrow or a year from now. But it won't happen until you hurt your wrist." His gaze flicked to my arm and I frowned.

"Your right arm is in a cast when the attack happens," he said.

Okay, that was detailed. I was starting to get freaked-out again.

"Badshah! Everhart!" Ashendell shouted. "You can chat later, we have a package to drop off!" We snapped to attention, stepping away from each other. I walked up to Tetra, who was limping, wincing with each step. Kohen widened his eyes as if telling me to say something.

"Hey, T," I whispered to her. "Have you ever thought about riding Ariyel?"

Tetra looked at me like I was insane. "She's not a horse. I would never disrespect her like that."

But the second I said it, Ariyel looked up at her, nudging her bad leg with her nose.

Tetra scowled at her. "No. I can walk," she ground out.

My gaze flicked to Kohen and I shrugged. My bestie was hardheaded sometimes, and it was important to me that she had her dignity. I didn't agree with the choice. I would think taking the weight off my painful leg in any way possible was a great idea, but I wasn't about to force her to do anything she didn't feel comfortable with.

"You're right," I agreed. "Your cane would probably get lonely."

She grinned at the joke and reached out to softly punch my arm. "My crystal cane is badass, I can't wait to get it back," she told me.

"*So* badass. I want to get you one with a top that pops off and reveals a hidden knife inside," I shared with her.

She laughed. "That would be awesome."

I glanced at Kohen. He looked disappointed that Tetra hadn't jumped all over his idea. It made me wonder if he really should be messing with the future. Like suggesting something before it was time. Who knew what kind of consequences that had. On the other hand, something like an attack on the school I would love to know more about and get every detail so that we could stop it.

We reached the train, where everyone else was waiting. It was over ten cars long.

Liana and Onyx landed, bowing low so that we could climb onto their backs. I slipped my leg into the stirrup and peered at Kohen. He did the same, and then we waited for all of our teammates to get into the back three cars. As the side door slid open, I saw the payload. It was a steel box about the size of a large boulder that could be carried by two men. The cadets filed in around it, their creatures climbing in with them. The train cars had a bunch of drilled holes in the upper half for airflow, and there seemed to be open hatches at the top, because Jace's security team began to climb out onto the roof, along with the rest of our battle team. Sans Tetra and Meera.

I was hoping that someone had talked some sense into her and told her to stay inside. Probably Anika; she seemed to have a soft spot for my bestie.

"What is the cargo?" Kohen asked Ashendell casually, indicating the steel crate inside.

"Assume that your clearance level doesn't allow you to know," she shot back.

Kohen pursed his lips but nodded.

Summer's team, who were in charge of navigation, pulled out their maps. "We will be traveling for roughly eleven hours, so get comfortable," Summer said.

I peered deeper into the backmost train car and noticed Tetra had pulled out her thin bedroll and elevated her foot on it as she sat on the floor with Ariyel on her lap. That wasn't a good sign. She must really be hurting.

They were pretty packed in there, especially with their creatures, but with the security and most of the battle team perched on the top of the cars with their swords at the ready, it made enough room.

I felt slightly antsy, mostly because I was worried about my best friend. This was a simulation. We knew at some point we would be "attacked" to test our readiness for war, we just didn't know when.

Our instructors all wished us good luck, then the train doors rolled shut and it took off, slowly at first and then faster. Kohen and I both held on as our creatures took to the skies, the cold wind biting at my skin, causing my fingers to sting.

After several hours of flying with no events, I scanned the landscape, noticing the way the tracks curved westward to the mountains of Golden Hills. One of our possible attack points was coming up just ahead.

"I should fly ahead and see if I notice anything suspicious," I yelled to Kohen over the wind.

He shook his head. "We stick together."

I rolled my eyes. "Fine, you can come with if you want."

He gave me a look. "I meant we stick with the train, with our fellow cadets."

"But—"

"No, Aisling," he said, like it was final.

I growled, digging my fingers into Liana's feathers.

'Bastard,' I told her.

I could almost feel her grinning.

'It's like Instructor Ashendell said, you need to learn what it's like to take orders.'

'Hey, how did you know about that?' I asked her. She wasn't there.

'You're a very loud thinker.'

I chuckled at that, and stuck with Kohen and the train like a good little soldier. If we failed this simulation, let it rest on him and the other leaders. My hands were clean.

As we approached the mountain, Kohen flew down to land atop the train and I followed. Liana's giant claws scratched against the metal as she lowered us on top of the second train car. "The mountain pass is up ahead," Kohen said to the other cadets, who had been perched on the roof this entire time. "Everyone get inside if you want to keep your head attached to your neck. Be alert for a possible attack."

The dozen or so cadets, with their creatures in tow, slipped down the roof hatches and into the three last cargo cars below.

Those who had flying creatures, like Alek's hawk and Dev's vulture, sent them skyward to fly with us and report back.

Kohen glanced at me: "I'm following the train inside the tunnel!" he screamed over the wind. "You fly over the mountain, and if anything happens, send word to Onyx through Liana."

I frowned. To fly *into* the tunnel was dangerous. Onyx was big, especially with his wings fully extended, and he'd have to follow behind a speeding train. But Kohen was my "leader," so I just nodded and Liana flew higher to position ourselves up and over the mountain.

Stupid orders. I had to take them and not complain.

Alek's hawk flew alongside Liana and I, while Dev's vulture stuck with Kohen. My creature threw Iniki, Alek's hawk, a few friendly glances. Liana, I had learned, had a very sensitive inner people radar. She either liked you or she didn't, and she knew in about four seconds which camp you were about to belong to. She liked Alek and Iniki, so that was good.

The first car of the long train sucked into the black tunnel and I held my breath for a second. I scanned the thick forest that covered the top of the mountain, searching for enemies. I waited for a glint of steel, or blond hair, a rustle of movement. I waited to see anything to tell me that our drill instructors were hiding in wait to attack us... but there was nothing. The last train car rolled into the dark tunnel and Kohen flew in after it as I sailed over the top.

Now would be the time. They would shoot a paint pellet at Liana and I to show their presence as a group of "rebels" leaped onto the top of the train coming out the other side...

But nothing happened. The train sailed easily through the tunnel and Kohen popped out the other side, giving me a thumbs-up, which I returned.

It meant that the first weak point we had assumed would be an attack was clear, but we still had the second. It was another mountain tunnel, about two more hours flight time away.

As the day drew on, I grew weary of flying. I had to constantly keep my muscles flexed so that I wouldn't slip or fall off, and it was exhausting.

'Lower me to the top of the train. I'm going to check on Tetra and the others,' I asked Liana.

She immediately started her descent. She landed

atop the moving train, her talons clicking onto the metal. I nodded to a few of my fellow cadets who stood atop the train car holding swords and bows and arrows at the ready. Alek was there, with Iniki on his shoulder.

"How's it up top?" he asked as I crouched down so that I wouldn't fall off the moving train.

Liana kicked off and resumed her place high above us.

"It's boring," I told him truthfully, and he grinned.

It had been slightly weird with Alek after he made his feelings known to me at Sleuth, but since then we'd fallen into an easy friendship. I think he realized that was all I could give right now.

Walking over to the ceiling panel that was popped open, I jumped down into the very back train car.

What I saw made my eyes widen a little. The cadets were playing poker, eating snacks, and chatting lazily. They had unholstered weapons and taken off jackets, letting their hair down.

I flicked my gaze to see Tetra sprawled over a few sacks of rice, napping.

"Hey!" I snapped rather loudly, and everyone present jolted into a more erect position, staring up at me. "We could be attacked any moment. We don't graduate without passing this simulation." I looked around at all the food wrappers and empty water canteens.

"You're not a leader, we don't have to listen to you," Summer told me.

"You're right. I'm not your leader today, but one day I'll be your leader for the rest of your life, so you better—"

"Okay!" Alek jumped down next to me, cutting off my sentence. "Let's clean up and look alive. Aisling is right, the attack could be any moment, and if we fail it's on you for not being ready."

A few cadets actually had the nerve to roll their eyes at him. Tetra had just woken up from her little nap looking guilty. I wasn't mad at her, but I was concerned that she still seemed to be elevating her foot. That meant it hurt worse than she let on.

"They split us into five teams for what reason? Navigation? The train is taking us where we need to go. This simulation is a joke," Summer said. I had to admit it seemed silly to make a team learn maps and be tasked with navigation when you intended to have a train take them all of the way. It didn't change the fact that they were being lazy and unready for the attack we all knew was coming.

"I SAID GET UP!" Alek barked so loudly and forcefully that I jumped, along with half the car.

His assertiveness was attractive at that moment, I had to admit.

"Alright, you heard him. Let's get things straightened up in here," Jace agreed, walking in through the hatch from the second train car. The doorway was open so people could move in and out freely. His shirt was unbuttoned, and was that chocolate on his face? Good grief, the son of the commander of my father's fleet and even he wasn't taking this seriously.

That got the cadets moving. They began to clean up their mess, fold away their cards, and get into a standing position. It seemed they respected Jace's authority more than Alek's. Or maybe just two people yelling at them was enough to get them to move their butts.

I knelt next to Tetra and peered down at her. She looked like she was having a *really* bad pain day. Semi-permanent wince, slightly sweaty appearance. Her creature nuzzled my thigh like she was trying to tell me something.

"How you holding up, T?" I reached out my hand like I would to a stray dog and her creature sat her chin inside my palm, allowing me to stroke her muzzle with my thumb. It was unheard of for a creature, and it meant she trusted me to take care of Tetra, which was an honor.

Tetra swallowed hard. "Not a great pain day, but I'll manage."

I nodded, looking to my right and lowering my voice to make sure I couldn't be overheard. "Did you try some of those pain relievers?" They were very hard to come by and pretty strong. She would be quite woozy after, and not very much help in an attack, but how much help could she be in constant pain?

She nodded. "Took half a pill about an hour ago, which is why I napped. It took the edge off but it still hurts." She flicked her gaze to her foot.

It was moments like this that I felt angry at the way the world was designed. Tetra, the most amazing person I knew, lived in constant pain and struggle, and she'd never hurt a fly. Meanwhile, there were murderers and terrorists who ran free while the good people suffered.

I sighed. "I'm sorry. Just hang tight. We'll see if there is a healer at the imperial base we're going to."

Healers were rare, humans who absorbed the power from their creature, but I knew of two in my father's Imperial Fleet and they were both out on active duty. If one of them was at this base, I'd pull every string possible to see if Tetra could see him. They wouldn't be able to heal her deformity, but they could take away pain and inflammation.

'Brace for impact, Aisling!' Liana's warning blared in my head.

"Brace for impact!" I screamed without question, and threw myself over Tetra's body, covering her creature as well. I grasped the tie-down strap loops, pinning them both under me, and that's when the train flew off the tracks.

TWENTY-ONE

The train lurched onto its side and my fingers ripped out of the loops I was holding as the weight of Tetra and her creature fell on top of me. Luckily, I was thrown into a pile of rice bags, but others were not so fortunate.

"Alek! Jace!" I cried out their names immediately as I knew they were in the car with me.

Wails of pain rose up throughout the small space.

'It's that smell,' Liana said as I tried to get my bearings. Tetra sat up. She seemed shaken but okay.

"Can you stand?" I asked her.

"Broken femur!" Alek called out as he did triage on one of the cadets.

"Head wound," came another voice.

"Dislocated shoulder," came another.

This was wrong. The drill instructors wouldn't do this.

'*Aisling. The smell,*' Liana called.

I shook myself, standing and helping Tetra and a few others out the roof hatch, which was now acting as door to the outside since the train had completely fallen on its side.

'*What smell, Liana? We have hurt people down here. Tell Kohen.*'

'*Cigars, whiskey, burnt ember, and cheap musk cologne. The people who tried to keep us from bonding. And I don't want to distract Kohen from the fight.*'

My head snapped to the sky and my jaw unhinged. The fight?

There were two other flying creatures above us, as well as Liana and Onyx, which made four. I couldn't see from here, but one was definitely a griffin.

A Talanagi.

'*Come get me!*' I told her. '*I can help.*'

I peeked my head into the train car and peered right at Alek. "We're under real attack. It's not the simulation. My best guess is the Luskins. Prepare for imminent conflict."

The color leached from his face, but he wasted no time in turning to the other leaders. "Triage the injured! Every able-bodied person outside with me. We are under real attack. This is not a simulation. I repeat, this is a real attack!"

Panic descended on the train cars, screaming cadets scrambling for their weapons, but I couldn't stay. Kohen needed me.

I spun just as Liana landed, and then we were flying.

'Luskins?' I asked Liana.

As we flew higher, fear washed over me at the sight of a blue dragon locked in battle with Onyx. Luska's version of The Wilds was called The Forbidden, and it was clearly teeming with Talanagi. Luskin soldiers had a higher concentration of them in their ranks, but I'd never seen it for myself since I'd never been in battle.

Kohen threw a fireball at the rider of the blue dragon, and now that I was close enough I could see a blonde with a typical Luskin braid that ran atop the crown of her head. But she wasn't wearing the Luskin army-issued military uniform, so this was all confusing.

Something moved in my peripheral vision and I jerked my body that way, careening Liana with me just as the older male rider atop the brown griffin threw some kind of energy wave at me. It knocked into Liana and I, and she rolled sideways in the air. I gripped the handholds of her harness and tightened my thighs at the same time in an effort to keep from falling off. I was still a little shaken after the train derailment and so my grip wasn't as tight as I had hoped for—my right wrist snapped with the sudden jerking motion. I cried out at red hot pain that splintered along my wrist and shot up to my elbow.

I slid to the side, but managed to stay on.

'Are you okay? I'm sorry.' Liana's voice was filled with compassion.

I had definitely just broken my wrist, but there was no time for dwelling on that.

'Fine,' I told her.

The moment Liana righted herself, I pulled up my bolt shooter that had been hooked to Liana's harness with my uninjured hand and fired off one of the serrated arrows. It sank into the rider's shoulder but he barely flinched. He was an older man in his fifties, and before I could reload, he tossed another energy wave at me, this one shaped like a net, glowing blue, just like the one used to trap Liana that night in the barn.

Liana dove out of the way, dodging the net, and popped back up in front of him.

At this confirmation that he was the one involved that night, rage filled me and my skin began to smoke.

This bastard tried to keep me from bonding to Liana! The heat simmered along my nerves, and a scream built in my throat.

'Get me close to him,' I ordered.

She flew right for him, crashing into his griffin and locking talons with it just as I exploded into a ball of fire. Heat and steam engulfed my face and skin. The orange and yellow wall then dissipated, the rider screamed in agony as he and his griffin flew away, on fire. They left a streak of smoke trailing in their wake.

A female grunted to my right, and then screamed. I

snapped my head in that direction just in time to see the blue dragon falling to the ground, Kohen's dagger imbedded in the rider's chest. She hit the ground with a thud, her body contorted and bent at all the wrong angles, dead.

My gaze went to her creature in anticipation. Once a human bonded died, the creature had only minutes to return to the habitat of The Wilds before...

The dragon slowly lowered to the hillside and I looked up at Kohen. He was panting, bleeding from a cut under his left eye, and watching me with a wild expression. I was holding my right wrist to my chest... and it dawned on me: this was the injury he spoke about that I would have when the school was attacked.

We descended to the ground as the blue dragon creature began to gasp for air. It made strangled choking noises as it stumbled forward, lying over the dead body of its human bonded.

The dragon's back heaved slowly and I looked away. I couldn't watch.

'Tell Kohen to end it,' Liana ordered.

"Liana says to end it," I told him, flicking my gaze back to the creature, who was somehow still alive. The instructor's creatures that had attacked me had died pretty quickly, but maybe the Talanagi were stronger, outlasting their bonded a little longer.

Kohen walked over to me with an emotionless expression, grasped the bolt shooter from my good arm, and shot the dragon in the back of the head. It went limp, fighting to live no more.

I peered into the woods. "Do you think there's more coming?"

Kohen shook his head, frowning as he stared at my wrist. "I think this was an assassination attempt, not a move to take our cargo."

I frowned. Why did people keep trying to kill me? I mean, I was the future empress and they were definitely Luskin, but… it didn't make sense. Why now?

"You're upset?" I asked. Kohen's jaw was clenched shut, nostrils flaring as he breathed deeply.

"Kohen, talk to me. What's wrong?" I stepped forward and reached out to probe the cut under his eye with my good hand. It might need glue or stitches.

His hand snaked out and grasped my fingers, which he pulled to his chest, laying them over his heart. The wild fluttering danced under my fingertips as I locked eyes with my father's sworn enemy.

"I couldn't protect you," he finally growled out.

Now it was my turn for my heart to beat frantically in my chest.

"I'm fine," I said. "I don't need you to protect me."

His eyes grew stormy, his dark thick brows drawing downward. "One day you will. One day you will *beg* me to protect you."

I yanked my hand back, fear spiking through me.

"Shit." He grabbed the sides of his face. "I freaked

you out again. I'm sorry. Knowing these things... it's a curse."

I nodded, suddenly grateful I didn't have his power.

"The others are hurt, we should go help," I told him, changing the subject. *One day I would beg him to protect me?* I wish I didn't know that.

We both got on our creatures and flew down to the train tracks. I leapt off of Liana and took everything in. It was truly like a warzone. The injured cadets had been dragged out of the train car and laid onto the forest floor. Alek's medical team was triaging them with the medic-kits, but you could tell they only had basic knowledge, nothing to handle this. There were never supposed to be serious injuries.

Kohen stopped at the tracks and growled, looking down. I followed his gaze, seeing the bolts that had been removed and the track that had been slid over to the side, causing the train to just fly off into the woods. We were lucky to be alive.

I strode over to the worst-looking cadet I could find. It was little Meera. She wailed into the fading daylight as she clutched her arm, which hung limply at her side.

With the medic manual in his hands, Alek stared up at me, panicked. "I think it's dislocated but I don't know how to..."

I nodded. I did. It was something Elaine taught me.

Kohen knelt next to Meera and met my gaze, then he peered at Alek and I noticed a slight surge of irritation there before it was gone.

"I can try," Kohen said. "I've seen it done before."

I shook my head. "I can do it." I knew she was special to him, and when you were popping in a dislocated shoulder you had to cause someone a fair amount of pain. He would stop out of compassion before getting the job done.

"Get her a stick to bite down on," I said, and Meera looked at me with wide, terrified eyes.

"I'm going to help you, and most of that pain is going to go away. It hurts because the bone is out of the socket. Once I put it back, you can move it and you'll start to heal."

She chewed on her lip and nodded, tears streaming down her face.

Kohen returned with the stick and put it into her mouth. Meera bit down and he peered up at me.

"Just hold her steady," I told him, but with a widening of my eyes that said *Pin her down.*

She was lying flat on her back, which was the perfect position for this.

"I know this is an awful scenario, but if anyone wants to learn how to relocate a shoulder, come watch," I yelled to everyone present.

Half a dozen bystanders, including Tetra, suddenly stood behind me, and I gazed down at Meera. "You're going to teach all these cadets how to do this so that they can help someone else someday. Okay?" I asked her.

"Okay," she managed to mumble around the stick.

I grabbed her floppy dislocated right arm with my uninjured hand and laid it flat out beside her as if she were a child making a snow angel.

"Lay the dislocated arm out at a ninety-degree angle away from the body," I told everyone, and then I grabbed her wrist. "And slowly pull." I began to pull on the arm, catching Kohen's gaze. He pinned her good shoulder and hip to the floor.

Meera screamed suddenly as I pulled her wrist firmly, causing tension in the shoulder. I gave it a tiny yank then and heard the click that the bone had returned to the socket. She exhaled in relief, her head lolling to the side as she spit the stick out, panting.

"You good?" I asked her.

She nodded. Then she lifted her arm slightly and wiggled her fingers. "Still sore but manageable. Thank you, Aisling."

I reached out with my good hand and tapped her thigh. "Glad to help."

I stood then, facing Alek. "Who else needs treatment? I can do sutures and—"

"You have a broken wrist," Kohen said, coming up beside me.

Alek frowned, his gaze going to my injured hand, which I clutched to my chest to protect it.

It hurt like hell, but I would suck it up.

Alek sat down and opened his medic kit. "Let me splint that until we can get you properly seen at base."

I flicked my gaze to Kohen and he walked away. Why did I equally love and hate how protective he was over me? Why was I thinking about kissing him in the middle of a horrible tragedy? Why couldn't I stop thinking about him telling me I would one day be his? That I was his best friend and he knew when our first kiss was. That I would beg for his protection and make love to him under a bed of stars. All of these future things were messing with my head and making me wonder if he was implanting feelings in my mind.

I hissed as Alek delicately placed my wrist in the splint.

He winced. "Sorry."

"It's fine, I wasn't ready," I told him, not wanting to appear weak.

"It looks like a bad break. Even with your rapid healing, you might need a cast to keep it from setting wrong."

Just like Kohen said.

I simply nodded.

This was my proof. My proof that everything Kohen said was probably real. I didn't know what to do with that.

Kohen stood at the center of our little shitshow, peering out at all of us bloodied and bruised with creatures that had limps and other injuries.

"As far as I am concerned, the simulation is still on.

We still need to make it to base camp with the cargo to graduate," he called out to everyone.

Silence.

"We were attacked by Luskin insurgents. If we wait here, won't the instructors come look for us?" Summer asked.

"Yes they will." I stood. "There is a protocol in place for this type of thing, but it doesn't include us graduating. They'll make sure we are safe and have a ride back to campus, where they will probably release us back to our parents as failures."

Groans rang throughout the group.

"Being in the Imperial Fleet means you are ready to die for your country!" I shouted. "For your emperor! It doesn't mean if something goes wrong you wait for help and ask for a ride back to mommy."

Alek clasped his case shut and stood beside me. "Aisling is right. This went sideways, but we still need to complete to graduate and get good postings. If you want to stay behind, or if you're too injured to travel, then so be it. You're at the mercy of the drill instructors' compassion. Or lack thereof."

Kohen walked over to the train car where the payload was located and disappeared inside.

Alek and Jace, clearly not liking him being the only one to see what it was, ran after him. The sound of metal scraping against metal filled the forest as I helped everyone make sense of their packs and we made sure we had rations and water—those of us who hadn't pigged out on it already while playing poker.

The boys appeared outside the train carrying the giant steel case. They strained under its weight, knocking into their shins as they walked.

"We've got at least six hours of walking, maybe more. How are we going to carry that for so long?" someone behind me said.

"By taking turns," Kohen grunted.

'*I can take it,*' Liana told me.

I snapped my head in her direction. "You're sure? It looks really heavy."

'*I could carry five grown men,*' she declared confidently.

"My creature will take it. We need to strap it to her back," I announced then. It would be a huge help.

It took us a full twenty minutes to get the large steel case onto Liana's back.

"What do you think is inside?" someone asked.

"A huge hunk of ember," Roc guessed.

"Weapons," another mentioned.

"Doesn't matter what's inside," Summer snapped. "It's going to get dark and we can only follow the tracks for so long before they curve to impassable territory on foot with so many injured. Then we'll have to branch out into the woods." She consulted her map.

"Let's move out! Look alert for any other attacks," Jace called out and started our group on the journey to the base. Some people were limping, holding hurt arms or busted ribs, but everyone moved as a group. No one was staying behind.

A wet muzzle dug into my palm and I peered down to see Tetra's creature.

I spoke too soon.

Tetra. She sat on the ground chewing her lip as she stared at the seemingly insurmountable task ahead.

I walked over to her as her creature nuzzled her leg.

"You can do this, T," I told her. "I'll carry you on my damn back with a broken wrist if I have to." I shook my splint in her face.

She gave me a sad smile—her fake smile.

"I can't. I should never have let them keep my name in the Lottery. I'm not cut out for this. I'm not as strong as you are, Ash."

I grabbed her cane, propping it up. "You are strong and you're *not* a quitter," I said, a little more forcefully this time.

She looked up at me and growled, an inhuman growl that was definitely more like her wolf.

"You push me too hard sometimes!" she snapped as she heaved herself up onto her cane.

"Because you're too damn stubborn sometimes and don't realize how strong you are," I snapped back. "So I clearly have to remind you."

She chuckled then, exasperated, shaking her head. "I love you, you idiot."

"Back at ya... idiot," I said without having to really

say the words. Sometimes I feared that the L word would sound weird coming out of my mouth. Like I might say I *lofe* you or something stupid.

With a grunt she started limping the worst I'd ever seen her. Her creature again shoved her muzzle into my free hand, as if trying to tell me something, but I couldn't talk to her.

"What's she trying to tell me?" I asked Tetra.

Tetra glared at her creature like she was a traitor. "Nothing."

I knew better than to pry. I'd gotten all I was going to out of this girl and I was just grateful she was up and walking.

I couldn't help but notice how Kohen was waiting up ahead with Anika. Waiting for me? Looking out for me? Or just being a good team leader?

When we reached them, I saw that Anika had taped up the cut under his eye and a spike of jealousy rushed through me. Did she like touching that perfect face? Had they ever dated? Had they ever kissed?

"All good?" Anika asked Tetra, who simply nodded, almost skipping to avoid putting any pressure on her leg.

Kohen stepped out from beside Anika and blocked Tetra's path.

"Ride your creature. That's an order, Thindrel," he snapped, looking every inch a commanding officer.

Tetra's head reared back at the same time as mine. "Excuse me?" she said.

"Yeah, what the hell? Don't talk to her like that," I warned him.

His gaze cut to mine. "This doesn't concern you, Aisling. Move along." There was something in his gaze, something that screamed for me to trust him.

This was my best friend we were talking about. My ride or die. But in my heart I did trust Kohen, even if I didn't want to.

So I walked away, Anika following me. I left him alone with Tetra.

I took twenty steps and stopped, but Anika grabbed my arm and forced me to keep going. "He's got this," she told me.

I peered sidelong at her. "You've known him long?"

A blush rushed to her cheeks, and I wanted to reach out and punch her for some reason.

"Only my whole life." The way she said it was like she was staking her claim.

She loved him, and it kind of killed me in that moment. I liked Anika—I wanted to hate her but dammit she was cool. Dark hair, mysterious badass vibe going on. I knew I couldn't have Kohen, no matter what his vision showed him, but I didn't want him to have anyone else either.

I quickly peeked behind me just in time to see Tetra climb onto Ariyel's back. I faced forward in shock.

He did it. He got my stubborn-ass best friend to do something that was good for her. It was a miracle.

In no time, they caught up to us and I peered at my best friend. That permanent pain wince was gone from her face. She looked relieved but also slightly embarrassed. Her small form fit perfectly onto her wolf, though her legs dangled awkwardly, so she tucked them up. She'd need a saddle eventually.

"Looking good, T." I gave her a smile.

She glared at Kohen. "An order is an order."

"Yep." He popped the P and glanced at me.

I'll be damned. Kohen Badshah was right about something.

WE WALKED in silence for about an hour. The terrain got rough, wrapping around the mountain to a sharp cliff, and then we had to head east to avoid falling off of it. It was slow going with the injured, and I was glad to see a few others riding on their creatures as well.

Kohen would intermittently talk with Summer and check that we were heading the right way.

When we stopped for a break, Anika reached into her pack and I could see the panic flare in her eyes.

"What's wrong?" Kohen asked her.

Her chest heaved. "I must have lost it when the train derailed."

He scanned her face and went pale. "Your med—"

"Shh," she hissed, widening her eyes, and guilt

crossed his features as he peered at me and anyone else in earshot.

"Your medical tape? For that cut?" he said.

She nodded, but it was clearly a cover-up for something else.

Tetra and I shared a look. I wanted so badly to talk to my bestie about this. What were they hiding? Was it those chewy candy things I saw her taking that day in The Wilds? They seemed pretty important. I wondered if they were medicinal, a drug maybe? If you had a drug problem, the Imperial Fleet would throw you out.

Kohen met me gaze, as if pleading me not to say anything.

"What did you lose?" I asked Anika. I wasn't going to cover for some druggie. My life might be in her hands one day, and if she had a problem it needed to get sorted out now.

Her nostrils flared. "Nothing."

'Kohen says drop it,' Liana told me.

Hah! He was sending me messages through Onyx.

'Is it drugs? I'm not covering for an addict,' I shot back through Liana.

Kohan hadn't dropped my gaze and the deep stare was having an effect on me. Why was he so gorgeous? And why did he have to tell me that our futures were intertwined? Now it was all I could think about. What he kissed like, how in the hell we would ever end up together, why I would beg him to protect me one day?

I wanted to know everything and nothing at the same time.

'*It's drugs, but not the kind you think,*' Liana said. '*It's medicine for a condition she is hiding from the Fleet.*'

I frowned then, and he widened his eyes as if begging me to drop it.

Liana added her own two cents: '*He's telling the truth.*'

Yeah. And hiding something from the Fleet.

"Let's move out. We are still under the clock," I announced, even though technically I wasn't one of the leaders. Kohen and Anika appeared relieved that I had dropped the subject, and everyone packed up their stuff.

Over the next hour I watched as Kohen walked extra close to Anika, keeping his hands stiff as if he were ready to catch her at any moment. Stupid, treacherous jealously rushed through me. I hated that I cared so much. He was literally the crowned prince of Imbria, the country that murdered thousands of my people in a terrorist attack. Our hostile takeover of their land made our peoples hate each other. We were enemies at best. I shouldn't be feeling what I felt about him, about any of them. Did it make me a traitor to the fallen Amerseans? The ones who lost their lives that night?

'*That was years ago,*' Liana said. '*Maybe it's time to move on and mend bridges. When you are empress one day, maybe your legacy will be uniting the peoples of Imbria and Amersea. Healing the past.'*

Either I was thinking loudly or she could read my mind. I didn't want to know if it was the latter.

'Maybe. Or maybe this is a long game he's playing.' I watched as Kohen sent another worried glance at Anika. *'Maybe he doesn't see the future. Or he does but he's lied about the parts where he sees us together. He's playing on my emotions so that he can get the ultimate revenge for my father killing his.'*

'If that's the case, I'll tear out his intestines with my talons and sprinkle them over the skies of Imbria.'

My eyes widened. *'Whoa, Liana, too dark,'* I joked, laughing in my head.

But I could feel the seriousness from her. *'If anyone threatens your life, I end theirs. That's a promise,'* she said, and the statement brought me comfort. Especially since there were so many people trying to kill me.

The trek was long, and my wrist still hurt, which told me it was healing wrong and would need to be reset and casted. Just like Kohen said.

I peered over at him just as Anika dropped to the ground with a thump. One second she was standing and the next she went limp, crumpling into a heap as her body hit the earth. Kohen reached for her instinctively but was unable to catch her.

The second she hit the ground, everyone stopped. Kohen fell to his knees and took her head in his lap just as her body began to convulse. Her eyes rolled into the back of her skull; her back arched and she thrashed around.

This must be related to whatever was in those chewy candies she was always taking, the ones missing from her bag now.

"Shhh." Kohen stroked her forehead and I wanted it to be me. I wanted to be the one he was touching, and I hated myself for it.

"Is she okay?" I knelt beside them both, guilt washing over me for even thinking she was a drug addict.

Dev and Nikhil started to do crowd control, pushing everyone back. "Alright, nothing to see here, give her some room," Dev said.

Little Meera popped up beside me. "She forget her meds?" she asked Kohen with a frown.

Kohen nodded, his face taut with anxiety as he stroked her face softly. "Lost in the train crash."

"How long does it last?" Tetra had slid off of Ariyel and limped over to Anika, sitting on the ground beside her and taking her hand. My best friend stroked her palm and I knew she felt a kinship in this moment. It wasn't the same as having a foot that didn't work properly since birth, but it was something... Neither of them were perfect by society's standards.

Kohen looked up at me. "It's been a long time since she's had an episode. Years. Meera made her the herbal chews, and as long as she takes one daily, they don't happen."

My compassion for Anika grew in that moment, and I pushed my jealousy aside.

"Are any of the herbs in the forest? I could ride Onyx to fetch them," I said, since Liana was currently saddled with our payload.

Meera shook her head. "To the best of my knowledge, the flower that stops the episodes only grows in the Imbrian Mountains."

Tetra whistled. "So what do you do when it runs out?"

The Imbrian Mountains were two days' travel away from the school. They'd have to get leave, and in order to do that they'd have to explain why.

Kohen shot Tetra a warning look. "We'll figure it out. Meera made her enough for a few months."

"But we will need to have a plan so that she doesn't run out once she gets posted," Meera said to Kohen in a low voice.

"I'll figure it out," Kohen said, and Anika's body suddenly went limp.

"She's coming out of it." Kohen sagged in relief.

Anika blinked up at Kohen, licking her lips as if she were thirsty. "Is Mother baking brownies?" She sounded as if she were in a dream.

I glanced at Kohen in alarm. The convulsions must scramble her brain afterwards.

He stroked her forehead tenderly. "You're okay. You had an episode."

She frowned, looking around at all of us. She appeared exhausted and I felt so bad for her.

Meera held her fingers to Anika's wrist. "Pulse is good."

Anika peered up at Kohen, reaching up to cup his face. "It's a pity you don't love me back. I could make you happy."

Kohen blushed, grasping her hand and pulling it back to her chest to set it there.

Then he looked at me, and he must have seen my jealousy, because his face changed at that moment.

He looked happy. Satisfied. Like he'd finally won me over.

"She gets confused for a bit after. She won't remember this," he said to us all.

But I would. I would never forget it. It was the moment I realized that I wanted Kohen Badshah for myself. That even if this were some incredible diabolical plan… I wanted him. Bad.

Tetra patted Anika's hand and then stood and motioned to me. "Let's give her some privacy."

I nodded, standing as well, and walked back over to Ariyel with her.

"That was scary," she told me in a whisper.

"Yeah, and when the instructors find out, she's going to be discharged."

Tetra chewed her lip. "Screw that. That's not fair. If she takes her medicine she's fine."

I shrugged. "Rules are rules."

"How would they find out? Are you going to tell?" Tetra asked me angrily.

"Relax. No. I won't, but everyone else watched." I pointed to the murmuring crowd of candidates.

I saw the moment grim determination crossed over her face. When Tetra thought there was an injustice, she made it her mission to bend the scales in favor of the innocent.

"Alright, LISTEN UP!" Tetra cried loudly, and for a second I saw her future as a drill instructor and with that set of lungs it looked good. Every single person glanced her way.

Oh no, what was she doing?

Her creature stepped up beside her and stood tall and proud.

"What just happened here with Anika... never happened," she growled. "She forgot her meds. It won't happen again."

Tucker opened his mouth to ask a question, and Tetra raised her cane, pointing it at him. "If *anyone* narcs about this when we get to base..." She let the silence linger and her wolf curled her upper lip, growling.

"Then what?" Summer crossed her arms and glared.

I noticed she was untouched from the train accident, which was proof karma wasn't real.

"Then you have problems with me." I stepped up beside Tetra. "Your future empress."

I might not agree with Tetra going about it like this, threatening our fellow cadets, but she was my girl and I had her back.

"Me too," Kohen called from where he was helping Anika up. She looked ashamed and more coherent now.

Onyx blew a streak of fire across the sky to prove his point, and Summer didn't say another word.

"This. Never. Happened," Tetra said again.

One by one, they nodded, and I looked at my best friend with pride. She'd done something good today for someone who would be looked at as weak by our society's standards, and I knew it was because she felt weak too sometimes, even though she was anything but.

When I met Kohen's eyes, I wasn't prepared for the look he gave me. An expression that said he was hungry and I was a meal.

What I wouldn't give to read that man's mind.

What game are you playing? I wanted to ask him. But I was afraid I was going to have to play to find out.

CHAPTER

TWENTY-TWO

With thirty minutes left on the clock, we reached the front gates of the Thunder Cliff Imperial Fleet base.

"They're here!" a soldier called to someone inside the gates as we limped our way inside.

Ashendell and a few of our other drill instructors ran out of a canvas tent with wide eyes. They didn't look as pissed as I thought they would. They looked... relieved.

Liana landed beside me and we began to unstrap the heavy payload from her back. The second we did, she took back to the skies with Onyx. I was learning that she was a bit of an introvert, and I respected that.

"Leaders, report!" Ashendell snapped.

Kohen, Roc, Jace, Summer, and Alek stood at attention and Ashendell waited.

"We were attacked, ma'am! Luskins we think," Kohen said.

Ashendell got up in his face. "How long ago? Permission to speak freely."

She was pissed, seething really. The word Luskin had lit something within her.

"Several hours. We—"

"*Several* hours? It would have only taken you a few hours to fly here on Onyx and report the attack. Why didn't you?" she asked, and I realized now she was peering at him with suspicion.

"I... it didn't even cross my mind. I wouldn't have wanted to leave my team behind."

She stared at me. "Same excuse?" She glanced up at Liana as if the firebird should have known better.

"We experienced some trauma, ma'am. I wasn't thinking clearly." It was the truth. My wrist, the dead Luskin girl, so many injured—I wasn't thinking.

Ashendell sighed. She glanced at my wrist and then straight into my eyes. "Next time, call for back-up," she snapped. "When you didn't show to our attack point, we found the derailed train and I assumed you were kidnapped. I have half the country looking for the emperor's daughter right now!" She then walked away.

Crap.

My father must be so pissed. I couldn't wait for that conversation.

"We brought the payload! Does that mean we graduate?" Kohen asked.

She stopped and turned around, heaving a big sigh. "That's what you're worried about right now? You get attacked by Luskins and you want to you know if you still graduate?"

Kohen nodded, and Ashendell couldn't help but shake her head.

"Yes, you all graduate."

Cheers and whoops rang throughout our little circle.

"Who should we get this to? It must be important." I tapped the giant steel container we'd pulled off of Liana's back.

Ashendell walked over, produced a key from her pocket, and opened the lock. When she flicked the lid open, I peered inside and held my breath.

"Are you serious?" I asked her.

"Rocks!" Kohen said, peeking over my shoulder.

A giant pile of dull gray boulders sat inside the steel case. It was worthless.

"You think we would trust rookies with something valuable?" Instructor Ashendell asked.

Again, she turned, and this time jogged back to the command tent, probably to get word to my father that I wasn't kidnapped.

Rocks.

A handful of medics ran up to us then carrying triage bags and called us over to a temporary tent that was set up in the east corner of the base. We lined up the wounded in order of most severely injured to least injured, and I took the time to look around at the famed headquarters that stood at The Wall. It was dark now, so I couldn't see the looming stone structure like I would in the daytime. I'd been here before with my father when I was sixteen and he'd begun to train me to take over for him in case he was assassinated. Yes, my father being murdered was something I'd had to contend with at a young age.

At the back-right section of the twenty-acre base were multiple redbrick apartment buildings, where the men and women were segregated. They held about a thousand soldiers in all if I remembered correctly. In the middle and towards the front gate was the command center, where Ashendell was right now. I hadn't been there in a few years, but I remembered it as a giant room with maps and radios and tables and chairs. There was also a mess hall, a gym, and a massive barn for creatures. This was one of the bigger bases, holding a thousand full-time soldiers in all.

Just as I was looking at the barn, about two dozen creatures bolted outside, and then their adjoining soldier bondeds burst out from the door of the command center.

They piled into trucks and then sped off out the open gates.

"Probably going on mission to find the people who

attacked us," I mused to Tetra, who stood on my right. Though one was already dead and one got away.

"Can I talk to you, Aisling?" Kohen's voice was like butter as it smoothed its way over me.

Tetra hobbled away to get into the end of the triage line, and I turned to face him.

Stars, he was good looking. He was one of those guys that was so handsome that you found yourself staring at him—like watching a piece of art and finding new beauty in it every time.

"What's up?" I asked, trying to keep my cool.

"Are you going to get in line for your wrist?" he asked. "Because in my vision you had a yellow cast on that arm." He pointed to my splinted wrist.

I frowned. There he was, treating me like I was his girlfriend or something.

"Why do you care what I do, Kohen?" I didn't mean for it to come out like that, but I was sick of this dance. The hurt that crossed his face made me regret my words instantly.

I lowered my voice. "You don't even know me, Kohen. Not really, and you say all this stuff about us in the future. You're so protective... I can't... if your visions are real—"

"They're real," he growled.

They probably were. I had accepted it at this point.

I nodded. "Then I don't want to know. I want things to play out however they're gonna play out without you telling me first. I can't know," I told him firmly.

His jaw gritted, nostrils flaring. "Fine," he growled, and walked away, taking the scent of sandalwood and cardamom with him.

I felt like the world's biggest jerk, but I couldn't handle him telling me how every step of my life was going to play out. It made me feel like I had no control, no choice.

It took over an hour for everyone to be seen by the medic. Once every last person had been treated, including Tetra, who they were unfortunately not able to do much for since their healer was out in battle on The Wall, I finally took my place in front of the medic. He was young, about my age, and had long brown hair braided down his back.

He removed my splint and hissed. "You have self-healing powers?" he asked.

I nodded and he shook his head.

"You should have been first in line. Rapid healing a bone at the wrong angle means you can have nerve damage and even loss of function."

My eyes went wide and I flicked my attention over to where Kohen was standing just inside the tent, almost looking smug.

Did he know that? I had told him I didn't want to know the future, so I guess that was on me. *Great.*

"What can we do?" I asked.

The medic's gaze flicked to his buddy, a handsome

twenty-something with blond hair, who shook his head. "Hell no, I'm not breaking the future empress' wrist," the buddy said.

I yanked my wrist back to my chest. "What?"

The medic with the brown braid winced slightly. "A controlled break with a cast. It's already started healing wrong. Look at your pinky."

I glanced down at my pinky and was horrified to see it at an odd angle and unmoving.

"Fine. Just do it," I told him.

He shook his head. "I don't do control breaks on rapid healers. He has all the expertise in that area." He looked back at Blondie, who was packing up his medic bag.

I opened my mouth to beg him when Liana landed at the mouth of the tent and stuck her head inside. As she dropped from the sky, the ground shook a little with her weight.

Both medics snapped their heads up to look at her.

"Holy shit, a firebird," Blondie said.

'Tell him to do the controlled break or I'll barbeque his face,' Liana threatened and I had to control my expression. I wanted to laugh, but I had a feeling it wasn't funny.

"My creature isn't happy with your refusal to do the controlled break. She's making some... colorful threats if you don't," I told him.

The blond dude's eyes went wide. "I mean, of course I'll do it. I'm just nervous your dad will kill me if I screw it up," he muttered, looking away from Liana and then back at me with fear.

I forgot the power my father had over these people.

I waved my good hand at him. "I hereby absolve you of any wrongdoing."

Tetra walked over with her cane and slipped something into my hand then. I knew what it was the second my fingers wrapped around the pill.

The tiny white pain pill I had smuggled in for her bad flare days. "No, you need this," I muttered, trying to hand it back.

She shook her head. "Trust me... you're gonna need it."

The medic's gaze fell to my hand which held the white round pill and he nodded. "If that is what I think it is... your friend is right, you should take it. We don't get the good stuff here."

Rebreaking an already broken wrist that had healed wrong sounded like hell, and we'd already been told we would graduate, so I didn't see the harm in taking the edge off. Without another thought, I popped the pill and swallowed it dry.

We sat around and waited another fifteen minutes until it kicked in.

'Medicines like that, and even alcohol, won't last long in your system because of your rapid healing,' Liana told me.

Good to know.

My body suddenly felt very heavy. I was sluggish in my movements, walking over to where the bone breaker sat.

I laughed to myself. *Bone breaker.*

"Okay, I think it's working," Kohen said with slight amusement at my laughing to myself. Everyone else had mostly scattered around the base checking things out but Kohen, Tetra, Alek, and Jace stood around me, watching with concerned expressions.

I pointed to Jace with my good hand. "Why are you still here? You don't care about me."

Tetra covered a snort-laugh and I realized I said that out loud. Crap, this pill was strong.

"That's not true," Jace said with a frown.

"This is going to hurt," the bone breaker said, slowly stroking the skin on my wrist as if he were pinpointing the exact place to break it.

"You don't deserve me," I told Jace bluntly. "So you should probably move on now. It's getting a little pathetic."

Alek's eyes widened at my bluntness just as Jace threw up his middle finger at me and stormed away.

"Maybe half a pill would have worked. I forget my tolerance has built up," Tetra said with a wince.

Oh who cares? Poor cheater got his feelings hurt.

Kohen was watching me like a loyal little dog, waiting to make sure I was okay. "And you!" I pointed to him just as the bone breaker snapped my wrist hard and sent pain shooting up my elbow. I screamed, the agony stealing my breath as I peered down. The bone breaker then made a little jerking motion and I gasped as another wave of hot sharp discomfort rocked me.

"That's good," he said, relieved. "It's straight now."

With agonizing effort, I wiggled my pinky and it did indeed move. The medic then went to work casting my arm. He pulled long wet strips from a package and wrapped them over gauze. I hated the fact that they were yellow. It took about thirty minutes, but by the time he was done my wrist was in a yellow plaster cast and I felt ready for a nap.

"Yank thoo," I said, and then frowned. "Thank you," I said slower this time. My brain felt scrambled.

The medic nodded. "With your advanced healing, that can get cut off in about a week," he said, and then left the tent.

"Alright, everyone gather round!" Instructor Ashendell called outside the tent. "We have a train ready to take you back to campus. We've also cleared the debris off the old tracks and repaired them. And I have a team looking into the Luskin attack."

Tetra and Alek made their way outside and I tried to stand, but then fell over. Kohen caught me, pulling me up against his warm body. It was like I came alive in that moment. Even heavily drugged, I felt every nerve ending in my body wake and respond to him. The pressure on my lower back, the way his hips pressed against mine, the splash of his breath on my face...

I looked up and he was peering down at me with a ravenous hunger.

"A coin for your thoughts?" I said, managing to get the words out in the right order.

He swallowed hard. "I'm wondering if by telling you about our future together, I have somehow compromised it. I'm coming to terms with the fact that it might all just be a dream now, a dream that I will have to live out in my head and never actually know in real life."

His words wrapped around my heart and squeezed.

"A coin for *your* thoughts?" he challenged.

My heart hammered against my chest as I swallowed hard, staring at his thick lips. "I simultaneously wonder two things, Kohen. One, what you taste like. And two, if you will one day bury a knife in my back like my father did to yours."

I didn't expect the whimper of shock that came from his mouth.

"Ash!" Tetra popped back into the tent.

She froze when she saw us so close together, but moved forward to grab me and pull me away from him. "Ashendell wants to make sure you are okay. Your dad is pissed and everyone is scared of losing their jobs."

I leaned on her offered arm, the one holding her

cane, and felt Kohen's hands fall away from me. By the time I made it onto the train, I was loopy as all hell, feeling the weight of sleep pull me under. I rested against Tetra, staring at Kohen and Alek, who sat in front of me, both wearing the same introspective expressions.

Then the slow rocking of the train lulled me to sleep.

TWENTY-THREE

Two days later, we graduated, and were all anxiously awaiting our orders for deployment. My father said the investigation into the train attack turned up nothing, and I could tell it bothered him that the enemy was able to get so close to me and leave no trail. We knew they were Luskin but that was all. Was the Luskin prime leader trying to take me out? If so, he must have spies in our city to know that I was attending the Imperial Fleet Training Center and exactly where I'd be on the train that day.

"You okay?" Tetra asked as she braided my hair down my back, interweaving the red and black sides. We were back at my house, having moved out of the training campus this morning. We would go to a graduation ball tonight at an event center near the training campus and then tomorrow morning we'd get our assignments and ship out to live on base somewhere across the country. Everyone would get sizeable weekly imperial coin payments for their service, some more than others, depending on how valuable they were to my father, and every two months we'd get one week off to travel home and see our families. It wasn't a bad gig to keep everyone we loved safe at home. A lifetime in the Imperial Fleet dedicated to fighting the war.

"Yeah." I smiled. "Just thinking."

Tetra's flare had subsided, and we'd all kept Anika's secret. She made it back to the training center in time to take her next dose of medication and all was well. She pulled me aside and told me that she hadn't had an issue in years. I didn't see a need to tell anyone so long as it wasn't a problem that inhibited her duty to the Imperial Fleet, and as far as I was concerned, it wasn't.

"Thinking about Kohen?" Tetra asked as she dusted my neck with shimmer powder. Tetra was always more into makeup than I was, so I let her give me makeovers all the time. The ball tonight was black tie, and Tetra had picked out a red dress for me that clung to my body like a second skin. I wore my locket with my mother's picture at my throat—thanks to Kohen. The yellow cast clashed a bit, but what was a girl to do?

Tetra was wearing an emerald-green dress that belled out at the knee, something her mother bought her with some of the coin from the hunk of ember Tetra had brought her from The Wilds.

I laughed. "No. But now I am. Thanks for that."

She grinned.

Kohen. The temptation I couldn't get out of my head.

"I've requested that my father give us assignments far away from each other. He agreed," I told her.

She stopped what she was doing, hand frozen over my cheek with blush. "You did?"

I sighed. "T, he's the prince of Imbria."

Period. Enough said.

She frowned. "I know. But... he's also like... so protective of you, and there's a vibe there. You guys are *electric*."

Tetra was a romantic.

I rolled my eyes. "So what? A vibe fizzles out. I need to be thinking long-term. Who will lead Amersea by my side when I'm empress one day?"

Tetra blew air through her teeth. "Man, you are so responsible. I'd be thinking: *How long can I have a secret affair with him until people find out and my dad makes me break up with him and marry someone boring for the good of the country?*"

I barked out in laughter. "Oh, Tetra, I love that the filter between what you are thinking and what you say is broken."

Now it was her turn to laugh. "But seriously, you never wondered what it would be like to kiss him?"

Kiss him. Bed him. Make beautiful babies with him. I'd wondered it all. And it all ended with me lying naked in bed with a knife in my back for allowing myself to trust the enemy.

"Have you ever wondered why he's so protective of me?" I asked Tetra. "Maybe he has some kind of long game."

She laughed. "Are you serious? You don't think he would have killed you by now if that's what he was looking to do? You've been alone with him plenty of times."

She was right. At the club in the closet he could have just strangled me and left me. In the alcove at school. In the woods. *So many places*. If he wasn't trying to get revenge on me for my father, then he could have.

Tetra grasped my hand, forcing me to look up at her. "I think Jace messed you up. I think you are having a hard time seeing that Kohen might just like you because you're hot, and smart, and powerful, and funny, and all the things."

I gave my bestie a soft smile, because she really was sweet to talk me up like that. "T, I don't live by the same rules as you. I'm the future empress. My father killed his dad. I can't."

Tetra nodded. "And he doesn't seem to care about that as much as you do."

Damn. She was really driving this home. Was she

right? Had I seen him as the enemy this entire time and he didn't feel the same?

Moments flashed through my mind, like when he stepped aside at the Lottery after Tetra's name was called so she could stand next to me. How he'd punched Jace for eating a French fry off my plate—but probably really because Jace cheated on me. How every step of the way he'd been sweet to me and I'd just punished him for where he was born and the history between our people.

I punished him for who his father was. I felt a little disgusted with myself.

I stared at the yellow cast on my wrist, the cast he saw ahead of time because he could see the future. Which meant everything else he saw between us was true too.

Why would he lie about that?

"You girls need to be home by midnight." My father's voice came from the doorway and I jumped. How long had he been standing there?

"I'm nineteen-years-old, Father. And a graduate of the Imperial Fleet now. Do I *really* still need a curfew?"

"You do while living under my roof," he replied flatly.

"Yes, sir," I said with a sigh. I was so ready to get my orders and ship out.

"Yes, sir." Tetra saluted him, but in a lazy way that I knew he hated, because the muscle in his jaw ticced.

"Aisling, can I have a word with you privately for a second?"

Oh boy.

I got up, putting a black coat over my slightly revealing red dress, and met him in the hallway.

Zuri was standing in the entryway outside his office, peering at me with her tail swishing. No sign that she was in distress, which meant I probably wasn't in trouble.

"I wanted to talk to you about your assignment before you hear about it tomorrow from your squad leader," my father said.

I braced myself, praying he was sending me to Sky Reach or Thunder Cliff, where I would get the most action and training. Even Evergreen might be okay.

"First tell me where Tetra is going. I want to make sure she's safe."

He nodded. He'd stopped questioning my love for that girl long ago. "I'm making her a drill instructor at the Imperial Fleet Training Center. She'll be safe right here in Riverine teaching cadets."

I sagged in relief. So the rumors were true. I felt like I could handle anything my father told me after that. I just needed to know Tetra was safe. "Thank you, Father."

He inclined his head in my direction. "And I'm sending *you* to Storm Haven."

I scoffed. I couldn't help it.

"So I can learn to knit?" I retorted. Storm Haven

was the safest base we had. It was the farthest from the war, basically a glorified storage unit for extra supplies that we packed and shipped on trains.

My father glared at me. "So you can stay alive and learn to one day take over for me."

"You never go to Storm Haven. How am I going to learn to take over for you if I'm counting meal rations and bottles of water?" It was pretty much all I'd be doing there.

"How can you take over for me if you are *dead*?" He matched my tone and I pursed my lips. "This is to keep you safe, Aisling. My decision is final," he said, then spun to walk away.

"Where did you post Kohen Badshah?" I called after him. I had to know.

His whole body stiffened and he turned back around to face me with one of his scary looks. The expression that said *Be careful you don't take this too far.* "Sky Reach," he said. "Because I don't care if he lives or dies."

With that, he stepped back into his office with Zuri, and I saw the glow of fire as he likely made a portal and went to some warfront.

Sky Reach. He was sending Kohen to the most formidable base in operation. A base that saw more casualties per week than there were hours in a day. I shouldn't care. My father did as I asked; he put us at separate postings. But the news tore a hole in my heart until it began to physically ache.

Sky Reach for a rookie? It was suicide. Sure Kohen had Onyx and was super powerful, but bombs went off at Sky Reach daily. The Luskins called it Easy Reach, because they could just throw firebombs over the border wall and hit it. It was one step down from sending him to stand atop The Wall and become a living bullseye.

Tetra knocked on the door casing behind me and I fixed my face from one of horror to excitement.

"Ready?" She smiled.

"Ready," I confirmed, ignoring my wounded heart.

Tetra was going to be safe, and I was going to focus on that and not on these new feelings that had bloomed in my stomach every time I thought of Kohen Badshah.

Because that scared me more than anything else.

THE BALL WAS ELEGANT, with a chocolate fountain, live band, and fancy linen tablecloths, but it was also really loud. Tetra went in search of a quieter room a half hour ago, but I was locked into a conversation about poisons with Meera against the far wall. She told me in detail about how she was able to make tasteless, odorless poisons that would kill a man in seconds. I still had yet to see any of the guys, including Kohen, and I wondered if they were hiding from me after I said all that stuff when I was on pain pills.

I was only slightly mortified. Jace deserved it.

"You should tell my father that. He could use that on the war front," I told her.

She nodded. "I mentioned it to my instructor at the training center but they didn't seem interested."

"Well, tell your squad leader once you get posted to a base. That might come in handy." Like in assassinating foreign leaders. I hated to think like that, but the Luskins started this war anyway, and if we took out Prime Leader Vlek it could all be over. He was the driving force behind the desire to expand his borders and steal our ember. It wasn't our fault our lands were rich with the stuff and they had little to none. They should buy it from us like everyone else, not attempt to steal it.

"I'm going to grab a drink," Meera told me and I nodded.

"I'm gonna go find Tetra!" I screamed back over the rock band blaring out of the speakers.

I went in search of my bestie, leaving the main ballroom and swerving down the hallway. This event center held weddings, birthdays, funerals, meetings, and much more. They had a main ballroom for bigger events and then tons of smaller rooms. I passed two closed doors before stopping near an opening to the game room, where there was a pool table, because I'd heard my name.

"Aisling is the hottest chick in our class," someone

said—it sounded like Alek but I couldn't be sure. I smiled at the nice compliment.

"Careful, Kohen's already pissed on her and marked his territory," Jace said. I'd recognize that voice anywhere.

"Screw you," Kohen shot back. "You're just mad that you had your chance with her and ruined it."

"Whatever, I'm just saying it's obvious you want Aisling," Jace said. "But you'll never have her. For one, her reputation would never allow her to be with a Badshah. And secondly, even if you got her, she wouldn't put out. So it's not worth the struggle in my opinion."

A bunch of male voices laughed in response and fury washed over me. Wouldn't put out? That's what he thought of me?

"Don't talk about her like she's some trophy to acquire!" Kohen's voice could cut glass. "If Aisling was ever my girlfriend, the last thing I would be thinking about was her 'putting out.' You're a piece of shit, Jace."

That was it, the final proof I needed to know that Kohen Badshah was good. He always had my back and stuck up for me. I'd read him wrong this entire time, and right then I wanted to prove Jace wrong. I didn't care about my reputation and I couldn't fight my feelings anymore. I was exhausted.

I strode into the room just as Jace opened his mouth to respond and everyone turned in my direction. Jace's gaze flicked to mine and I could see the panic there. He was with Tucker and his other cronies. Kohen looked like he'd been attempting to play darts with Nikhil before Jace had confronted him.

Kohen's gaze locked on mine. I walked straight towards him with purpose, never taking my eyes off of him.

"Hey, Aisling," Jace laughed nervously from my left. "We were just going to play a round of—"

I pushed Kohen hard until his back hit the wall, and then my lips crashed into his in a passionate kiss I wasn't prepared for. Pressing my body flat against him, my heart beat frantically between us as he smiled against my mouth. My fingers wrapped around the back of his neck and I hungrily opened my lips to deepen the kiss as desire bloomed inside of me. His fingertips trailed at my lower back and heat flushed along my body.

Holy crap! I'm kissing Kohen Badshah... in public. And I didn't care.

His hands came around my hips, digging my pelvis into his and I moaned. As our tongues swept against each other, it felt like the climax of my secret unspoken desire. For so long I had pushed down these feelings, fearful of bringing them to the surface, but now they burned their way to the top, bright and hot. It was as if time stood still, the world fading away as we surrendered to the sweet intoxication of our first kiss. I exhaled into his mouth and he swallowed it, as if wanting to capture everything about the moment, even my breath.

"Holy shit," Jace said beside me, as Kohen pulled my bottom lip into his mouth and sucked it. Desire bloomed deep in my gut and I finally pulled away from him, panting. Kohen was grinning ear to ear, which in turn made me smile.

I spun, facing Jace. His jaw was unhinged as he stared open-mouthed at me.

"That was so much better than in my dreams," Kohen declared to the room, and I decided that was a good note to leave on. I knew he meant his visions, not his dreams—and I had to agree, it was pretty epic. Reckless. But epic. The only thing ruining it right now was the sad look on Alek's face as he watched from the corner of the room. I hadn't meant to do that so publicly. Something had just come over me.

Strolling out of the room, I ran down the hall in search of my bestie. There were probably going to be consequences to that kiss, especially if word got back to my father.

But I didn't care. It was worth it.

I couldn't find Tetra inside so I stepped out into the garden and passed a couple making out. Where did she go?

Tetra giggled and I spun, eyes wide.

She was the couple making out. With Dev.

"Umm," I said, as she spotted me, laughing into

Dev's chest as he grinned down at her, red-faced. "Sorry, I'll leave you to it."

I ran back inside to give them privacy, beaming and happy for my bestie, when I slammed into someone's chest. I knew the moment the scent of cardamom and ginger washed over me that it was Kohen. After our kiss, I wasn't sure how things would go, but when I looked up into his eyes and saw yearning there, I couldn't help but grin.

"You think you can just kiss me like that and walk away?" he breathed, stepping closer to me as I backed up. My butt hit the brick wall and Kohen raised his arms, boxing me in and leaning against the wall on his forearms. Delicious anticipation danced on the tip of my tongue, waiting for him to kiss me, but he simply looked down at me with adoration and a sort of reverence. It was as if he was cataloguing all of my features, never having been this close to me before. I hadn't really been paying attention before either, but seeing him now in his full black suit made my stomach flip over.

"My stars, you're beautiful, Aisling," he breathed. Leaning forward, he dragged his lips across my neck and my legs went weak as tendrils of desire skated from my nape to my navel. "And that kiss..." He pulled back and looked at me with a halfcocked grin. "...was almost as good as the look on Jace's face after you left."

I smacked him and he dropped one of his hands, threading his fingers through mine. He pulled my left palm over his chest and I felt his heart beat wildly against my fingertips.

"Aisling Everhart?" he asked.

"Yes," I practically panted.

"I crave you every moment of every day." The words barely left his mouth before his lips were on mine. Now that we were alone in the dark hallway, I held nothing back. My lips parted as our tongues stroked each other's in a perfect rhythm that had heat building up in my core. I reached under his shirt, stroking the skin that was tightly pulled over his abdominal muscles. A carnal need came over me, one I'd never had with Jace. I wanted more of Kohen, I wanted all of him. I moaned, breathless, when he pulled away from me suddenly.

I was shocked to see horror on his face. He was staring at the wall beside me as if in a trance. Was he having a vision? It looked a lot like the one he'd had when he had been returning his practice blade and touched Anika.

"It's happening soon," Kohen said dreamily.

I frowned. "What is?"

He looked out the back garden in the direction of the training center. "The attack on the training center. I just had another vision. You need to get Tetra home. Everyone needs to get home and lock their doors."

Chills ran up my spine. We were close to the training center campus, if an attack was about to happen there—too close.

"Kohen, if you know there is going to be an attack on the campus tonight, you *have* to tell my father."

He reached up and grabbed the side of my face gently, forcing me to stare into his blue eyes. "Aisling, believe me when I tell you that your father *cannot* be trusted with knowledge of my gift."

My stomach sank. "Do people die? Our people?" I asked him.

He sighed. "Yes."

I couldn't just let someone die to protect one person. "Get everyone to go home. I don't care what you have to say. And promise me you will personally take Tetra home," I begged.

He frowned, reaching out to brush the bottom of my lip with his thumb, sending shivers down my spine. "Why, what are you going to do?"

"Don't you already know?" I countered.

How much did he see?

He swallowed hard and shook his head. "I don't know what you do. I only know that right now is the last time I kiss you for a long time."

I frowned. "Wh—?" Before I could question him, his lips were on mine again in a greedy kiss that I matched. My hands gripped him tightly, running over hardened muscle as his tongue slicked across mine, making heat run down my chest and settle between my thighs.

Stars, have mercy on me. This man was liable to

make me explode. By the time he pulled back, I was breathless.

He looked so sad and I wasn't sure why.

"I want you to remember something, okay?" he breathed.

All I could do was nod.

Leaning forward, he pressed his lips to my ear. "Remember that no matter how things may seem, everything I do is to protect you."

I frowned, and then Tetra and Dev stepped into the room holding hands and laughing. I broke apart from Kohen, remembering the urgency of his message about the attack.

"Get her home," I told him.

He nodded, and then I pulled my fingers from his and ran out the front door of the event hall with Tetra screaming after me. Liana was already there, waiting with her head down and wings tucked in so I could leap onto her. I had to ride sidesaddle since my dress was so tight.

'Don't tell me you are about to do what I think you are,' Liana said.

'Am I a loud thinker or are you a mind reader?' I asked her as she took flight and headed for my house.

'What's the difference?' she asked, and despite the current situation, I couldn't help but laugh.

'So are you doing what I think you are?' she asked again, a seriousness in her tone. *'Are you going to tell your father that you see the future?'*

So she *could* read my mind.

'*Yes,*' I said without hesitation. It was the only way to try and save lives without endangering Kohen's.

'*I advise against that,*' she said, and I could feel her worry through our bond. We didn't disagree on much, and to my knowledge we'd never really argued. But there was a first time for everything.

'*Noted. But I have to do this, unless you have some other way to warn the soldiers at the campus that an attack is incoming without putting Kohen's life at risk by revealing his gift.*'

She was silent, and that was that. Sometimes as a leader you had to do hard things for the good of all. My own father told me that.

Liana landed in front of my house and I leapt off of her. '*I'll be right out here waiting for you,*' she said.

That made me nervous. Was she expecting some kind of retaliation from my own father? Sure, he would be pissed I had kept such a gift from him, but he'd protect me.

Right?

'*Then why haven't you told him you can control minds?*' Liana asked.

That wasn't fair. I planned to take that to the grave and never use that magic again unless I absolutely had to. That was one of those powers you didn't tell anyone about. Even Tetra. To do so would put everyone who knew at risk. It was a forbidden power that no one should have, least of all a future empress who was going to be in control of the entire Imperial Fleet one day.

But so was the gift of seeing the future. To tell my father about it now would anger him. He hated lying and secret keeping. I wasn't naïve, I knew he'd be pissed, but I hoped he'd lay it aside and put our people first. I was his daughter after all.

"Aisling." My father's voice came from behind me just as I was about to knock on his study door.

I spun to find him in his robe watching me with a scowl.

"I know it's late. I'm sorry if you were sleeping but it's an emergency."

The scowl lifted to curiosity and concern.

I glanced down the hallway as Valor peeked her sleepy head out of the triplets' room.

"Can we talk in your office?" I asked him.

He pulled the key out of his pocket and unlocked the door. The moment we slipped inside, Zuri included, I launched into a ramble.

"I'm sorry I've kept this from you but I've been too scared to tell you and now it's a matter of life or death. There is going to be an attack on the training center campus tonight, like any minute, and we have to—"

"Stop," he said, eyes wild. "Take a deep breath."

I did as he asked and he took off his robe, revealing black military fatigues. Then he walked over to the cabinet in his office that held his armor. He began to suit up, which let me know he was taking this seriously.

"How do you know? What intel do you have?" he asked.

It never occurred to me that I could just say I had gotten some intel, but at this point I wouldn't even know where to begin with that. What intel and where did I get it at a graduation party?

"I can see the future," I blurted out, and my father froze halfway into putting on his chest armor.

The glare he gave me sent chills down my spine. "What?"

I would rather die than have to live this lie out right now, but there was no other way. I was hoping he would be too busy focusing on the fact that an attack was imminent than interrogate me. But I forgot about Zuri. She pranced around me in a circle, sniffing at my legs as if my lie was like a pungent odor.

"I... had a vision tonight, just now. I assume it's a latent gift acquired from my creature. I saw the campus being attacked. Tonight."

Zuri shared a look with my father and he slowly clicked his chest armor on, peering at me in a calculated way that made my skin crawl. "You have foresight and you kept this from me?" There was a growl in his tone but it was also laced with hurt.

I swallowed hard. "I'm... telling you now."

He sighed, pulling his blade from the cabinet and slid it into its scabbard at his waist. "Stay home and protect your sisters," was all he said as the fire portal began to open in his office.

He believed me, and he was going to help.

"I want to help. Liana is just outside. I could—"

His head snapped in my direction. "Stay at home! That's an order. You and your sisters are the most important thing in this world to me."

He'd never said anything like that in all the nineteen years that I'd known him, and it shut the retort in my mouth.

"Yes, sir," I said, as emotion clogged my throat. Sometimes I thought my father regretted having children and the emotional burden they were. Other times, I thought he just didn't know how to handle emotional burdens and he was so stern because he cared so much and didn't know what to do with that.

The campus' courtyard became visible just beyond him, and I watched as he strode through the ring of fire and into it. A group of soldiers ran over to him and he began to bark orders. Just before the portal shut, Zuri peered back to glare at me, and I knew in that moment that my father had sensed my lie, but also maybe some truth because he'd gone on my word and rallied the troops. He believed in most of what I said and was going to help because I'd asked, and that meant the world to me.

I spun to go check on my sisters, then saw Elaine standing in the open office doorway in her robe.

"I normally don't eavesdrop, but I heard your voice and wanted to make sure you were okay and…"

Crap.

"What did you hear?" I asked, my heart hammering in my chest. Lying to my father was one thing, but to Elaine? I couldn't.

"Enough," she said with a frown. "Aisling, how big will the attack be?"

I had no idea, because I was a freaking liar and I'd never seen the vision.

"Enough to lose lives." Hadn't Kohen said something like that?

"Will it spill over into the city?" She peered back down the hallway at my sisters' room. "Should we flee with the girls?"

I didn't know if it would spill over. In fact, I didn't know anything, and if it did come close to our house…

"Yes. You should take the girls and go to the country house in Cedar Creek for the night," I told her, rushing to pack a bag for them.

"*We,*" she said, frowning at me.

I looked over at her and gave her a soft smile. This woman was like a mother to me. She should know by now what I would do. "You didn't raise me to run from trouble."

She opened her mouth to speak, but I pulled her into a hug. She was stiff for a moment, before wrapping her arms tightly around me.

I love you, sat on the tip of my tongue, but my

father had contaminated those words, making me feel weak for even wanting to say them, so I just held on to her tighter. It was my non-verbal *I love you.*

When she finally pulled back, she was smiling. "You will make a wonderful empress someday."

I beamed at the compliment.

Within ten minutes I had changed into my Fleet-issued fatigues, and had the triplets and Elaine packed into the car with Elaine in the driver's seat. She wasn't used to driving as we normally had Verik, but she knew how.

"I'll send word when it's safe to return," I told her.

Victory, Valor, and Virtue all peered at me with identical expressions of fear.

"What's going on?" Virtue murmured, hair mussed from sleep.

"What aren't you telling us?" Valor asked.

"Come with us," Victory begged, grasping my good hand.

I reached into the open car window with my good arm and squeezed all of their hands. "Mind Elaine. And be strong. I have to stay and help Father. I need you safe," I told them methodically, trying to keep emotion from my voice.

I moved to step back and then thought better of it. What if this was the last time I saw any of them? It was a dark wild thought that permeated my mind.

The words I was so afraid to say fell out of my mouth in fear, fear I would die and never say them to anyone. "I love you all," I spoke into the car in a rush, freed in that moment.

Victory smiled but the other three appeared shocked at my words, like they were dirty.

"Go," I told them.

With that, I stepped back and Elaine gunned it, zipping onto the main road and heading for our country estate. I'd spent many summers in Cedar Creek fishing in the pond behind the house and going for long walks in the forest. It was sparsely populated and near the Evergreen Fleet base in case something really bad went down. They'd be safe there. Safer than here.

When I spun around, Kohen was landing Onyx right next to Liana, who was still exactly where I'd left her. I hoped my father would agree with my sending the girls away. I needed to keep them safe, and if this attack was from Luska, they might target the emperor's home. His family. I was still confused how this attack was going to go down. If anyone from Luska wanted to attack Riverine, they'd have to fly the entire length of our country or come up on shore. Our scouts with flying creatures would have seen them and sounded the alarm. Unless they found some weakness in our defenses. Maybe the Cove. I had overheard my father speaking last night in his office about the Cove being a weak point of ours that we needed to shore up.

"What are you doing here?" I asked Kohen.

"I got Tetra home safely," he told me. "But your

father called for all fleet troops to report at the campus. So I don't know how long she will stay there."

Because she was now Fleet. We all were.

Shit.

"And I had another vision," he added as he gripped Onyx's reins and prepared for flight.

"Tell me," I begged.

He frowned. "You said you didn't want to know the future, that you wanted to just live out—"

"Tell me!" Did Tetra die? No, that was too dark. I couldn't fathom it.

He sighed, looking at the ground. "You and I help fend off the attack. It's an air assault, and we rain down fire from the sky."

My heart brightened. "We help? Great. Let's go."

He reached out and grasped the top of my shoulder, forcing me to look up at him, and I was startled by what I saw in his blue eyes. "But someone you love dies," he said, and I froze, dread sinking into my bones.

"Who?" I asked, my heart practically beating out of my chest.

He shook his head. "I don't know but... I saw you sobbing with a body on the floor behind you. It was blurry—hard to explain—but it can only mean one thing." He looked away, as if he couldn't meet my eyes. It must be hard to see me like that in the future. Like watching one of those films they projected at the park on the weekends.

Sobbing? That didn't sound like me. I'd purposely

hardened my emotions so that I would never be affected in that way. I didn't care about many people, and the few I did were safe. Tetra was home. The triplets were on their way to the country.

Unless it was him? Would Kohen dying cause me to sob?

The very thought made my heart seize in my chest, and I realized in that moment that I had allowed myself to fall for him. Much deeper than I ever should have permitted. Now there was no way back from it.

"We gotta go," Kohen said, gripping the reins of his dragon.

I nodded, peering over at him. How had we gone from kissing an hour ago to riding into battle with each other now?

Stars have mercy on us.

I mounted Liana and we took off into the night and headed for the training center, which I was dismayed to see was now on fire.

CHAPTER
TWENTY-FOUR

It was chaos. I'd sat in many war council meetings with my father this year to learn how things worked, and they'd given detailed reports of battles along our borders. But never had I seen it in person. Fire, smoke, arrows, swords, bodies, blood, screaming, creatures tearing into each other. Death. So much death.

The attack must have happened the moment my father stepped onto campus, because it was already far along. Imperial soldiers raced across the lawn, shooting arrows up at the sky, where I saw over a dozen flying Talanagi—dragons, griffins, a winged horse, a winged lion, creatures that I didn't even have names for. It was incredible and terrifying all at once.

Some of these Talanagi were carrying large baskets in their talons the size of cars, and inside of those baskets were Luskin soldiers wearing their red uniforms. *So that's how they did it.*

Before Kohen and I could do anything, they lowered the baskets to the ground and the soldiers scattered like ants. My father was in the center of the campus lawn, slashing through the Luskin intruders with his sword as Zuri ripped out their throats.

Would he be angry if he knew I was here? He had called for all Fleet to report to campus. But somehow I knew that didn't mean me. That he'd want his successor and daughter safe. But I couldn't just sit here and allow this attack to happen.

"Anika!" Kohen shouted down below, and my attention was drawn to the ground. Anika was still in her beautiful dress from the ball with Alek, Dev, and others in tow. They held swords and fanned out along the campus with their creatures, joining the battle without question. I was just glad that Tetra was not among them.

'Let's help them out,' I told Liana, and she beelined it for the flying creatures on the field. They had dropped the soldiers off in the baskets and were now taking to the skies with their bonded riders. Liana flew closer to a cluster of them and breathed a stream of fire as I pulled out my bolt shooter from where it was clipped on her harness. A couple of the riders fell off their creatures, aflame, and ran away, but some of the creatures were uninjured and now gunning for us. Liana flew higher, pulling them away from the

campus. I had nine bolts loaded, and I fired in rapid succession at the wings and necks of the dragon, griffin, and flying lion that were now coming for me. My aim was true, and two of the creatures lost their ability to fly, with three serrated bolts embedded in their wings.

But the red-scaled dragon with its blond female rider was evading my every blow. There was a crest embroidered on her jacket but I wasn't close enough to see what it was. It was some official seal, likely designating her as a commander of some sort.

She raised her fist and I prepared for her to throw fire or an energy blast or something. It took me a second to realize I could no longer breathe. The wind was being sucked from my lungs as Liana dove away from her and flew in another direction to put distance between us. When we got about a hundred yards away from her, I gasped for air, feeling Liana doing the same beneath me, her ribcage widening under my thighs.

Holy crap. The red dragon rider could manipulate the very air in my lungs!

Then that feeling was back, like I couldn't breathe, and I peered behind me to see the psycho grinning ear to ear as her red dragon raced through the sky after us with half a dozen Talanagi in tow. Liana turned her head and breathed a stream of fire, but the red dragon was too fast.

I pulled for my own fire power, but without being able to breathe, it was hard to concentrate. Liana was erratically flying every which way to lose her, but the red dragon rider was on us like glue.

'*Thrall her or we are both going down—and you may not come back,*' Liana told me as black dots danced at the edges of my vision.

I hadn't ever wanted to use that again.

Where the hell was Kohen? Alek's hawk? Everyone else?

I saw then, in the distance, behind the goons chasing us, that there were a dozen more flying Luska fighters, all riding Talanagi and chasing down Kohen as he tried to reach me. How did they have so many?

Power built in my core, like an electric zapping along my skin, as Liana began to lose altitude. Without oxygen, she was growing weak, and couldn't outrun this red dragon rider and her team. There were too many Talanagi. They were so fast and powerful. We were woefully unprepared.

I felt like I was going to lose consciousness any second, and the power inside of me snapped.

'*Stop!*' I screamed mentally, with no air left in my lungs as I spun to face the red rider and threw out my hand. Two glowing silver threads shot from my palms and wrapped around the heads of the red dragon rider and her creature.

Instantly, the pressure on my lungs was gone and I gasped for air, my throat burning as I coughed and sputtered. Liana gasped beneath me as well, and flew farther away from the red rider. The soldiers who had flanked her were suspended in midair, staring from her to me in confusion, no doubt wondering what was going on with their leader. I still had no idea if the little silver rope could be seen by others. The red rider was open-mouthed, unresponsive with my silver cord still engaged around her head.

That's when her posse came for me. Anger saturated their features and they flew after us with determination. The cord finally snapped, disappearing from my hand, and I shot what bolts I had left at the advancing soldiers.

A blur of brown flew up next to me and I noticed Iniki.

"Tell Alek I'm okay. Focus on the ground fight. I'm going to take out their wing crew," I told her.

She nodded and then dove downward.

Liana brought me closer to Kohen, who was igniting fires across the sky as best he could, but he was clearly overwhelmed. There were so many of them. I felt that well of power inside of me growing as my anger simmered to the surface.

"Kohen, land and help the others!" I screamed to him over the wind just as a streak of fire came from one of the dragon riders, heading right for him. Onyx ducked, dropping him down ten feet in the air.

Kohen peered up at me, a knowing in his gaze. Had he seen this? Did he know my plan? He must have, because he nodded once and then dropped to the ground. That was very unlike protective Kohen to just leave me in danger. He knew.

'I will lead them on a bit of a chase to get them to cluster together,' Liana said. So she had read my mind and she knew my plan as well. Good, everyone was on board.

I gripped the handles of Liana's harness as she went into her super speed mode, which drew all the Talanagi in the sky into a chase with us.

I peered down at the ground. Amersean soldiers were running back and forth across the campus, screaming orders and engaging the Luskins. But there seemed to be fewer red coats than before, so I thought we were winning the ground front.

And then the air was sucked from my lungs.

Dammit.

Red dragon rider was back in action. I peered behind me and counted *thirteen* Talanagi in all.

I hoped most of them were not impervious to fire.

Because like Instructor Ashendell said, I was a human bomb.

And I was about to go off.

'Now!' I told Liana and she suspended in midair, allowing the others to catch up with us. They whooshed alongside me just as I exploded.

I pushed the limits of my power this time. Heat engulfed me, and my vision was overcome with flames. Fire crawled across the sky and I pinched my eyes shut as screams rose up around me. My eyes popped open just in time to see the tidal wave of fire lap against the Talanagi pursuing me and ignite their riders into flames. All except two—the red dragon rider and a green dragon rider. They seemed to be protected and flew away unharmed, clearly giving up the fight. Meanwhile, their fellow soldiers burned in the sky as they flew in frantic circles.

The sight was sickening.

'Take me down,' I ordered Liana.

She did, and when I landed it was a relief to see we had won against the ground assault too. The red coats were dead or taken prisoner. Medics were starting to triage the wounded.

Instructor Ashendell was there suddenly, holding a bow in her hands.

"Take them down and put them out of their misery," I told her, pointing to the sky.

The lead instructor followed my gaze and nodded. "Archers! With me!" she cried.

A group of a dozen soldiers rushed to her side and took a knee. They shot their arrows into the sky as I leapt off Liana and ran to the battlefield. "Kohan! Anika! Dev! Alek!" I just started screaming the names of those I knew were here, leaping over dead bodies and scanning their faces for my friends.

It wasn't until I saw Ariyel limping over to me with ash on her fur that Kohen's vision about someone I loved dying rose up into my mind.

"TETRA!" I bellowed, until my voice was hoarse,

doing a full three-sixty, scanning the field frantically. My heart raced as bile rose in my throat. *No. No don't take her. Not her. Anyone but her.*

My eyes filled with tears, spilling over onto my cheeks, and I knew this was the moment from Kohen's vision. If anyone could thaw my heart and soften me to tears, it was Tetra. My beloved best friend.

Someone crashed into me from behind, squeezing me tightly. Her blonde hair half covered my face and I saw her cane drop to the ground as I spun and held her so hard I thought I might break her.

"I thought you were..." A tear slipped down my cheek and I felt relief. Kohen was wrong. He must have seen the moment up until now—with tears in my eyes and dead bodies all around me—and assumed someone I cared about died.

I pulled Tetra back and looked her over.

"You okay?" I asked, wiping all evidence of weakness from my face. She looked good—no blood or signs of damage.

She nodded, scanning me. "The sky lit up like the fire sky in The Wilds! Was that you?"

"Yes." I took her hand in mine. "Where is everyone else?"

Word got out that the attack was over and people began to leave their hiding spaces, crawling out of bushes and from behind buildings.

Anika limped over to us with a torniquet cinched tight on her upper thigh. Her lion creature nuzzled her bad leg. Dev, Jace, Alek, Meera... they were okay. I sagged in relief.

"Wait, where's Kohen?" I asked.

"I'm here," he called from behind me, and I couldn't explain the amount of relief I felt.

I spun to him, and there was alarm etched all over his face.

"Where's Nikhil?" he asked Anika.

"Dead." Her voice was hollow as she stood there and stared at Kohen with an empty expression. "He saved me."

"No..." Kohen's voice cracked and my heart broke in that moment. Nikhil... the funny ladies' man had grown on me. This was what Kohen must have seen that day in the woods when he said his friends were hurt and he didn't know who survived.

"False retreat! False retreat!" Instructor Ashendell screamed, and we looked up into the sky to see the red and green dragon rider barreling towards us.

I sucked in a breath. There was no time to think of a strategy or do anything as they descended from the sky and flew right at us.

Tetra suddenly hopped on one foot and threw herself in front of all of us.

"No!" I screamed as fire and arrows bore down from the dragon riders on our little group of survivors.

I flinched, waiting to be struck with the rain of steel when Tetra threw her arms wide and a pearlescent shield burst from her hands, covering us all like a dome. The fire splashed across the dome, bringing heat but nothing else. The arrows snapped and hit the ground, useless.

The red and green dragon riders circled for a second attack, but Liana and Onyx took to the skies, chasing the riders off.

I turned to my best friend with wide eyes. "Holy crap, Tetra, you can do that?"

I knew shield making was her gift, but in practice she'd never gotten it bigger than the size of a tire.

Her hands shook a little, her face ashen with shock. "I guess so."

Anika and everyone rushed forward then to hug and thank her.

'Onyx and I are chasing them off. They are heading west to the Cove.'

I flicked my gaze to Kohen and he nodded to show that he knew as well, but something seemed off about him. His expression was pinched, as if he were expecting something.

'Keep me posted,' I told her, and frowned at Kohen.

The double doors to the main training center building burst open and Admiral Caruso rushed out, face whiter than a sheet.

Her eyes scanned the carnage outside and rested on me. I froze, chills racing up my arms.

It wasn't until that moment that I wondered... *Where is my father?*

Admiral Caruso rushed over to me and I straightened my back, standing at attention. We all did.

"The emperor is dead. I need to swear you in."

Her words were like fog in my brain. They made no sense. Everything was muffled and confusing. The emperor couldn't be dead. The emperor was my father.

My breathing grew ragged. Tetra slipped her hand in mine but I shook her off.

"What? I didn't hear you." I extended my left ear to Admiral Caruso.

Compassion washed over her face and she swallowed hard. "Your father is dead. You are the leader of Amersea now, Empress Aisling." She saluted me and my whole body went numb.

"Where is he?" This was a lie. She was mistaken.

"Inside the building, in the mess hall, but—"

I took off running, leaping over fallen soldiers, bursting through the double doors. The halls of the campus were bathed in blood and soot. It was clear many soldiers tried to barricade themselves in here. I turned the corner and sprinted into the mess hall, where I skidded to a stop. Slumped over on his side, on the floor, was my father. No significant blood marred his suit, no sword was in his back, just a thin bit of foam on his lips and some small cuts on his arms.

Zuri was lifeless on his lap, and every wall I'd built up inside of me crumbled in that moment.

"Daddy!" I sobbed, rushing forward as I was

reduced to what I used to call him as a small child. His ashen skin and graying hair made him look so old in that moment. It killed me.

Tears filled my eyes so quickly, I had to blink rapidly to clear them as my chest heaved and my throat burned. A sob ripped from me as I screamed in horror. I couldn't remember the last time I'd cried like this. Maybe when my mother died giving birth to the triplets. It felt like I was drowning. I never got to tell him I loved him. He was a hardass, strict, cold, but he was my father, the only parent I had left.

"Don't leave me. I'm not ready," I whimpered to him.

I heard footsteps and spun around just in time to see Kohen. He looked heartbroken for me, and I suddenly became angry.

"You knew!" I screamed at him, rushing to beat him on the chest. "You knew it would be him and you didn't tell me!" I punched his chest like a wild animal and he just held me as I broke down, letting every emotion I'd stored up over the years fall out of me in a messy heap.

"Step away from the empress!" Admiral Caruso barked from behind him, and Kohen released me. I wiped my eyes, trying to get myself together as she walked down the hall with Instructor Ashendell. Caruso took one look at Kohen and flicked her head at the exit, indicating that it was his time to leave. "You no longer have clearance to be around her."

'I'm coming,' Liana told me. She knew. She saw everything through me and she knew.

Kohen took one more agonizing look at me and left back down the hall he came.

The admiral grasped both sides of my shoulders and held my gaze. "We've just sustained the first attack on record in the city of Riverine. Our great safe capital. The people will be rocked by this news and by the passing of their emperor. I need to swear you in, and I need you to be strong. For the soldiers out there and the families at home. For all of us."

I sucked up my last tear, rebuilding the walls around my heart, and nodded to her.

I peered down at my father's lifeless body. "Find me the bastard that did this. I want their head on a spike in the middle of the square." My voice was hollow. I felt dead inside.

"Yes, Empress," she vowed.

Whatever shred of innocence I had left died in that moment. All I cared about now was revenge on whoever just took the only remaining parent my little sisters and I had.

Book two, *Lies that Bind*, can be preordered on Amazon. Check LeiaStone.com for the latest news.

ABOUT LEIA STONE

Leia Stone is the USA Today bestselling author of multiple bestselling series including Matefinder and Wolf Girl. She's sold over three million books and her Fallen Academy series has been optioned for film. Her novels have been translated into multiple languages and she even dabbles in script writing.

Leia writes urban fantasy and paranormal romance with sassy kick-butt heroines and irresistible love interests. She lives in Spokane, WA with her husband and two children.

www.LeiaStone.com

JOIN THE FAN CLUB

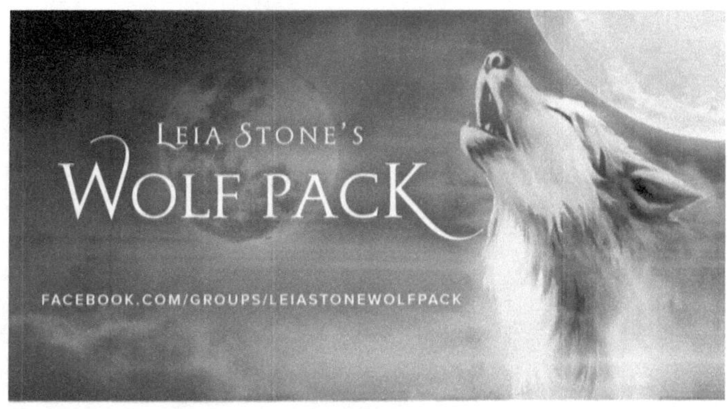

Get involved, make some friends, and get exclusive sneak peeks before anyone else.

News:

Also join my Newsletter! (Link on my website Leias tone.com) I only send one out when I have a new release or something exciting.

Shop:

Shop in my store! (LeiaStoneBooks.Com) I have special editions and ebook bundles and more!

 *Leia*

BOOKS BY LEIA STONE

LEIASTONE.COM/BOOKS

FANTASY

Vampire Hunter Society

Shifter Island Series

Wolf Girl Series

Daughter of Light Series

The Titan's Saga

Supernatural Bounty Hunter Series

Dream Wars Series

Fallen Academy Series

Dragons & Druids Series

Matefinder Series

Matefinder: Next Generation

Hive Trilogy

NYC Mecca Series

Night War Saga

Water Realm Series

The Kings of Avalier Series

Gilded City Series

ALL TITLES

LeiaStone.com/books

Acknowledgments

A huge thank you to my editors, beta readers, and sensitivity readers for your steadfast work on this project. It truly takes a village to get every single book out into The Wild. You see what I did there? I have to send out a huge thank my readers for buying my books and turning this passion into a career that supports my family. I'm literally living my dream. And finally thank you to my amazing and supportive family for sharing me with my characters. And to God for this truly remarkable gift you have given me.